✓ _Really Good!_

Uncertain ... g
pursued, S ... he
rooms toward the front of the house,
flung open the door and, without
even blinking, launched herself at the
man who was standing there.

"Barto!"

Halted by his tall form, Sydony breathed his name against
the soft lapel where she buried her face. A vague memory of
security blossomed into a reassuring sense of safety. It was
no wonder, for the hard body she clung to was as strong and
solid as an oak. It smelled good, too, like horses and leather
and something else. She had never noticed Barto's scent
before, but then, she hadn't been this close to him in years.

* * *

The Dark Viscount
Harlequin® Historical #918—October 2008

The Dark Viscount

DEBORAH SIMMONS

HARLEQUIN®

TORONTO • NEW YORK • LONDON
AMSTERDAM • PARIS • SYDNEY • HAMBURG
STOCKHOLM • ATHENS • TOKYO • MILAN • MADRID
PRAGUE • WARSAW • BUDAPEST • AUCKLAND

ISBN-13: 978-0-373-29518-0
ISBN-10:   0-373-29518-9

THE DARK VISCOUNT

www.eHarlequin.com

Printed in U.S.A.

With thanks to my fellow author Terri Valentine
for her support, encouragement and friendship.

Chapter One

Sydony watched dark clouds skitter across the sky with a wary eye, aware that the approaching storm made for an ominous arrival at their new home. The heavens seemed bigger out here, the elements of nature more powerful, or perhaps it was just the strangeness of the countryside that gripped her as she gazed out the carriage window. Her brother Kit would say she read too many Gothic novels, yet there was no denying that their destination was a far cry from the neat brick house they had called home for so long.

The sad truth was that she and Kit were orphans—not the wretched sort forced into the workhouses, but orphans none the less. Their mother had passed away when they were still young children, and she was remembered fondly, if not well. But their father had died less than a year ago, and the wound was still fresh.

An especially deep rut in the road flung Sydony against her brother, and she was grateful for Kit's solid presence. They had come to lean on each other more since the accident, by both choice and necessity. Their father had been a scholar—a man of books, not business—and, since his death, they had been forced to tighten their purses.

Although only two years Sydony's senior, at nineteen Kit had kept a clear head. He had never succumbed to the lure of gambling or drinking to excess that made so many of his peers fools and paupers or worse. He might sometimes tease Sydony that she was their only real asset, a beauty who would fare well on the marriage mart, but they had neither the heart nor the funds for a Season in London.

So they had remained together, continuing to lease the house where they had lived with their father. But not long after his death, the owner pressed them for more money. Apparently, he was leery of two young people running a household, and, truth to tell, their various stipends and resources were stretched thin. But where were they to go?

It was then, when things looked rather dismal, that their sagging fortunes finally took a turn for the better. The news that they had inherited property from a distant relative seemed like a windfall. They sold off their furniture, packed up their belongings, and set out immediately for their new home. But now, as Sydony watched leaves chasing across the bleak landscape, denuded oaks stark against the sky, she wondered whether their circumstances had sunk even lower.

She caught sight of a sprawling stone structure rising in the distance just as the heavens burst. The storm was upon them, and so, now, was their future. Sydony drew a deep breath as she clung to her seat. The rough road that had seemed nearly impassable before was not improved by the downpour.

'That must be Oakfield! Do you see it?' Kit said, leaning forward and pointing eagerly.

'Yes,' Sydony murmured, squinting into the sheets of rain. 'Though this hardly seems a promising welcome.'

Ever the optimist, Kit ignored her dismay. 'Well, at least we've found the place before the road washes away.'

'Now, that's a lovely thought,' Sydony said. Their lifelong neighbour Lady Elizabeth Hawthorne had warned them that the site sounded remote, but Sydony had not thought it beyond the reach of modern highways.

Kit laughed, and Sydony set aside her misgivings as the coach halted in a thunder of splashing hooves. Without waiting for the coachman, Kit pushed at the door, but the wind and rain were so fierce that he had to use some force to thrust it open. Heedless of the elements, he leapt down and turned towards her, his hand extended. But when Sydony stuck her head out, she faltered, blinking against the wetness and gaping at the scene before her.

The world outside was thick with the unnatural twilight of the storm, blinding rain making it hard to see beyond the feeble glow of the carriage lantern. But there was no mistaking the hulking darkness of a building that rose behind the figure of her brother, eerily forbidding, and yet somehow familiar, as if Sydony had seen it in dreams...

'Syd!' Kit yelled, and she turned her attention back to her brother. By the time her slippers touched the gravelled drive, her cloak was whipping around her and the hood had been thrown back from her face. Ducking, she held on to Kit's hand as they dashed towards an arched entrance.

'Look! It's medieval,' Kit shouted, pointing upwards, and Sydony lifted her face to see a vague outline of battlements. She paused, once again, to stare at the forbidding façade of old stone laced with even blacker shadows. Either it was crumbling to pieces or it was covered in some sort of growth that made for an altogether unpleasant aspect.

'Hurry, before we're both soaked,' Kit urged, dragging Sydony inside.

It was too late for that. Sydony's gown was already plastered to her legs, the cold and wet seeping into her bones. For once, she found it difficult to share her brother's enthusiasm. Being male and of an age that sought excitement and new experiences, he viewed the move as a big adventure, while Sydony longed for the familiar and a routine that might have chafed before, but now would be welcomed.

As they stood under the archway, Kit banged upon the door, but there was no answer to their summons. When their coachman Henry deposited a trunk upon the doorstep, Kit waved him away. 'See if you can find a stable around the back,' he shouted over the storm.

Henry nodded and hurried back to the coach, obviously eager to locate a dry berth, while the Marchants were left standing before the massive doors, rattling the knocker.

'Maybe they can't hear us,' Kit said.

The thought was no comfort to Sydony, who

shivered under the onslaught of rain and glanced around her dismal surroundings. 'It looks deserted,' she said.

Indeed, it did, for no lights glowed warmly at the mullioned windows. The walkway was overgrown, as was the grass and shrubbery. The solicitor had written a warning that the house had not been kept up over the past few years and that additional staff would be needed. Now, as Sydony stood in the pouring rain, she pondered the exact meaning of 'additional'.

Finally, Kit tried the door, which swung open after a brief struggle. Inside, all was dark and quiet, with little light filtering in from outside.

'Hello?' Kit called out. His voice echoed in the old-fashioned hall with its stone flags. Although open, the space smelled musty, and Sydony was struck by a vision of their cosy cottage with its wood floors, brightly painted walls and cheerful, airy windows. Despite her father's dusty piles of books, it had always been filled with the scents of beeswax and flowers, fresh or dried.

'Well, even if there's no one to greet us, here we are at our own place, Syd. What do you think of our good fortune?' Kit said, spreading his arms to encompass the dreary area.

'Astounding,' she said, tongue firmly in cheek.

As she had anticipated, Kit chuckled at her tone before hurrying to drag in the trunks.

Unfastening her cloak, Sydony went in search of the kitchen, but she found no comfort there. Although no servants were about, the place looked as if they had but recently left in the midst of their labours. Several bowls and utensils cluttered the work table, yet when Sydony reached out to touch them, her gloved finger became marked with dust.

It was almost as though the inhabitants had exited suddenly, but when? Sydony shook her head. If so, they had left no food about to spoil or draw vermin, Sydony noted with a quick glance into the shadowy corners. Even the kitchen was gloomy, and as she glanced about Sydony saw that a window high in one wall had been boarded over. No wonder it was dim.

Thankfully, a window in the other wall remained intact. Stepping towards it, Sydony wiped it with a gloved hand and leaned forwards to peek out. At first she could see only blackness, but then a face swam behind the pane. She let out an involuntary shriek before she recognised their own coachman.

Her heart pounding, Sydony drew a deep breath and straightened as she moved to open the nearby door. Although hardly missish, it seemed she was not immune to the odd mood set by the deserted residence.

'Sorry, miss,' Henry said, stepping inside. He slipped off his hat and shook the rain from his shoulders. 'Didn't mean to give you a fright.'

'Certainly not,' Sydony said, knowing how Kit would roar with laughter. She had thought a childhood of boy's pranks had inured her to everything, but the new surroundings were enough to unnerve anyone.

As if on cue, Kit appeared in the doorway, a sturdy implement in hand that he must have snatched up from a fireplace. 'Are you all right?' he asked. 'I thought I heard something.'

'I'm afraid I gave Miss Marchant a turn,' Henry said.

'It was nothing,' Sydony muttered, and, for once,

Kit did not pursue it. They had more important things to do.

'I didn't see any of the crates we shipped ahead,' Kit said. 'Did you see anything in the stables?'

Henry shook his head. 'My boy Clarence is settling in the horses, but I didn't see hide nor hair of anyone. The place looks like it hasn't been used in many a year.'

'Well, we shall just have to set up our own stables,' Kit said.

'I hope you'll be able to find some decent grooms-men way out here,' Henry said, looking down at the hat in his hand.

'You're welcome to stay on, of course. You and Clarence both,' Kit said, though Sydony knew they had discussed this before.

'Thank you, sir, but it just isn't my home here. I'll miss the team and all, though.'

'Of course, we shall take care of them, personally, until we can hire some trustworthy,' Kit assured him. 'And you must let us know how you get on at the Fieldings'.'

'I will, sir.'

Before things turned really maudlin, Sydony cleared her throat. 'Well, since there seem to be no servants about, I'll see what I can muster up for our dinner. You and Clarence come on back to the kitchen once the horses are bedded down.'

'Shall we look for a room for you?' Kit asked.

'No, sir. We'll be just fine out in the stables. There's a separate area with cots.'

'Very well. Thank you, Henry,' Kit said. He looked like he wanted to say more, but it had all been said. Sadly, their groomsmen, their cook and their maids had elected not to move to parts unknown. And right now, Sydony could not blame them. Lest she be tempted to take the mail coach back with Henry and Clarence, she set to work. Throwing her cloak over a chair, she stripped off her gloves and went searching for edibles, while Kit started a fire in the open hearth.

Before long there was a nice blaze going, which put forth both warmth and cheer, though the room itself was not exactly homely. Sydony told herself that a good scrubbing and some bright paint would help, though there was no altering the fact that the house was old, with its own style and quirks. A more pessimistic sort might deem it a medieval horror right out of the most popular novels, but Sydony refused to acknowledge the possibility.

For Kit's sake, if not her own, she needed to keep such thoughts at bay. Besides, everything would look better in the morning, she told herself as she shook out a cloth and laid it upon a corner of the work table. They would eat here, for, despite her good intentions, she hadn't the heart to tackle any other room at the moment.

Kit found some lanterns that added more light, which improved the atmosphere, and Sydony was grateful. Not knowing what lay ahead today, she had asked for a packed basket when they stopped for luncheon, so there was cold chicken, salted ham, wedges of cheese, a fat loaf of bread and apples for their supper. Thankfully, at some point water had been piped into the house, and Kit produced a bottle of wine that was most welcome.

But when all four of them were seated, it was a sad little group, everyone well aware of their parting on the morrow. Henry made obvious his disapproval of the whole situation, muttering about a godforsaken place without a soul to even greet them properly.

'Now, Henry, you are talking about my country estate,' Kit said, while slicing himself more cheese. 'Don't you think I'm suited to be a gentleman farmer?'

'More suited to be that than a gentleman scholar,' Sydony said, and they all laughed. But even Sydony's wit and Kit's good humour could not entirely relieve the sense of a gallows bird's last meal that hung over the company.

That mood only grew stronger after the coachman and his boy left for the stables and Kit and Sydony went in search of some beds. It was full dark outside, though the storm had abated, as they made their way back to the hall, its musty smell more pronounced after the relatively odour-free kitchen.

'Look at this wonderful staircase,' Kit said, as they approached the steps that led from the ground floor up to the first. It squared off, leading up to an open landing, before turning upwards again, its dark wood carved into intricate patterns that seemed a bit busy to Sydony. However, she was loathe to discourage her brother. Someone had to see the bright side of this experience, and Kit was obviously bursting with some sort of male pride of ownership that failed to move his sister.

When they reached the landing, Sydony lifted her lantern towards the looming darkness. 'What is this?' she asked. The glow illuminated heavy wooden planks that appeared to be been nailed across the wall.

'Maybe they're covering a broken window,' Kit said.

'In a place like this, there might have been a stained glass one that would cost a lot to replace.'

'But a window in the kitchen is boarded up, as well.'

'Could be more than one has broken over the years,' Kit said.

Sydony lifted a finger to touch the raw wood, so out of place among the trappings of a medieval manor house. It seemed that someone had gone to an awful lot of trouble to cover up every inch of what lay beneath, but perhaps that was to keep any air from entering. The house was draughty enough without a gaping hole in the wall.

Upstairs, as they wandered from room to room, Sydony noticed more unusual window coverings, this time heavy wooden interior shutters. 'The place is closed up tighter than a drum,' she muttered.

'Maybe Great-aunt Elspeth had an aversion to light,' Kit joked.

'Or perhaps a cyclone came through, blowing out one entire side of the house,' Sydony said drily.

Oddly enough, it did seem that one side of the house, especially, was battened down, and all the windows facing that direction tightly shuttered. Curious, Sydony tried to open one, only to find it nailed securely. 'Why, you can't even loose them.'

'Maybe the place was shut up after Great-aunt Elspeth died,' Kit answered, obviously not too concerned.

Sydony turned round, trying to get her bearings. 'But it's mostly the rooms facing the rear of the house, as did the landing on the stair, that are completely covered.'

'Maybe the winds are fierce from that direction,' Kit said.

'But there must be closed windows behind them,' Sydony said. Lifting a hand in front of the shutters, she felt no draught. 'Why nail them shut?'

'She probably thought they rattled. You know how old ladies are,' Kit said, over his shoulder. 'It doesn't look like these rooms have been used in some time, so she might well have had them shut up.' Obviously uninterested, he was already moving on, but Sydony couldn't rid herself of the notion that something wasn't right.

Why would anyone nail shutters closed, and only those in certain rooms? She shook her head, turning to follow her brother, but the sensation lingered, fuelling her growing uneasiness about the turn of their fortunes.

When they had finally found suitable rooms, Sydony unpacked some clean linens and made up the beds. Kit was surprisingly helpful, although he jested about pursuing a life in service as an upstairs maid. Though her brother remained cheerful, Sydony knew he must be dismayed at the general condition of the house, which should have been prepared for their arrival by a staff set to greet them.

'No doubt the solicitor misunderstood our arrival date,' Sydony said to cheer him, though she wasn't so sure.

Surrounded by a few of her own possessions, Sydony settled in to sleep with the knowledge that Kit was right in the next room. And yet, the fact that they were the only two residents made the strange house seem preternaturally quiet, as did their location, far from any neighbours, known or unknown. Only the wind howled its welcome, keeping her awake long into the night and moving into her dreams, where unnatural Gothic settings shifted and transformed into her new home.

* * *

The silence woke her. At least that's how it seemed. Perhaps the foul wind had finally abated. More likely, it was the lack of the usual morning bustle, servants lighting fires and fixing breakfasts, that made Sydony blink confusedly. Here in her new surroundings, all was quiet, except for a faint whistling through the window frames.

For a long moment Sydony lay there as awareness seeped through her. In days past, Rose would be opening the curtains and chiding her to get up and join her father, who would be breakfasting over a book, and everything was as familiar to her as her own reflection. But those days were gone, and as pressure formed behind her eyes at that acknowledgement, Sydony blinked and sat up.

She had Kit and a home and was grateful for both. She even had windows without shutters in this new room of hers, Sydony thought with a smile, and she saw that the morning had dawned bright and clear. The events of the night seemed dreamlike now, a product of weariness and darkness and isolation. She was determined that today would be better, and she hurried through her toilet to go downstairs, only to find Kit already at the work table in the kitchen, eating what was left in the hamper.

'We need to find some chickens and steal their eggs,' he said, with his mouth full of cheese, and Sydony felt her heart swell. When he pushed a steaming bowl towards her, she leaned over to give him a kiss on the cheek.

'What's that for?' he asked, between forkfuls.

'Can't a sister give her brother a nice greeting?' Sydony asked.

'You're just glad that I found some tea,' Kit said.

'You know me too well,' Sydony said, reaching for the bowl. She could do without some things, but not her morning tea.

'How did you sleep?' Kit asked, and Sydony hesitated. No doubt her brother had snoozed like the proverbial log and would take personally any complaints that she had not.

'It is a bit peculiar, being so quiet,' Sydony said, as tactfully as possible.

'We'll get a new staff soon. Then it will sound more like home. And you won't have to cook for us,' Kit teased.

'I can cook quite well, thank you,' Sydony said, making a face. And it was true. Growing up without a mother, she had often shadowed the servants at their tasks and had learned enough to make do, if necessary. The sudden loss of her mother also had made Sydony aware of how quickly circumstances could change, and she became determined to fend for herself, whether in the kitchen or on horseback or behind the barrel of a pistol.

'Will we be able to afford enough servants to keep this up?' Sydony asked, taking in their new home with a wave of her hand.

'It is larger than I anticipated,' Kit said. Rising to his feet, he walked to the window as though concentrating on the grounds, not the house. Typical male. 'Well, we are to inherit some money, too, so I hope we can manage to run the place, as well as tidy it up a bit. We shall know more when the solicitor arrives.'

'*If* he arrives,' Sydony said.

'I've got to take Henry and Clarence to catch the mail coach in Oak's Hollow, which is where our man has his office, so I'll stop in and make sure he's planning on attending to business,' Kit said.

'And find out if he has the household goods we shipped ahead,' Sydony said. 'I'd hate to have Father's books go missing.'

Kit nodded, then grabbed up the coat he had slung over a chair and shrugged into it. 'Maybe you had better come along. I don't like leaving you here all alone.'

'Rubbish,' Sydony said. The answer was automatic, a response she had made countless times before to her brother, and yet she realized that the circumstances were different now. She was alone in a strange, empty house, with nothing but bleak moorland surrounding her.

'Fine, then,' Kit said, without glancing her way. 'I doubt that you'll have any trouble, but Grandfather's duelling pistols are up in the room I slept in.'

The offhand comment was not comforting, and Sydony opened her mouth to tell him that she might join him, after all. But he was already slamming the door behind him, leaving her to the dusty stillness. The companionable moment they had shared in their kitchen seemed all too brief, and even the room itself fell into shadow, as if a cloud had passed over the sun.

She could still reach Kit before he left, Sydony knew, and he would not mock her for joining him. However, a lifetime of keeping up with her brother and demanding her own independence made her loathe to give in to feminine fears, even if it meant defiantly staying in a house with enough peculiarities to make a Gothic heroine swoon.

Although Sydony wasn't the swooning type, she wondered whether she ought not try to catch up with her brother. Pushing back her chair, she slipped on her cloak and stepped outside, intending to call after Kit. She saw him striding toward the stables, but paused at her first real glimpse of her new surroundings.

Instead of neatly clipped lawns and tilled rolling hills, Sydony saw tall grass sadly in need of a trimming and barren moors rising into the distance. With a shudder, she turned round, in search of some pleasant aspect. There had to be a garden somewhere, she told herself, as she stepped along a weedy gravel path that led towards the rear of the house.

She had only taken a few steps when she saw something, a huge mass of dark green that made her pause. 'What is that?' she called at Kit, pointing.

'It's a maze,' Kit shouted, with a smile and a wave.

He continued on his way, and Sydony did not stop him. She was too busy looking ahead towards the maze. She'd heard of such things, of course, and had even seen a small one at the pleasure gardens near her old home, but the thought of owning one sent a quiver of delight up her spine. She hurried on until the path ended, then hesitated only briefly before lifting her hem and trudging into the damp grass.

As usual, she resented Kit's more sensible costume of breeches, boots and greatcoat. He had often told her that she could dress like a man for all he cared; though tempted, Sydony had never succumbed. She had been quite the tomboy when younger, trailing after Kit and his friends, determined to keep up. But over the years, she had come to realize that she was, by nature, different, and had tried to adopt more seemly behaviour. It was not too difficult, especially when her former companions revolted her with some masculine prank. She would never be content to sit and sew, but neither did she care to stride around in breeches, shearing sheep or shooting birds.

Although her slippers were already wet, Sydony continued walking until she reached the rear of the house. There, a crumbling terrace of sorts was surrounded by what had once been a garden. And behind it all, great dark hedges rose so high that they seemed to block out all else. Shivering at the sight, Sydony pulled her cloak tighter around her against a sudden chill in the air. The overgrown greenery held a certain allure that compelled her to seek out its secrets, yet at the same time, its wild, ominous aspect warned her away.

'Don't go in there!'

Sydony jumped at the sound of her very thoughts shouted aloud, but when she turned it was only Kit, calling to her from the path.

'You're liable to get lost, and we've got to meet the solicitor.'

Normally, his high-handed male order would make her bristle, but Sydony nodded in agreement. Still, her brother made no move to leave. Obviously, he was waiting for her to return to the house; with a sigh, she walked towards him.

'We'll have plenty of time to explore later. But business first,' he added, flashing her a grin.

Sydony nodded. There had been a time when she had been the more practical one, but now she was proud of him for taking on so much responsibility.

And just how practical was she? As she watched him leave, Sydony knew full well she ought to go with him. But now, there were more interesting things to investigate at Oakfield, including a maze that was situated behind the house, but could not be viewed from any of its windows.

Chapter Two

Sydony returned to the house with a new purpose. Soon she was searching each room that looked over the rear of the property, but every window was either shuttered or boarded over. Even the doors in the drawing room that led to the crumbling terrace had been blocked. She could wait until Kit returned, but was too impatient for a glimpse of what lay beyond the gardens. Although the maze was nothing except a mass of tall shrubbery at ground level, from higher up in the house, she should be able to view the pattern itself.

Turning on her heel, Sydony decided to look for a crowbar or some tool that she could use to pry free the wood panels. But when she reached the stairs, she remembered that last night Kit had pointed out battlements, rooftop outlooks that were not uncommon in medieval dwellings. A giddy excitement rushed through her at the prospect of standing above with the entire labyrinth laid out before her, its secrets finally revealed.

Although Sydony glanced about for a way upwards,

the main staircase did not resume its path, and a quick reconnoitre revealed no other steps. There had to be a way to reach the roof from inside the house, and such a stair should have an opening on every floor, yet all Sydony could find was a door that might or might not take her to the top. And it was locked.

Her new search for a key sent her back down to the ground floor, where she discovered two more locked doors. She was hot and dusty by the time she wandered into what looked like a library—without the books. The room was dark, heavily panelled and lined with shelves, but they were bare, much to Sydony's disappointment.

With a sigh, she told herself she had no time to read anyway. In fact, she ought to be cataloguing the contents of the house or taking a broom to it instead of chasing after phantoms. And, yet, as new owners, shouldn't she and Kit be able to view every facet of the building, including whatever was closed off?

With that thought in mind, Sydony renewed her search for keys and tugged at the drawers of a tall secretary that was one of the few furnishings in the room. At first glance, they appeared to contain only old letters and receipts. Still, she checked every nook and cranny, digging through the papers until her fingers brushed against metal. With a cry of delight, Sydony pulled out a ring of keys that had probably been carelessly tossed into the drawer.

She stood, intent upon hurrying upstairs at once, but fought against the compulsion. Logic dictated that she try the nearest doors first, so she sought out those on the ground floor. And if one opened on to a servants' stair that led all the way to the battlements, so much the better.

Unfortunately, it was not that simple. As Sydony stood in front of the first door, trying key after key, her impatience grew. But just as she was tempted to turn aside, she heard the click of the lock that heralded her success. Still, she had to struggle with the door, which seemed to have swollen in the wet weather. Putting all her weight behind her efforts, she leaned back and pulled until the heavy wood swung open with a banging and knocking sound that seemed to ring throughout the house.

Sydony peered into the gaping dark as the smell of cool, damp air greeted her. But just as she leaned forwards, something else rushed out of the blackness, and she fell back with a shriek. Even as she told herself that the thing was probably only a bird, her dislike of the other distinct possibility—that it was a bat—sent her running as far away as possible. Uncertain whether she was being pursued, Sydony raced through the rooms toward the front of the house, flung open the door, and, without even blinking, launched herself at the man who was standing there.

'Barto!'

Halted by his tall form, Sydony breathed his name against the soft lapel where she buried her face. A vague memory of security blossomed into a reassuring sense of safety. It was no wonder, for the hard body she clung to was as strong and solid as an oak. It smelled good, too, like horses and leather and something else. She had never noticed Barto's scent before, but then, she hadn't been this close to him in years.

And with that thought, Sydony realised just how stiffly her rescuer was standing beneath her grip, his chin lifted and his arms rigid at his sides. Far from giving her comfort, he was uncomfortable himself, a discovery that sent embarrassment knifing through her. Sydony stepped back, away from him. Yet even as she loosed her hold, Sydony felt a pang, as though she were letting go of something vital and precious.

Or perhaps one night in this medieval monstrosity had completely unhinged her mind. It had certainly affected her behaviour. Trying to regain her good sense, Sydony drew a deep breath of autumn air that bespoke recent rain and dead leaves, instead of Bartholomew Hawthorne.

'Pardon me,' she said, though her behaviour was unpardonable. It might have been accepted, or at least tolerated when she was a small girl tagging after her brother and his best friend. But that friend had drifted away and had grown into a man. And not just any man, mind you, but a lord of the realm: Viscount Hawthorne.

Sydony could feel her face flame. 'Something gave me a fright, a bird probably,' she muttered. But even as she spoke, she knew how ridiculous that must sound to someone who had once known her well. She had been resolutely fearless in her younger years, and now she was running from a bird?

Barto's cool gaze flicked over her, making Sydony raise a hand to her hair. *Something* had flown at her, for it was in disarray that no amount of surreptitious smoothing could remedy. Under her visitor's impassionate scrutiny, she realised just how unkempt she must appear. Her simple day gown was mussed and dirty, and smudges marred her skin. All she needed was an apron to complete her impersonation of a scullery

maid. Still, there was no need for Barto to look at her
in such a condescending fashion. Stung, Sydony raised
her chin.

'What are you doing here?' she asked baldly.

Instead of appearing dismayed by the question, Barto
simply lifted a dark brow, as though remarking on her
poor manners. When had he become so aloof? Sydony
wondered. Even more disconcerting, when had he
become so attractive? Barto had always been handsome,
but then, so was Kit. Girls had always gaped at them,
but Sydony had taken little notice. Until now.

Had he grown into his face, maturing into this masculine beauty, or had familiarity blinded her to his
looks? If so, that familiarity was long gone. Sydony had
seen him at her father's funeral and at his father's, as
well, but only for brief moments, and before that, it had
been years since she and her brother had spent long,
careless days in his company.

He was tall now, towering over her, despite her own
height, and his shoulders were wide. His deep brown
hair was burnished and well cut, although a little too
long to be fashionable. But it was his face, at once
known and yet different, that made Sydony's heart beat
faster. Unfortunately, its dark perfection was marred
by the mocking tilt of his lips, which told her he was
well aware of her study.

'My mother said that you had moved. She misses
you, of course, and was naturally concerned that your
new home be as you'd hoped,' he said, finally, in answer
to her question.

'Well, it isn't,' Sydony said, irritated by the glint in
his eye. Barto probably knew all too well just how

handsome he was, and she refused to flatter him with any further study.

'The residence is deserted, with no staff at all, so we could hardly provide the hospitality to which you are accustomed, *my lord Viscount*,' Sydony noted. She had intended to scorn his fine title, but the oddness of addressing Barto by his father's name took the force from her words.

Barto's dark brows lowered, and Sydony remembered his temper, although she saw no crack in his elegant façade. 'I assure you that I am not made of spun sugar,' he said, coolly. 'Nor will I melt away without the benefit of luxuries.'

Sydony doubted that. Once upon a time, she had fed this man mud pies, but now he was used to the best of everything, and she could not even offer him biscuits. If she had seen some hint of her former companion, Sydony would have given little thought to the change in circumstances, but there was no warmth in this meeting. And if he treated her so coldly, what if he looked down his aristocratic nose at Kit, flush with excitement over his property?

'I'm sorry, Ba—my lord,' Sydony swiftly amended. 'We are not at home to visitors, as yet. But do give your mother my greatest regards and tell her that we are well and arrived safely.'

Sydony tendered a terse smile, but Barto obviously would not be dismissed on the threshold like some tradesman. Again, though the exterior remained unchanged, Sydony saw the flash in those dark eyes, and she was tempted to shut the door, rather than face his displeasure. Yet she stood her ground, her own temper flaring at the untenable position he had put her in. A gentleman would take her rebuff with good grace.

But Barto had never been a gentleman.

Well mannered when he chose, he was too used to getting his own way to have the natural charm of someone like Kit. And right now the set of his mouth made her suspect he was going to argue with her, rather than give way. She was wondering how on earth to get rid of him when the decision was taken out of her hands.

Indeed, they had been so intent upon each other that neither one had noticed Kit's approach. But now Sydony heard the sound of a team driven a little too fast. No doubt Kit was concerned to see her alone with a visitor, for he slowed as soon as he neared Barto's coach, the crest clearly visible. Jumping down from the carriage, he bounded up the walkway with an grin of delight. Sydony tried to catch his eye, to warn him against effusive greetings, but it was too late.

'Barto!' Kit exclaimed, reaching out to thump the new viscount on the back in the friendly gesture of boon companions. 'This is a welcome surprise!'

Good-natured Kit probably took no notice, but Sydony saw the stiffness in Barto's stance, as well as his blank expression, and she bristled. If he had no intention of pursuing an old acquaintance, then why did he not take his leave? Surely his mother would demand no more.

'I'd invite you to stay, but I'm afraid we're a bit at sixes and sevens here,' Kit said.

'So your sister explained.'

'But I stopped by the solicitor's, and he is to follow

shortly,' Kit said, turning to Sydony. 'I insisted he come out here as I didn't want to leave you alone any longer than necessary.'

Barto shot her a strange look. 'You were here alone?'

'I told you the place was deserted,' Sydony snapped.

A dark brow lifted, perhaps a signal of astonishment; in the world of Viscount Hawthorne, 'deserted' probably meant a staff of twenty.

Ignoring the exchange, just as he had their past squabbles, Kit continued, 'And he has the household goods we sent on ahead, which he didn't think should be stored here.'

'Certainly not when the door is open to all and sundry,' Sydony said.

'And you here alone,' Barto said, his lips curving downwards. He eyed Sydony in a manner that disconcerted her, but went unnoticed by her brother.

'Ah, well, you know these country folks,' Kit said, with a shrug. He turned to Barto. 'Come in. I'm afraid we can't offer you anything, but you must see the palatial estate since you are here.'

Not trusting herself to witness Barto's disdain, Sydony hurried off to make herself more presentable. She refused to change her gown, but she shook out the skirt, washed off the smudges, and fixed her hair. It would have to do.

Exiting her room, Sydony found the two men before the locked door on the first floor. 'See here, Syd,' Kit said. 'We were hoping this might lead up to the battlements,' he added, although Barto looked as though he harboured no such desire.

Having been distracted by the viscount since his

arrival, Sydony abruptly remembered her earlier preoccupation with the maze, and her excitement returned. 'I found a set of keys,' she said, pulling the ring from her pocket with a flourish.

Barto raised a dark brow yet again, which probably meant her enthusiasm was unladylike. But Sydony ignored him and turned to her brother. 'In fact, I had begun to try them on the locked doors when a bat flew out of the cellar at me.'

Aware of her irrational fear, Kit eyed her closely. 'Are you all right?' he asked, having long since stopped tormenting her with creatures, both real and fake.

'Yes. Luckily, our guest arrived to rescue me,' Sydony said, her tone laced with sarcasm. She declined to elaborate on the circumstances, which could only cause her renewed embarrassment. But, hopefully, Barto realised that she had not run into his arms in avid greeting or with hopes of pursuing their acquaintance.

While the two men watched, Sydony began trying the keys in the lock, one by one, but none fit. 'How odd,' she murmured, struck once more by the peculiarities of their new home.

Meanwhile, Kit took the ring from her and attempted the task himself, in the manner of males everywhere. Since brute strength was not required, Sydony thought his efforts wasted, but said nothing. After all, he was her brother and much beloved.

'The place has been shut up for a long time,' he noted, when his attempts failed, as well. 'For all we know, some rooms might be blocked off for a reason.'

'Such as an infestation of bats?' Sydony suggested.

Kit grinned, but she didn't bother to glance at Barto, whose circle probably outlawed smiles as beneath them.

'The solicitor will have a full set,' Kit said, handing the ring back to her.

'Not if it's the same one he used to lock up the house.'

As usual, Kit ignored her dry comment, but Barto gave her a studied look. Perhaps, if she truly offended his arrogant sensibilities, he would leave. Momentarily diverted, Sydony considered ways in which to do so, but she was hard pressed to come up with something worse than what she had already done—running into his arms to clutch at him like a long-lost lover.

Lover? Sydony froze. She had no idea why that word came to mind. She had run to him just as she would have her brother or her father or perhaps even the younger version of Barto—for comfort from a fright. Any other interpretation was ludicrous.

Her face suddenly flushed, Sydony turned and headed down the staircase. To her relief, when she reached the open area, the solicitor had arrived, and she had a good excuse to avoid her old neighbour as she and Kit adjourned to the library.

As Kit led them inside, Sydony glanced curiously at Mr Sparrowhawk, who looked more like a sparrow than a hawk, except perhaps for his large hook nose. Otherwise, he was small and bony and rather drab. He also appeared to be nervous, his dark little eyes behind spectacles darting about, as if he expected something to jump out of the shadows towards him at any moment.

Maybe he knew about the bats.

Sitting down on the very edge of a straight-backed chair, his hands clutching the satchel in his lap, the solicitor cleared his throat. 'Well, obviously, you found the place without any problem,' he said.

Or assistance, Sydony wanted to add.

'As I made clear in our correspondence, as your father's son and heir, you, Mr Marchant, are now the owner of the property of Oakfield, which includes a manor house, stables, various outbuildings, gardens, orchards and a substantial amount of acreage, formerly in the possession of one Elspeth Marchant. Here is a complete list, as well as the various accounts available to you.'

The solicitor presented papers for Kit's signature, impatiently tapping a finger while her brother read through them all. He seemed intent upon concluding his business rapidly; when he gathered up the documents, Sydony leaned forwards.

'Do you have a set of keys for us?' she asked.

Mr Sparrowhawk looked startled, whether by the question or Sydony's presence, she could not guess.

'The building was unlocked and unattended when we arrived, and since you are holding some of our goods, I thought you might have a set of keys, as well,' she explained.

'I do,' he replied, as if her words had reminded him of the fact. Reaching into his satchel, he handed over a heavy ring to Kit, seeming glad to be rid of it.

Mr Sparrowhawk then cleared his throat. 'I apologise for missing your arrival,' he said. 'I'm afraid I confused the time.' He glanced down, as though unable to look at them, and Sydony wondered just how successful the man could be.

'And the servants?'

Mr Sparrowhawk eyed his knuckles intently. 'I did make an effort to find you some staff, but without knowledge of your circumstances and needs, I hesitated to—'

Sydony cut him off. 'We need someone immediately, Mr Sparrowhawk, two housemaids, at least, and a cook.'

'And a groomsman,' Kit added.

'It is a rather remote location,' the solicitor muttered, shaking his head.

'But I assume it was staffed before? What happened to the former employees?' Sydony asked.

Mr Sparrowhawk frowned. 'I'm not certain, but I shall make inquiries.'

'As well as send on the rest of our household goods?'

He nodded tersely, moved even closer to the edge of his chair, as though anxious to make his escape, then paused. 'I do have some other business to present to you,' he said. 'As your solicitor, I am bound to report that I have received an offer on the property.'

Sydony's opinion of the man rose immediately. If someone was interested in the house, she and Kit might take the money from the sale and return home, or at least to their old neighbourhood, where they could buy or lease something else. Sydony leaned forwards, hardly daring to hope, but when Mr Sparrowhawk named an amount, she slumped in her seat.

'Why, that's not half the worth of the house, let alone the property,' Kit said.

'Yes, well, I am only reporting it.'

'Perhaps if we formally put the place up for sale, we might get a more reasonable offer,' Sydony suggested, without glancing at Kit.

Mr Sparrowhawk cleared his throat. 'As you can see, Oakfield isn't quite what it used to be. And yet, as you say, it is still worth a goodly amount. But there aren't many buyers around here with that kind of money.' His bony hands gripped the satchel tightly.

There was something he wasn't saying, Sydony could tell. 'Is there anything wrong with the house?'

The solicitor appeared flustered by the direct question. 'Well, um, there are many old stories, as I'm sure you'll hear. I wouldn't pay them any mind. You are young and just may turn the place around.'

'From what?' Sydony asked.

She could hear Kit stir beside her. 'From a bit of neglect, which I'm sure we can remedy,' he said, his firm tone obviously meant to silence her.

Sydony ignored it. 'Can you tell me why all the windows facing the gardens have been secured, either with boards or shutters that have been nailed shut?'

Mr Sparrowhawk's beady eyes looked as though they might pop from his head, and for a moment Sydony thought he would not answer at all. But after a long pause, he cleared his throat. 'Did you know Miss Marchant well?' he asked.

Sydony shook her head. They had rarely seen their father's Aunt Elspeth, though she sent them religious tracts, rather…well…religiously on their birthdays.

'She seemed a very pious woman,' Kit noted.

'Yes. Quite devout,' Mr. Sparrowhawk said, looking down at his hands. 'But she was also getting on in years and developed some peculiar notions.'

Sydony eyed the man expectantly.

He lifted a finger to loosen his collar. 'Yes, well, as

to the windows, I understand that Miss Marchant didn't care for the maze. She claimed she saw lights bobbing about in it and did not want to look upon it. She was a superstitious woman.'

'But why would she be superstitious of a maze?' Kit asked, obviously bewildered.

'As I said, she developed some peculiar notions,' the solicitor repeated. 'I understand that she thought someone was breaking into the house, though she reported no thefts. And there was talk of her wanting to burn all the books, though I don't know whether she did or not.'

With that, Mr Sparrowhawk stood, apparently having said all he intended on the subject. 'Now, if you will excuse me, I have other business to conduct this after-noon.'

He slipped out of the library quite neatly, but was prevented from reaching the door by Barto, who stood as though waiting for an introduction.

The change that came over the bird-like fellow at the mention of Barto's title annoyed Sydony, even though she should have expected as much. In childhood, there had been little distinction among the three companions, except for their treatment by some of the servants. But now the gulf between them was obvious as the formerly reticent solicitor fawned over Barto in a manner Sydony could only term sickening.

'Mr Marchant was just showing me through his new acquisition, but since you were in charge of the estate, I'm sure you'll want to go through the house with him to make sure that all is as it should be,' Barto said.

Mr Sparrowhawk looked as though he would like

nothing less, but dared not refuse a viscount. And so all four of them began trudging through the residence, the solicitor glancing over his shoulder as though expecting someone else to appear. A member of the non-existent staff, perhaps? Sydony was beginning to wonder whether prolonged association with Oakfield directly affected the mind.

Her own was a muddle of annoyance with the general state of things, worry over staffing the large house, and homesickness. Drawing a deep breath, she tried to clear her thoughts as she followed after them, listening to Barto ask the questions of a knowledgeable property owner.

Just when the solicitor seemed on the verge of escape, the viscount held him up with another pointed question concerning the dearth of servants. Red-faced and bowing, Mr Sparrowhawk dutifully promised to send someone out immediately.

'Very good. I shall hold you personally responsible, then?' Barto asked, in a tone that Sydony barely recognised as his. It was not loud or forceful, but ripe with the expectation of having his wishes fulfilled. Unsaid, but implicit, was the promise of swift and merciless retribution, should he not be obeyed.

That silent vow she remembered from her childhood, as his will and her stubbornness had often clashed. Not without her own resources, Sydony's revenge had often involved public embarrassment of the young peer, the recollection of which made her flush with mortification.

Now, however, she was sullenly grateful for his expertise. There was no denying that Barto got things done. He had power, but that was not all of it. He was more determined than Kit, who had a casual outlook on life. Why demand a trip through the house? her brother would ask, if she pressed him. What did it matter? It really didn't, but still, she was grateful to the viscount.

Anyone who could find her servants was someone to be reckoned with. But why had Barto gone out of his way to help them? Sydony could not think it kindness that drove him or even any pledge to his mother. What, then?

As if reading her mind, he turned toward her and Kit. 'I'll have my groomsmen stable the horses. And my valet can ready a room, with your permission?'

Sydony could only gape while Kit agreed.

'You're staying?' she said.

Barto nodded, a dark brow lifting at her question.

'But there isn't any staff or foodstuffs!'

'Actually, I did bring some supplies in from the village,' Kit said, turning to follow Mr Sparrowhawk out the door.

Sydony was left standing with a smug-looking Barto. The curve of those full lips was slight, but enough to remind her of his small victories over her in their youth. Sydony's eyes narrowed. 'Very well. I hope you are comfortable, *my lord*,' she said.

'Surely it can be no worse than the time we spent lost in the wilds of Sherwood Forest,' he said, that lovely mouth quirking at the corner.

Sydony blinked, first in confusion, and then with recognition as the long-forgotten incident returned to her mind. That was when Barto was going through his Robin Hood spell. Having read all that he could upon the subject, he gathered his small band together for excursions into the vast tracts of wood that were part of his birthright.

Sydony never wanted to be Maid Marian, so she took up a variety of roles, including Friar Tuck. That day, Kit had twisted his ankle, and so Little John had limped home, but Barto and Sydony had gone on. He had dared her to follow, and she would not refuse a challenge.

He never admitted they were lost, of course. And when darkness fell, he made them a bed of leaves and told her that this time she was Maid Marian, captured and forced to spend the night with the brigands, but she was not to worry as he would keep her safe. And Sydony had never felt so secure as with the boy she fought with and tagged after, unwanted.

Suddenly, Sydony wanted to weep for that boy and for a sweet memory that the man he was now had ruined. But she would not allow how much it had meant to her, would not give him that further triumph, and so she again blinked, banishing the moisture that threatened her eyes.

'Indeed, for at least we shall have a roof over our heads,' she said. The words came out brittle and hoarse, with more emotion than she intended. And just as if they were children again, Sydony was seized with an urge to push him hard for his taunt. She could happily imagine knocking him to the stone floor, his elegant garb damaged along with his pride.

But, besides the fact that she was too old for such behaviour, Sydony suspected that he would not be so easy to move these days. And something else made her wary of touching him again, something that ran far deeper than her battered emotions: a fear that this time she might not let go.

Chapter Three

Bartholomew Hawthorne, sixth Viscount Hawthorne, waited until his former neighbour was well out of sight before slipping off to the stables, where he found Hob keeping watch. Ostensibly, Hob was a groomsman, but his expertise went far beyond handling horses. His shadowy background of pugilism and military service, rumoured to include some spying for his Majesty's government, was just what Barto wanted after recent events.

'Well, my lord?' Hob asked, from a darkened corner of the old stables.

'Well, indeed,' Barto said, looking around at the building that was even more neglected than the house. 'Would you like a room in the servants' quarters, though I dare say they aren't much better?'

'No. I'd prefer to keep to myself, me and Jack,' Hob said, referring to the man who was sorting through some old tack. Jack had been part of the hire, as Hob didn't want anyone else aware of his movements. 'Did you find out anything?'

'Not much,' Barto said. 'If they've come into a fortune, it certainly isn't visible.'

'Hmm. The fellow's an open sort. What about the lady?'

Barto thought about Sydony with something akin to chagrin, a sensation that rarely visited him. Of course, he had stepped out of the bounds of good taste by mentioning the night he had spent with her, no matter how young they had been at the time. But the look on her face when he mentioned that night had startled him. He had not meant to draw blood with the reference, merely prove that he could survive without the usual comforts.

'She seems to think I can't do without my luxuries,' Barto said, a tinge of asperity creeping into his voice. Did she think him a pampered, fat, titled buffoon, like the Prince Regent himself? The contempt lurking in her green eyes had managed to pierce his usual aplomb, making him want to respond in kind.

But the contempt hadn't always been there. When she rushed from the house, Barto had seen a flash of surprised recognition and pleasure before she threw herself at him. For a moment, the years melted away, and Barto knew an urge to gather her to him and weep—both with the joy of reunion and with a grief that he had not even revealed to his mother.

The feelings were wholly unexpected, but when Sydony Marchant put her arms around him, Barto wanted nothing more than to lose himself in her embrace. It had taken all his discipline not to keep her close, but his will had held. He was thankful for that discipline when he considered what had followed: a complete turn of mood that culminated in her apparent disapproval of his plans.

'It could be that she doesn't want me to stay here,' Barto mused aloud.

'Any idea why?'

Barto shook his head. She had turned and stalked away without the slightest attempt at gracious excuses, leaving him to watch the slight sway of her hips, a sure indication that Sydony Marchant had grown up. Although he had glimpsed her at the funerals, he'd been too sunk in his own misery to notice. But now, in much closer quarters, the changes were very apparent.

Sydony had always been boyish, a smaller, more delicate version of Kit. Although she was still slender, she could not be mistaken for a lad with those round breasts, gently curved hips, and that luxurious mop of hair. Mop was right, as her tomboyish ways still left her looking more dishevelled than any proper female should. So why did he feel a sudden interest in seeing her even more dishevelled?

Barto frowned at the thought, which he found both repugnant and vaguely incestuous. Although they had no blood ties, a childhood spent in close contact with Sydony Marchant made her seem like a relation, which would explain his fury over her being here alone and unprotected.

He glanced at Hob. 'Did you find anyone else around?'

'No, sir. Not a soul, and it looks like the place has been abandoned for a while.'

Had Barto known of their solitude when she threw her arms about him… But he hadn't, and he had been chased by too many females intent upon the promise of a comfortable living and a title not to wonder whether

Sydony would presume upon their old acquaintance to secure her future. The idea seemed laughable now, after the abrupt change in her attitude, but what had caused the change? His failure to return her embrace? Kit's arrival? His subsequent plans to stay? Or was it something more sinister?

Barto's expression hardened at the reminder of his mission, and he turned his full attention to Hob. 'We're going to need some help…'

To Sydony's surprise, they soon had more supplies and the crates that had been shipped ahead, as well as a cook, a maid and a man to help with unloading, lifting and general repairs. Throughout the afternoon and evening, Sydony hurried from one task to another, consulting with the new servants and doing what she could to make the place more presentable, but her mind kept drifting back to one thing. And it wasn't the maze.

Try as she might to dismiss him from her mind, Barto lingered in her awareness, drawing her attention like a nasty boil of which she could not be rid. It seemed that everything she did made her consider his reaction, which only annoyed her further. She was torn between her desire to improve the house, so that he not disparage it, and a wish that he be as uncomfortable as possible, so that he would leave.

Even Sydony recognised the impulses as contradictory.

She acknowledged that the manor had begun to look better already. Cleaning and airing and light did much to improve the place, though Kit would not hear of removing the ivy that clung to the exterior. He claimed the vines added character, while Sydony thought they just made the building dark and eerie.

Barto said nothing. For Kit's sake, Sydony had hoped that the easy familiarity that once existed between the neighbours would return, but that had not happened. The friendship of two boys who seemed to share each other's thoughts had been replaced by a mannered distance imposed by Barto.

He stalked around the their home with a coldness and arrogance that Sydony found unbearable. Although she told herself that she was outraged on Kit's behalf, she was more angry with herself, for noticing the man at all.

Indeed, far from cheering her, the presence of their former neighbour seemed only to heighten the sensation of being cut off from all she knew, the servants, friends and villagers, the country dances and small social pleasures of her former life. Although remotely situated in their new location, Sydony was surprised they had received no invitations from the local gentry or welcoming visits from neighbours. But for Mr. Sparrowhawk and the arrival of the servants, it was as if the Marchants were alone.

And now, as they sat in the hastily cleaned dining hall, Barto's presence cast a pall over the table, making her tense and aware of all her shortcomings, or, rather, the *house*'s shortcomings.

Oblivious to any undercurrents, Kit chatted away about the place, while Barto contributed his opinions. To Sydony's surprise, he appeared to be very knowledgeable about managing property. When had he come to care about drainage and tenant farmers and enclosure laws? Although he probably could use all that information to run the family seat, she thought he'd lost all interest in his future responsibilities when he went off to school. Were the rumours of him being sunk in dissipations in London just that, ill-founded gossip?

'Are you living at Hawthorne Park, then?' she asked.

Barto's dark gaze skimmed over her, as though he had forgotten her very existence. 'Yes. I have been home for some time.'

His cursory response irked her, and Sydony was tempted to ask why he had not paid them a visit before they moved. But the maid entered the room at that moment with another course.

'The cook is to be commended,' Kit said, as he dug into a piece of boiled beef. He was happy with simple fare and lots of it. Although he was nearly as tall as Barto, Sydony swore he was still growing. 'I think she will do nicely for us.'

'But she won't stay above a month,' Sydony said. 'She is moving away to live with her daughter.' Or, at least, that's what she had told Sydony when pressed. The woman was terse and uncommunicative, so Sydony could only hope for someone more agreeable in the future.

'Have you talked with all of them, the new servants?' Barto asked.

'Of course,' Sydony said. Did he think her a useless henwit? Or did he imagine that Kit had suddenly developed an interest in running a household? As the sole female, she had been in charge of their home for years.

Barto did not glance her way when she answered, but looked to Kit. 'It appears that Mr Sparrowhawk was not exaggerating his difficulties, for they seem rather reluctant to be here.'

'The servants?' Kit asked, with a look of surprise.

Sydony frowned. 'That is not true. The maid is fresh and eager for her first position.'

'Perhaps because she does not know the house, but the other two are less enthusiastic,' Barto said.

Sydony blinked at him. Had he always been so obnoxious, or had he acquired the habit when living in London? Perhaps it was his newly elevated rank that made him an expert on every subject, even her own staff.

'I don't know about the cook or the maid, but I talked to the fellow, Newton, and he did seem a bit peculiar,' Kit admitted. 'When I said we needed someone to clear brush, he was quite adamant in refusing any outside work.'

'Perhaps he has an aversion to fresh air,' Sydony said.

Barto ignored her jibe, as though she hadn't spoken. 'Apparently, there's some sort of history to the house, but I can't discover exactly what. No one is very talkative.'

Although Barto's words confirmed her own suspicions, Sydony did not want him ruining Kit's pride of ownership with vague insinuations. 'I think I should appreciate a house that has been talked about,' she said.

'Most definitely, especially if there is a delicious scandal attached,' Kit said with a wicked grin. 'Perhaps an illicit affair.'

Sydony nearly choked at the thought of Great-aunt Elspeth being involved in something so tawdry, but she fell in with the spirit of the moment. 'I think I would prefer a duel,' she suggested.

'Or orgies along the lines of the Devil's Club.'

'Kit!' Sydony sputtered in shock, while her brother laughed at her outrage. But Barto didn't join in the play. Apparently, he was too dignified to engage in such silliness, because he looked annoyed, if not affronted, by their amusement. But he said nothing further on the history of the house, and Sydony was glad when the conversation veered in another direction.

She couldn't help wondering just what Barto had discovered, but even if there were some sort of story to the house, what could they do about it? They could not sell, except at a great loss, so they must live here and make the best of it.

And they did have the maze, Sydony thought as she remembered the mysterious labyrinth that Aunt Elspeth had so disliked. Suddenly, Sydony wondered if the hired man's aversion to exterior jobs had any relation to the overgrown hedges behind the house. At the thought, she drew in a sharp breath, and was glad to see that her brother was too deep in conversation with Barto to notice. Of course, if she suggested such a thing, Kit would say her imagination was running wild, a result of reading too many Gothic novels. But didn't they always have a dark, mysterious villain?

Sydony glanced surreptitiously at Barto. Handsome, cool and stiffly polite, he was too elegant and collected to qualify. No doubt, he would be at ease even in the finest circles, which made her wonder what was he doing in their dining hall. Why did he insist on staying? And why would a nobleman concern himself with another's servants at all, let alone question them about the house he was visiting?

Sydony frowned, unable to piece together the puzzle that was Viscount Hawthorne, but she had the feeling, just as she'd had with the solicitor, that there was something their old friend wasn't saying.

Although it was late by the time Sydony heard Kit come to bed, she drew him into her room for a private conversation, their first real chance to talk since he had left the house this morning. Pulling him over to a seat by the windows, she listened as he spoke enthusiastically about his plans for the property and Barto's suggestions. But at the mention of the new viscount, Sydony studied her brother closely.

'Don't you think it odd that he arrived here immediately after we did when he hasn't approached us for years?' she asked.

'No,' Kit said. Leaning back in the upholstered chair, he crossed his arms behind his head and stretched out his long legs. 'He's been busy. And you heard him—his mother had only just informed him of our move.'

'But common courtesy requires that a visitor, especially an uninvited one, wait until their hosts are settled into the new residence.'

Kit grinned. 'I'm afraid that men don't think along those lines. And since when are you a stickler for etiquette?'

'I'm not,' Sydony said. 'But Viscount Hawthorne should be, given his vaunted position in society.'

'He's human, Syd, just like he's always been,' Kit countered.

'And how would we know what he is now or has

been over these past years? We saw little enough of him once he went off to Eton, to be among his own.'

Kit snorted. 'He had no choice, Syd. He wasn't blessed with a father who held the public school system in contempt, like we were. I was lucky to be tutored at home, rather than be tormented by older boys and sadistic men with little or no interest in teaching.'

Sydony glanced at him sharply. 'What? Is that what Barto endured? Did he tell you so?'

Kit shrugged, obviously unwilling to share a confidence. 'It's what everyone endures and why Father took our studies upon himself.'

'Beyond his own love of scholarship,' Sydony noted, with a smile. She *was* grateful for their father's habits, which had given her the opportunity to learn more than most females.

'I suppose that you saw him more often than I did,' Sydony mused.

'Who? Barto?' Kit asked.

Sydony nodded, but Kit only shrugged again. She knew that they had sought each other's company often enough when younger, devising ways to exclude her. And they probably had continued the practice long after she stopped chasing after them.

'When I did chance upon him, he seemed so much older. Harder,' Sydony mused.

'He was always more mature,' Kit said. 'From birth he had the responsibility of nobility hanging over his head. That vast estate and the people it supports were always destined to be his, and it weighed upon him.'

Sydony looked up in surprise once more, but Kit

appeared uncomfortable. 'I hardly saw him in the later years, either,' he added.

Sydony frowned. 'Yes, I imagine he had other pursuits.' They had heard of wild times in London and his mother's concern for his future. But now she wondered just how much of it was true.

Again, Kit snorted. 'Well, they seem to have done him no harm.'

Sydony refused to admit that Barto bore no ill effects from any sordid adventures. 'No, they appear only have made him more arrogant.'

'Lud, Syd, what have you got against the fellow? He's always had his duty hanging over him, and he never seemed pleased about the prospect.'

'He looks eager enough now to play the lord.'

Kit threw up his hands in exasperation and stood.

'I just think his sudden desire to visit is odd, that's all,' Sydony said.

'You think everything is odd,' her brother called over his shoulder.

'If I do, it's because…everything here is,' Sydony whispered, though Kit was already closing the door.

She nearly called him back, but the knowledge that he was weary after their long day kept her silent. With his exit, the night drew in around her, and Sydony felt a sudden pang of loneliness. She tried to dismiss it as she prepared for bed, for, were she at her former home, she would still be by herself. No one would be joining her here in the darkness.

Yet her father had always been available, like as not nodding over a book in his study at all hours. The servants were well liked and of long standing, though she would not have disturbed their rest. And there were her friends and neighbours, who sometimes shared extended visits. Of course, Molly was married now, as was Eliza, but Sydony had remained close to them until the move. Theirs was a small set, not polished or grand in the manner of Viscount Hawthorne's London circle.

Thoughts of her unwanted guest made Sydony feel even more bereft, for she found herself missing the boy she had once known, replaced now by a stiff and arrogant nobleman. She swallowed a lump in her throat as she remembered his earlier taunt about Sherwood Forest.

Not only was she far from her home and all that was familiar, but this stranger was ruining treasured memories of her childhood. Crawling into bed, Sydony turned on her side and finally let herself weep for all that was lost.

During the long hours until morning Sydony tossed and turned through distressing dreams in which huge hedges walled her in and Barto stood by, doing nothing to help her. She woke up gasping for breath, having buried herself under the covers, but she swung out of bed, determined to avoid another night of such torment.

Today she would satisfy her curiosity about the maze, once and for all. The mysterious greenery couldn't haunt her sleep if she faced it in the daylight. She had the ring of keys from the solicitor, as well as a workman to remove the shutters that barred her view. Either way, she was going to see the source of her curiosity, and, by doing so, put it to rest.

Sydony's heart picked up its pace as she headed down to the dining hall, eager to tackle the secret of the labyrinth. Hurrying into the room, Sydony startled Kit by demanding the keys without preamble. Caught with a mouthful of breakfast, he pointed soundlessly toward the library, where she found her brother had piled the papers that Mr Sparrowhawk had given him.

Muttering to herself at the habits of men, Sydony gathered them together, lest they become mixed in with the stacks of old receipts and miscellany that were already crowding the secretary. Then she snatched up the ring and headed back up the staircase, nearly running into Barto, who was descending, elegant as always—thanks to his valet, no doubt.

Thanks were surely due someone, Sydony thought, for Barto was a sight to behold. He didn't dress like some of the peacocks she had seen on her rare visits to London, but with an understated sophistication that made him look…well, beautiful. For some reason, Sydony's pulse started pounding at that revelation, but the mocking lift of one of his dark brows quickly brought it back to normal.

'Pardon me,' Sydony said as she hurried past him. Better she be obsessed with the maze than her old neighbour, no matter how handsome he had become. Pushing Barto firmly from her mind, Sydony reached the door on the first floor and tried the new set of keys, her excitement growing with each attempt. But, just like yesterday, none of those on the ring worked the lock. In disbelief, Sydony went through each another time, to no avail.

Thwarted once more, she could do nothing except return to the dining hall, where Barto had joined her brother. His greeting at her entrance was perfunctory, and again, she wondered just why he was here. Perhaps he would leave today, Sydony thought with a mixture of pleasure and vague disappointment. If she were disappointed, she told herself, it was only because the reasons for his visit would remain a mystery.

As she filled her plate, Sydony considered the possibility that he might be hiding from someone—a pack of creditors, perhaps. The new viscount might have amassed gambling debts from his forays to London, and who would look for him here?

This new theory made him seem the villain of her nightmares, and she studied him closely as she took her seat. Would he lift a finger to aid her, if needed? Thankfully, she would never be in a position to find out.

A sharp glance from the subject of her scrutiny made Sydony lift her fork and turn to Kit. 'I shall require your man today.'

'Sorry, but you can't have him,' Kit said as he stood to fill another plate. 'I'm setting him about repairing some loose boards in the library. It looks as though someone tore up the floor at some point.'

'What?'

Kit shrugged, as if to admit that nothing about Oakfield Manor made sense.

'But I was hoping to get those shutters taken down,' Sydony protested.

A look from Kit told her he did not deem her fascination with the rear of the property as important as a dangerous stretch of flooring. He was right, of course, and yet Sydony felt a growing urgency to investigate the maze. Perhaps she ought to just go out there and try to wind her way through it? Excitement surged through her at the thought, but one glance at the windows, where a steady rain beat against the panes, made her change her mind.

'None of the keys will open the locked door on the upper story, so I cannot get up there,' she complained.

'Perhaps the battlements are closed off for some reason,' Kit said.

'Mr Sparrowhawk said nothing of it.'

Kit snorted. 'The man said nothing of anything unless Barto wormed it out of him.'

'Since we did not go up there during our inspection of the house, maybe you should contact him,' Barto said. 'It could be dangerous.'

Sydony frowned. No doubt he was too sophisticated to share her interest in a mere garden maze.

'You mean that someone might have fallen from the roof? That could give rise to your ill rumours about the house. You know how accidents make people nervous,' Kit said.

'The battlements might be crumbling, but, no, I don't think that's the sort of thing that would cause such talk,' Barto said.

'Well, I'd send a note round to Sparrowhawk, if I could spare my man. I wish he would send more prospects out here. I must have a groomsman. Perhaps I'll ride into the village later.'

'Don't bother. I'll send one of my men with a note,' Barto said, and Kit nodded in gratitude.

'Surely the floor won't take all day. Perhaps he can help me with a few of the shutters when you are finished,' Sydony said.

Kit shook his head. 'Your obsession will have to wait, Syd.'

Sydony could not blame him. Still, she felt a sharp sense of disappointment. Perhaps it would clear off later, enough for her to…

'May I be of service to you?'

Sydony's head jerked at the sound of Barto's voice, so smooth, so deep and so unexpected. Her pulse pounded again, inexplicably, as she realised just what he had said. 'I beg you pardon?'

'The shutters. Can I help you with them?'

Sydony smiled at the thought of the elegant nobleman toiling like a commoner. 'Well, perhaps you could volunteer another one of your groomsmen, as it will involve some labour.'

Barto lifted one dark brow in mocking question. The man was insufferable, Sydony decided. 'But if you are intent upon doing it yourself, you will need some tool to pry them open, for they are all nailed shut.' Although she expected him to demure, once again, Barto surprised her.

'I'm sure I can find something to use,' he said. The dark look he sent her was a challenge, and one Sydony remembered well from her childhood. In those days, she would have returned his bold gaze, rising to whatever dare he put to her.

But now she shivered, her pulse racing once again. Although she nodded in agreement, Sydony refused to meet his eyes, fearful not only of what she might find there, but of her own response.

Chapter Four

Sydony led Barto into one of the bedrooms at the rear of the house with a decided lack of enthusiasm. She was anxious to see the maze, of course, but she would prefer not to be beholden to her guest. The prospect made her uncomfortable, as did extended time alone with her former neighbour.

'Look,' she said, pointing to the windows. 'They are all shut and nailed, as well.'

'I can see that,' Barto answered, in a dry tone. 'But I think I can manage them.'

Sydony recognised the sarcasm, so she waited expectantly. But instead of moving towards the window, Barto set down the heavy pry bar that the workman had provided. 'You don't have to stay. I imagine you have other matters that require your attention,' he said.

Sydony's eyes narrowed. Was her company repugnant, or did he think to escape an onerous duty as soon as her back was turned? Would he make his valet do the chore? Although just a few minutes before she had dreaded being here with him, now Sydony felt compelled to remain, if only to see the job done.

'Yes, I do have much to occupy me, but I am too curious as to the outcome here,' she said, in a dry tone of her own.

One of Barto's dark brows shot up, and the set of that gorgeous mouth told her he wasn't pleased. Then why had he volunteered? The man and his motives were a complete mystery to her. He turned away, and, for a moment, she thought he was going to quit before starting. Instead, he began shrugging out of his dark blue morning coat.

'Excuse me,' he said, stiffly, 'but Thompson will have my head if I ruin the material.'

Automatically, Sydony stepped behind to assist him, as she would Kit, but the elegant garment was more fitted and Barto suddenly seemed taller than her brother. Moving nearer, she drew a deep breath that filled her head with Barto's unique scent and made her lose her grasp. She tried again, pulling the material off wide shoulders and away from a torso that was different from her brother's. When had Barto grown so hard and muscular?

Sydony found herself staring at his back, and she stepped away, taking the coat with her. But when Barto turned around, her attention was caught by his chest, encased in a subtly designed waistcoat. Lest she stare again, Sydony forced herself to look past his elegantly tied cravat to his face, but his dark gaze captured hers with a ferocity she had never seen before. Breathless and witless, she felt like a stranger facing a stranger, her will no longer her own. That alarming thought jolted her from her trance, and she turned to hide her confusion.

Laying the expensive material over the back of a chair, Sydony smoothed it several times as she tried to regain her composure. *What had just happened?* Only a lifetime of refusing to back down made her turn around, her heart pounding so loudly she suspected Barto might hear it. Although she was relieved to see that he had started his task, the atmosphere had changed. No longer was he a former friend from her childhood, but some new and frightening creature, capable of affecting her in ways she'd never thought possible.

Skittish now, Sydony wondered if she should leave. She realised that she was alone in a bedroom with a man in his shirt sleeves, and there was no servant even within shouting distance. Not that she expected Barto to attack her, she thought, stifling a hysterical giggle. The very thought was absurd, and yet she had no idea what had just passed between them.

Sydony glanced nervously in his direction as he pried at the shutters with apparent ease. When had he become so strong? She remembered a scrawny boy with a tangle of brown hair, but now his hair was dark and sleek, as was Barto himself. Wary of eyeing him too closely, Sydony occupied herself with walking about the room, removing dust covers and inspecting the contents of a tall dresser, until she heard him speak.

'I don't think you'll be able to salvage these,' he said, and Sydony turned to see the expanse of glass revealed by his labours. The old window was dirty, and she hurried to wipe at it, resisting a temptation to call the maid from her duties. Although the panes needed proper cleaning, Sydony still could see through them since the rain had stopped. She looked eagerly below, where a mass of greenery caught her eye. It was much larger than she imagined, and, despite being overgrown, there was a definite pattern.

'There it is!' Sydony whispered. Filled with excitement, she grabbed Barto's arm, as she might have years ago, and pointed with her other hand.

'What?' he asked, as though startled by her enthusiasm.

Sydony glanced up at him in surprise. Had no one mentioned the hedges? She opened her mouth to explain, but the flicker of interest on Barto's usually impassive face told her that he had seen it, too.

'A maze,' he murmured, and they shared a moment of wonder that made Sydony forget her earlier discomfiture.

'You'd need a scythe to get through some of the passages,' Barto said softly.

He was probably right. The hedges were so thick in spots Sydony could not easily discern the path, a twisty, tangled route that made her shiver. 'But there's certainly no mistaking the centre,' she said, awed by the huge tree, obviously ancient, that stood like a sentinel in the middle, its branches spreading out over the surrounding plantings.

'It's too wet to go out there now,' Barto said.

'Yes,' Sydony answered. She glanced up at the man standing beside her, and for a moment the years fell away. They shared a look from their past, one that promised adventure and daring, right here in her own garden.

'Well?'

The sound of Kit's voice jarred Sydony, and she

realised she was standing far too close to Barto. She was still clutching his arm, too. Releasing her hold, she stepped back, just as Barto did, and turned, unaccountably flustered, to face her brother.

'Can you see it?' Kit asked. His open expression gave no hint of anything except curiosity.

'We can,' Barto said. The tone of his voice made Sydony glance at him, and she realised that whatever had passed between them was gone. His face once again looked impassive—cold, even—and she felt a sharp stab of disappointment.

'Duece, it's huge,' Kit said, moving between them to look out over the lawn.

'And dangerous. You wouldn't want to get lost in there,' Barto said, just as though he hadn't been tempted to brave it.

'Yes! Don't go investigating by yourself, Syd,' Kit warned.

Sydony frowned. 'Well, you're not going without me,' she said, in an echo of her youthful protests.

Kit laughed. 'No, we should all go, to try to map it out. But we'll probably need an army of gardeners to trim the hedges, or we'll be scratched to death.'

Her brother's choice of words made Sydony shiver, and the maze that had seemed so intriguing took on a threatening aspect. It was only the gloom of the weather, Sydony told herself as she peered out into the mist. Although the rain had stopped, the trees still dripped, and the constant wind made it appear as if there were movement among the greenery. In fact, Sydony could swear she saw something black in the dark hedges as she squinted through the dirty glass.

'Syd!'

Reluctantly, Sydony turned away from the panes toward Kit, who must have been speaking to her. But instead of looking exasperated, he wore an expression of suppressed excitement. 'Come away from the window. I want you both to see what our man found in the library.'

Although Kit was keyed up about something, Sydony was loath to leave the labyrinth she had waited so long to view. Perhaps she could try to put the pattern on to a sheet of paper… But Kit was already heading toward the door, and Sydony watched as Barto snatched up his coat and shrugged into it without breaking his stride. Obviously eager to follow Kit from the room, he disappeared without a backwards glance.

The moment they had shared definitely was gone. In fact, Sydony wondered if she hadn't imagined it.

Barto moved alongside Kit, intent upon putting some space between himself and Sydony Marchant. He blamed the close quarters for the heat he had imagined between them. She had made her animosity clear since his arrival, and his sudden, unexpected hunger when she removed his coat was no more than a typical male reaction. No doubt, he had gone without a woman for too long, but he hadn't the heart for it since his father's death and everything that followed.

With that sharp reminder of his purpose, Barto dismissed all thoughts of Sydony from his mind. She might have grown into a beauty, but he was not here for a dalliance. He had too many questions, and even if the Marchants were not involved in the answers, he had no intention of seducing a gently bred female whom his mother had asked about.

Keeping his countenance, as well as his unwelcome urges, under rigid control, Barto followed Kit into one of the lower rooms. It was deserted except for the workman who stood near the doorway, wearing an odd expression. As Barto passed by, he gave the fellow a sharp glance. Though the man kept his face downcast, it was almost as if he were terrified. Had something startled him, or was he simply as queer as Dick's hatband? Barto didn't think much of Sparrowhawk's hires. But was it the fault of the solicitor, or was something deeper at work?

When Barto moved into the room he could see some unusual ruptures in the floor, which went beyond the ravages of time. Indeed, the wood was torn in places, and, upon inspection, appeared not to be the result of accidents or animals, but of a pry bar.

'I wanted to make sure that there weren't any other bad spots while we were repairing in here,' Kit explained. 'So I had our man Newton there pull up the carpet.' He gave a nod towards the man who still stood near the doorway, as though held there by no will of his own.

Scanning the space, Barto saw that the crates and furniture in the room had been pushed to the side, so that a large, worn rug that had covered one section of the floor could be rolled up. Beneath it was an expanse of wood that differed little from the rest of the planks, except for one small area where the secretary had stood.

'What is it?' Barto asked. At first glance, there appeared to be cuts in the flooring, perhaps where planks had been replaced. But when he stepped closer, Barto saw the marks were actually grooves in the wood.

'It looks like a trapdoor!' Sydony's voice rose in excitement from behind him, like a phantom from his past. The ladies Barto knew these days would never show emotion in public. But Sydony always had been a strange one, more boy than girl, more stubborn and reckless than any other female.

'It's not big enough for a trapdoor,' Kit said, as Sydony crowded in beside them, and Barto saw disappointment cross her face. She appeared to make no effort to hide her feelings; after the intrigues he was accustomed to, Barto found her lack of guile refreshing—if it were real. Then again, Sydony might just have grown up to be a better actress than any of the *ton*.

'But, still, it might be a secret hiding place. It's big enough to hold papers, I'm sure,' she said.

'Or books,' Barto noted, watching the siblings for a reaction.

'I doubt if it's big enough to hold all the books that must have resided here,' Sydony said, drily.

Changing his assessment of her bluntness from refreshing to annoying, Barto ignored her. 'Were there ever any books on these shelves?'

'Not when we arrived,' Kit said. He crouched down before the section of flooring and ran his hand over the edges, then looked up suddenly. 'Come to think of it, didn't Father receive a large shipment of books not that long ago?' he asked, turning his head toward his sister.

'Father was always getting shipments of books,' Sydony said. 'And anyway, I thought Sparrowhawk said Elspeth had them all burned.'

Barto studied her carefully. Was she impatient to investigate this spot, or was she deliberately being dismissive? Barto looked at Kit, but he appeared to have lost all interest in the topic and was bent over the flooring again.

'There's no catch as far as I can tell,' he said, his fingers probing the area gingerly.

Barto walked over to the secretary and rifled through the drawers to find a heavy letter opener. 'Try this,' he said, handing it to Kit. 'If that doesn't work, I left the pry bar upstairs.'

'I hate to ruin the surface,' Kit said.

'I'm afraid that someone else has already done that,' Barto reminded him, and both Marchants followed his gaze to the places where the flooring had been pulled up.

'You don't think someone was looking for…this?' Sydony asked, surprise clearly written on her face.

Barto lifted a brow. 'I think that's pretty obvious.'

'But if you knew where it was…'

'And if you didn't?' Barto asked. 'Perhaps whoever was searching didn't know the hidden compartment was underneath the rug, with heavy furniture lying atop it.'

Kit turned towards Barto. 'The solicitor said that our great-aunt claimed that someone was breaking into the house. But no thefts were reported.'

'He acted like she was addled, but maybe she wasn't,' Sydony said.

Barto glanced around the room at the old mullioned windows set deep into the walls, presumably an easy entrance for a would-be thief. And unreliable or disbelieving servants attending an elderly woman they thought addled would provide little protection. And yet, something didn't fit…

'Why wouldn't the would-be thief just come in after her death?' Barto mused aloud. 'By all accounts, the place was abandoned and deserted.'

'Maybe he did. Maybe it's empty,' Sydony said, looking down at the spot in the floor.

But Barto suspected that the average thief wouldn't trouble to return the room to the way he had found it. And yet, maybe the thief wasn't average. Or maybe what he was looking for was already gone…

Barto watched as Kit levered the opener into the corner and the plank popped upwards, with no apparent damage.

'Is it empty?' Sydony asked, stooping beside her brother.

'No,' Kit said. Lifting the end further, he peered below. 'It's quite deep, actually, and I can see something in there.'

'Books? Papers?' Sydony asked, and Barto wondered why she seemed focused on those things. You'd think a woman would hope for a box of jewellery or a hidden hoard of coins or gold.

'Hold on,' Kit said, reaching into the space. His movements sent up a cloud of dust, and Sydony inched backwards, waving a hand in front of her face, which was probably just as well, considering what Kit pulled out of the hole.

Although dirty and blackened, the object appeared to be a skull. A human skull. Barto watched Sydony in case she started to drop into a swoon, but she didn't even shriek at the sight. Again, she proved that she was not the typical female, that perhaps she was as brave as he remembered.

The shriek, when it came, echoed from outside their

small circle. Barto looked up in surprise to see the workman, who had remained standing silent and as far from them as possible, stifle another wail.

'You don't suppose he's anything to do with this, do you?' Kit asked.

Barto shook his head. 'More than likely the fellow is thinking of abandoning his employment.'

'Why? Because of an old skull?' Kit asked, grinning at him, and Barto felt the same sensation he had known earlier with Sydony. The years fell away, and he and Kit were just two boys, digging in the dirt and gleefully sharing their mischief. Except Barto wasn't sure just how much they shared these days.

Schooling his features, he leaned over the opening. 'Is the rest of a body down there?' he asked.

'I might need a lantern, but I don't think there's anything else down there,' Kit said. He set aside the skull to peer into the blackness, but he had barely moved when another wail pierced the silence.

Again, Barto looked to the workman, who was so pale, he seemed frozen to the spot by fright. Finally, he lifted a shaking arm to point toward the skull. 'It's his,' the fellow mumbled.

'Whose?' Kit asked, sitting back on his haunches.

'*His.*' The workman's voice was low and ragged.

'Well, whoever he is, he's been dead for a while, from the looks of his skull,' Kit observed.

At his words, the workman looked like he was going to faint dead away and Sydony shushed her brother fiercely. 'Do you know whose this is? Is it someone who lived live here at one time? Are you saying the man was never buried?' Sydony asked.

Barto suspected the workman was incapable of answering, but now that Kit had remarked on the age of the relic, Barto stooped to look at it more closely. He had seen bones before, mainly at the Royal College of Surgeons, where some members were always eager to share grisly learning tools. This one was old, and unusual, if he wasn't mistaken. Pulling out his handkerchief, Barto rubbed away some of the dust to reveal its unique properties.

'What the devil is that, a hole in the head?' Kit asked.

'Yes,' Barton said. 'Apparently, our departed friend was trepanned.'

For a long moment, the room was so quiet that Barto could hear the intake of Sydony's breath. Then the silence was broken by the sound of the workman's boots echoing on the hard floor as he fled the room.

'Should I go after him?' Kit asked.

Barto lifted a brow. 'Even if you could catch him, I don't think you'll be able to convince him to return.'

'Damn. Who's going to finish the work?'

'What do you mean—he was trepanned?' Sydony's voice rang out so loudly that both Barto and Kit both looked at her in surprise.

'How can you two calmly discuss repairs when there is a skull secreted in our floor with holes drilled into it?'

For a moment, Barto wondered whether Sydony had succumbed to the ways of her gender, but she appeared to be more angry than hysterical.

'Calm down, Syd. There are all sorts of strange things in buildings that are this old,' Kit said. 'Maybe it's some saint or another. Lots of medieval churches have famous relics and bones.'

'Not with holes drilled in them,' Sydony said. She

turned toward Barto with a look of exasperation that was so familiar he felt another giddy slip of time. Only firm resolve kept him from finding it endearing.

'The holes weren't drilled,' he said. 'Trepanation is a form of surgery, and different instruments are used.'

'But why?' Sydony appeared shocked, and Barto hardened his heart against those wide green eyes.

'Probably to treat head wounds. Maybe mental illness. I'm not a surgeon, but I don't think it's a common procedure.'

'And the patient lives?' Sydony asked.

Barto shrugged. 'Sometimes.'

'But this…thing obviously is old,' she said, making a face as she eyed the lump of bone. 'When would it have been done?'

'Who knows? And this fellow's not telling,' Kit said.

'But the workman, Newton, seemed to think he knew who it was,' Sydony said. 'We should talk to him.'

'Good luck with that,' Barto said, drily.

Sydony sent him a sharp look. 'Kit—'

But Barto quieted her with a gesture. 'Someone's here,' he said, as the sound of horses' hooves and wheels could be heard outside. In an instant, Kit had snatched up the skull, as if to return it to its hiding place.

'Don't put it back in the floor!' Sydony cried.

'Yes, find another hiding place. And I think you should cover up the spot, as well,' Barto said. 'Let's keep this discovery to ourselves.'

Kit snorted. 'You don't think our man Newton isn't going to spread the tale everywhere?'

'Maybe,' Barto said. But he remembered the man's face, pale and stricken with terror. 'And maybe not.'

Sydony rose to her feet. 'Put it in there for now,' she said, pointing to an old carved cupboard. 'And I'll tell the maid not to clean in here just yet.'

Once Kit had stored the skull, he and Barto rolled out the carpet to cover the place where they had found it, just as they heard a carriage go past toward the side of the house.

'There. That's that,' Kit said, dusting off his hands.

'No, that is definitely *not* that,' Sydony said. 'I still want to know why that thing was hidden in the floor of this house.'

Kit looked like he was going to say something, but Sydony cut him off. 'Don't tell me that old houses routinely have unburied body parts lying around. And that skull isn't the only strange thing about this place. Did you see that workman's face? I intend to do some digging—'

Kit burst out laughing, and Sydony flushed. 'Some *investigating*,' she amended. 'Something's dreadfully queer here.'

Privately, Barto agreed, but he said nothing. He had his own investigation to tend to, and this was just one more twist in the maze it had become.

Chapter Five

Since the carriage had gone to the side of the house, Sydony hurried toward the kitchen to welcome either a delivery, or, hopefully, another servant. With Newton gone, they had only the cook and the maid and lots of work that had to be done. When she reached the kitchen, Sydony saw the cook peering out the window with a rolling pin clutched in one thick fist, almost like a weapon.

At Sydony's entrance, she turned. 'It's only Mr Sparrowhawk's conveyance,' she said, and went back to her baking without another word.

Sydony supposed it wasn't the cook's job to go to the door, but she felt a twinge of annoyance, especially since she could already hear the carriage leaving. Had they even knocked? Surely, the solicitor's men wouldn't leave anything without checking with someone. Perhaps they had gone on to the stables instead. Sydony opened the door to see for herself, only to step back in surprise. Before her stood a squat woman with a small trunk, her conveyance gone.

'I'm Mrs Talbot,' the older woman said. 'Mr Sparrowhawk said you'd be needing me. I served as housekeeper for Miss Marchant.'

'Oh, yes! Welcome. I'm Miss Sydony Marchant. Elspeth was my great-aunt,' Sydony said, gesturing the woman inside.

'I know who you are,' Mrs Talbot said in a flat tone that did not convey pleasure. She was shorter and not as heavy as the cook, but she looked even more dour. In fact, the two exchanged an odd look as soon as Mrs Talbot stepped inside.

'I never thought I'd be here again,' she said, setting down her trunk with a grim expression. 'I was at my daughter's and wasn't inclined to come back, but the solicitor said you were nice young people, responsible, with a need.'

Sydony nodded, unsure what to say. They definitely needed help, but she would prefer more cheerful employees.

'I wouldn't stay on before, you know,' Mrs Talbot said. 'I left right after it happened.'

'After what happened?' Sydony asked.

Before the housekeeper could answer, a loud thump made Sydony jump. She turned to see the cook leaning over to pick up her rolling pin from the floor. 'Sorry,' the woman muttered, but she sent Mrs Talbot another odd look.

Sydony glanced at the two sharply. Were they hiding something, or was she imagining things? That business with the skull had left her nervous as a cat.

'After Miss Marchant died,' the housekeeper said, but she wouldn't look Sydony in the eye. Was there more she wasn't saying? Sydony didn't have a chance to ask as Mrs Talbot headed toward the basement door. 'If I could have my old room back?' she said.

'Of course,' Sydony said. 'I'm sure that can be arranged. There's only the cook and the maid, and Mr Newton. But I don't think he'll be staying, after all.'

Another pregnant look passed between the two older women, and Sydony had reached her limit. 'What is it?' she asked.

'What, miss?' the cook asked, in a belligerent tone.

'I'll just put my things away and get right to work,' Mrs Talbot said briskly, leaving Sydony frustrated and wondering, again, what had just happened.

Sydony spent the rest of the day working with Mrs Talbot to restore the house to a state of cleanliness, if not to its former glory, though she couldn't picture the place as glorious. It was not the sort of house that appealed to Sydony, who liked light and airy rooms, but she was determined to do her best to make it livable.

Busy with the servants, Sydony did not see much of her brother or their guest. But when there was a lull in activity, her thoughts drifted to Barto, and she wondered if he had left. She knew there was no reason for him to stay or to visit at all, but would he go without bidding her goodbye?

The man he had become would easily do so, Sydony decided, and that knowledge chafed—just another reason she wanted him gone. Sydony didn't like the feelings he engendered in her, which consisted mostly of indignation, if she didn't count the incident with the shutters, *and she didn't*.

She had enough problems adjusting to a new house and a new life without Barto reminding her of her old home and a past she could not reclaim, as well as annoying her with his aloofness. Better that he go back to his world and let them settle into theirs. As she made her rounds of the rooms with Mrs Talbot, Sydony acknowledged that the viscount had been helpful, especially with the solicitor, but what more could he do?

'The shutters are gone.' The housekeeper's dark tone nearly made Sydony jump. She looked up to find that the woman had stopped in the doorway of one of the rear bedrooms. Peeking over her shoulder, Sydony saw she was right. The room that had been so gloomy before was bathed in light from the tall windows. Slipping around the stationery woman, Sydony moved toward them.

'Yes, B—that is, Viscount Hawthorne must have come back to take them all off,' Sydony said over her shoulder as she walked to the deeply recessed windows. The shutters and all evidence of them had been removed from the room, and Sydony looked out to where the dark mass of the maze lay below, an enigma even from above.

'This was her room, Miss Marchant's,' Mrs Talbot said.

At her words, Sydony turned, but saw that the housekeeper remained at the threshold, as though reluctant to enter. 'Then I shall make it mine,' Sydony said, perhaps in defiance of the housekeeper's demeanour. Did something odd pass over the stoic servant's face, or was Sydony imagining things again?

'As you wish, miss,' she said, with a curt nod. 'I'll send up the maid.'

As soon as she had gone, Sydony turned back to the window and tried to count the turns in the labyrinth below, but it was so overgrown she couldn't be sure of them. The whole property had obviously been neglected for some time, even before Elspeth's death. In fact, one area by the hedges appeared dead and blackened.

Had there been a fire? Maybe that's where her great-aunt had burned the books from the library, an act so appalling it could hardly be that of a sane person. Sydony shook her head, finding it difficult to associate the Elspeth of infrequent letters with the woman who had lived here. She had always seemed eccentric, but...

'Are you moving in here, miss?'

Sydony started at the voice, and realised she must have been staring outside for some time, lost in thought. She turned and nodded to the maid, a friendly country girl, eager for an opportunity to work.

'I just made up the next room for the viscount,' she said, cocking her head at the sight of the windows. 'Said he liked the view, what with all those shutters gone.'

Sydony looked at Nellie in surprise. Barto must have removed the shutters from the other bedroom at the rear of the house, as well. But why would he change rooms? Sydony planned to live here for the rest of her life, unless they could eventually sell the house, while Barto shouldn't be staying at all.

Sydony knew a swift surge of annoyance at her guest and his presumption, followed by a sense of unease. Now she would be further from her brother and closer to Barto, in the very room where earlier...what? *Nothing*, Sydony told herself. Viscount Hawthorne was cool and distant, not burning with some inner heat. Suddenly, she was struck by a flash of memory, of discovering the many layers of her young neighbour, only to push it aside. Layered or not, Barto was no longer her concern.

'It already looks better with the light coming in, doesn't?' the maid asked as she started to make up the bed with fresh linens.

'Yes. I'm not sure why my great-aunt insisted on covering all the windows at the rear of the house,' Sydony said.

'My da was here early on, back when she used to keep a carriage and all. Said she went right barmy, but who could blame her?'

Obviously, Nellie had not been raised for a life in service, but Sydony couldn't be choosy. Besides, she liked the girl's straightforward speech and was eager for any information about her new home, even a servant's gossip.

'He was none too happy to have me come out here, either, but there's too many of us at home for him to feed.' Nellie straightened and flushed, as if she'd said too much.

'Why didn't he want you here?' Sydony asked. Perhaps the girl's father thought all the Marchants were 'barmy'.

Nellie shrugged and continued with her work. 'He said the place hasn't ever been right.'

Sydony waited expectantly as Nellie shook out a pillow.

'Because of the Druids.'

Sydony blinked.

Nellie straightened again and put her hands on her

hips. 'My da always told me they'd get me, if I wandered too far from home. But I don't think they're really around here any more. Do you?'

Sydony could only shake her head. *Druids?* 'I'm afraid I don't know much about them. Do you?'

'Not really. I suspect it was something he said to scare us children into behaving.'

'But why do you suppose…Druids?'

'Oh, the maze, of course.' Nellie in her usual matter-of-fact tone. 'It's where they held their ceremonies.'

Sydony blinked again. She could just imagine what Kit would say to such talk. 'Perhaps he told you that just to keep you away from it, so you wouldn't get lost inside,' she suggested. She could imagine local children drawn to such a place and concerned parents warning them away.

Nellie shuddered. 'Oh, you couldn't catch me going near it, nor anyone else from hereabouts, either, miss.' She tilted her head toward the rear of the house and lowered her voice. 'That's been their place since long before our time. Centuries, probably. It's best to leave it to them.'

With a conspiratorial nod, the maid went back to her work, but Sydony stood where she was, stunned to silence. If Nellie didn't appear so simple and sincere, Sydony would have suspected the local girl of having one over her. But the rest of the staff were too grim to be in on any jest, and the maid appeared to fully believe everything she had just said.

And yet, just because Nellie believed in it, it did not make her tale true. Superstitions abounded among country folk, with residents of each village clinging to their own lore and legends. In fact, All-Hallows Eve would be coming soon, and, no doubt, the people in this area had particular celebrations that she and Kit weren't familiar with.

Sydony moved to the window and looked down at the maze that twisted and turned upon itself, like a giant serpent. Surely, the dark hedges couldn't be that old? But Sydony knew nothing about Druids, except for the vague notion that they worshipped trees. The thought sent her gaze skittering toward the centre of the labyrinth, where the ancient oak stood sentinel, and she shivered.

It was nearly time for supper when Sydony snatched a few moments to slip into the library. She realised, with a start, that the skull must still be there, hidden in the cupboard, and made a mental note to have Kit move it. But to where? She wondered whether they ought to notify the authorities, but Barto had been insistent that they keep the find secret. As a landowner and peer, did he know something they didn't?

With a shake of her head, Sydony moved towards one of the crates of books that had been shipped from their old house. Although intent upon finding information, she was seized by nostalgia as soon as she looked inside. Lifting out a thick volume, she could remember it lying open across her father's cluttered desk. The image filled her with such a longing for home that she nearly sank to her knees.

Swallowing hard, she put the book aside and lifted out others, general and arcane, searching only for those that might mention the ancient Celts and their like. She could quickly set aside the ones she recognised, but others, that her father had acquired shortly before his death or kept stacked away from his overflowing shelves, required a closer examination. So consumed was Sydony with her task that she didn't hear anyone else come into the room.

'They're back, then.'

The sound of a voice made her drop the book in her hands, and Sydony realised she truly was as nervous as a cat to jump at every noise. There was something about the house, perhaps its unfamiliarity, that put her on edge. Or maybe it was the fact that there were skulls hidden in the flooring and rumours of Druids gathering on the grounds. Surely that was enough to make anyone anxious.

But no skeleton stood in the doorway, only Mrs Talbot, though she looked even more grim than usual as she stared at the crates. 'Who is back?' Sydony asked. Had some additional workers arrived?

'The books,' Mrs Talbot said. Although the house-keeper never appeared to change expression, Sydony could sense her tension, as if the very air reverberated with it.

'What, these? These are our books from home,' Sydony said, then caught herself. 'From our old house. Our father was a scholar and a great collector of volumes.'

'Yes.' The housekeeper just stared as though seeing a ghost. 'That's why I sent him her books. I thought I was doing right…'

Sydony blinked in confusion. 'Whose books? Great-aunt Elspeth's? But I thought she had her books burned.'

'She wanted to. She said they were evil and must be destroyed, but I didn't do it. I thought she just wanted to be rid of them, that if they were gone, she wouldn't think someone was breaking in to steal them—' Mrs Talbot broke off, seemingly unable to continue. Indeed, it was the longest speech Sydony had ever heard the woman give.

Sydony glanced at the telltale marks where the floor had been pried. 'You think someone was looking for *books* here?' *Not a dead man's head?*

'When they were gone, Mrs Marchant no longer complained of thieves breaking into the house,' the housekeeper said, though she did not answer Sydony's question.

Sydony dusted off her hands. 'But you think that these thieves will return, now that the books are back?' She eyed the crates, not quite sure what, among the old volumes, could be that valuable.

'I don't know, miss,' the housekeeper said.

Was it really books someone was after, or the skull? Sydony shook her head, utterly bewildered by the whole business, not to mention the Druids.

'But if you didn't burn them, what's the blackened area by the hedges that looks like the remnants of an outdoor fire?'

Mrs Talbot's expression hardened, as if closing her off from further conversation. 'That's where she tried to have the maze burned down.'

'*The maze burned down?*' Sydony echoed. Why would anyone seek to destroy the garden labyrinth, especially with a fire that might move to the house, endangering lives and property? As the realisation struck her, Sydony took a deep breath.

'Mrs Talbot, did the maze drive my great-aunt mad?'

'No,' the housekeeper said. 'It killed her.'

* * *

Unwilling to speak in front of Barto, Sydony said nothing at supper. Of course, she did not want the new viscount to think ill of the Marchants' home and relatives, or any more so, at least. But there was something else that made her hold her tongue: her nagging mistrust of Barto, his sudden appearance and his extended visit.

During the meal their guest spoke to Kit in generalities that might have been the conversation of a stranger. To Sydony's surprise, neither man mentioned the skull, which she would have thought paramount in everyone's mind. Apparently, now that they were adults, the two weren't interested in such things and instead doted upon the weather and preparations for the upcoming winter.

Annoyed, Sydony felt like taking to her room, but she wanted to speak with her brother alone, and so joined them in the parlour, where they cracked open a bottle of port from the cellar. Yet Barto did not seem inclined to drink, and as the evening progressed, he stalked about the room like some cat on the prowl, refusing to play a hand of cards or read the books offered to him.

'Perhaps when you have unpacked your father's library, I shall choose a volume,' he said, pinning Sydony with a dark stare.

Since he so rarely acknowledged her, Sydony was aware of Barto's piercing gaze, but not its cause. Had he overheard her conversation with the housekeeper? Perhaps he had quizzed the woman himself, having already admitted to interrogating the servants yesterday.

Sydony could not be sure, but his abrupt interest in books seemed too much of a coincidence to ignore.

'You are certainly welcome to root around in the crates, if nothing here strikes your fancy,' she said.

'Indeed?' Barto lifted a dark brow. 'Perhaps I will.'

'Is there a specific volume you are looking for?' Sydony asked. Did he know of some valuable tomes among Great-aunt Elspeth's hoard, or was he just making conversation?

'Why? Is there one you recommend?' he countered.

Sydony's reply was cut off by Kit, who must have noticed the cat-and-mouse game going on between the two of them. 'Oh, enough of books! Come play a game of chess with me,' Kit said, urging Barto over to the set he had brought from home.

But, again, their guest declined, preferring to pace around the confines of the dimly lit room some more before finally taking himself off to the stables to check on his horses.

Glaring suspiciously at his departing back, Sydony turned to Kit. 'And what exactly will he do there at this time of night?' she asked. Had he really gone off to the stables or was he in the servants' quarters below, asking more questions?

Kit shrugged. 'He just wants a walk.'

Sydony made a noise slightly more ladylike than her brother's characteristic snort. 'He seems to have been doing plenty of it in here.'

'Admit it, Syd, you are just as restless. You two aren't going to start snapping at each other, are you, like you did when we grew older?'

Sydony blinked at her brother. She did not remember

snapping at Bartholomew Hawthorne as they grew older, probably because he was never around *when* they grew older.

'Come trounce me at chess instead of sitting there glowering after Barto,' Kit said.

With a sound of disgust, Sydony rose from her chair. She was not glowering, and, if she were, why not? The only time their former neighbour spoke to her was to make some kind of veiled insinuations.

Seating herself across from Kit, Sydony absently set up her pieces. At least Barto's disappearance gave her the opportunity she had been seeking all evening. 'I've been wanting to speak to you alone,' she said, her voice lowered.

'I think that can be arranged,' Kit said, whispering dramatically.

Sydony restrained herself from slapping him on the arm, as she would have done in the past. 'I'm serious. You would not believe what I've heard today about our new home and the relative who left it to us.'

'Don't speak ill of the dead,' Kit intoned, then he flashed a grin. 'Or those who have provided for us orphans.'

Normally, Sydony would have laughed, but not tonight. 'Listen, Kit. I had the oddest exchange with the maid this afternoon,' Sydony said. After relating everything that Nellie had told her, she leaned back in her chair expectantly.

But Kit was sceptical. 'Country bugaboos, Syd. I wouldn't make much of it.' He paused, his hand over a pawn, and cocked his head. 'But why do Druids sound familiar?'

Sydony thought he was making another jest, but then she, too, was struck by a memory from their old life, a snippet that she had forgotten. 'Wasn't Viscount Hawthorne, Barto's father, part of some group, a Druid clan or whatever?'

Kit snorted. 'I think that was just an excuse to lift a few glasses with other gentlemen.'

'But don't you think that's an awful coincidence?'

'What? That there are still groups that call themselves Druids?' Kit did not look convinced.

Sydony frowned. 'I wonder if Barto is one, too,' she mused aloud.

'What? A drinker?'

'No! A Druid.'

'Why don't you ask him?' Kit said casually as he captured her knight.

'No!' Sydony's answer came out more sharply than she intended. 'And don't say anything to him just yet. I want to do some digging first.'

Kit looked like he wanted say something about her continuing suspicions of Barto, but he just shook his head. 'Well, let me know if you find any more bones.'

Although Kit made light of her concerns, he hadn't heard the maid's speech, so matter of fact and yet so eerie, about their new home. 'But she warned me away from the maze, just as if the Druids still used it,' Sydony insisted.

Kit snorted again. 'Syd, nobody can get in there, the way it's overgrown.'

Sydony frowned. Kit was probably right, and wouldn't they notice, if a group of Druids was trooping about the property? No doubt the lore had been passed down for years, as Nellie said, even centuries. 'I suppose it can't really go back to the original Druids,' Sydony murmured.

'It's probably a familiar landmark known around here, so someone must know a bit more about it than our maid does,' Kit said. 'You know how Father believed in getting information from the experts.'

Sydony nodded slowly, only to be reminded of her conversation with Mrs Talbot. 'Speaking of Father, the housekeeper claims she sent all of Great-aunt Elspeth's books to him,' Sydony said, repeating what the woman had said.

Kit looked up from the game, paying more attention to this conversation than he had the Druids. 'Father did get a shipment of books not long before…the accident,' he said. 'I remember he said he'd found something of interest to the viscount.'

'Really?' Sydony leaned forwards, curious, because the neighbours, although friendly, did not spend a lot of time together or share many pursuits. 'What was it?'

'Who knows?' Kit said. 'Probably something on the peerage or estate farming, which might come in handy now, come to think of it.'

'I wonder if Barto knows about it,' Sydony mused.

'I don't see why,' Kit said. 'He wasn't home.'

That was true enough. Although Sydony would like to think that Barto had come here to steal a priceless book from them, even she wasn't that imaginative. 'But you don't believe anything will happen now that the books are back, do you?'

Kit snorted. 'I think our housekeeper's as queer as Dick's hatband. How can books be evil?'

Sydony shrugged. 'I gather it was our great-aunt who held that notion, so you can't really blame Mrs Talbot,' Sydony said. She eyed her brother closely. 'But might there be something valuable in amongst the books that someone would break in here to look for again?'

Kit shook his head. 'Don't start sounding like Great-aunt Elspeth, or I'll have to take away your religious tracts.'

Sydony smiled, but refused to be distracted. 'But when we found that…thing hidden in the library, Barto thought someone might have been looking for it.'

'We don't know how old those pry marks are,' Kit said, as he moved his knight. 'They could have been made years ago, long before Great-aunt Elspeth lived here.'

Sydony eyed him askance, until he shrugged in surrender. 'All right, they probably aren't that old. But even if they are more recent and somebody was looking for something, I doubt they were after some old skull or book,' Kit said. 'Word probably got around, as it does over the years, that there was something hidden in the house and no one except an elderly lady and some undependable household help around to protect it,' he said, and Sydony knew just what he was doing. In his most reasonable voice, Kit was trying to convince her that she shouldn't be concerned about the weird happenings in their new home.

'Maybe a couple of young boys on a dare, or the local thief, made some efforts to find a possible treasure. And maybe Great-aunt Elspeth saw the damage, and all she could think of was that someone was after something in the library. Hence, a book. For someone as addled as she sounds, getting rid of the books would get rid of the problem.'

Kit looked her in the eye as he made his move. 'We are all perfectly safe here,' he said. 'Except for you.'

And then he grinned. 'Checkmate.'

Chapter Six

Early the next morning Barto rode out alone to look over the property. Although Hob had offered to go with him or follow, Barto had left the groomsman to watch the house. And as he approached the stables, he was pleased to see his man step out of the shadows.

'Any activity?' Barto asked as he dismounted.

'Just the usual. I think they're still eating breakfast, but I can't tell too much from out here. We'll be able to keep a better eye on 'em when we have someone inside,' Hob said. 'Did you see anything?'

'Just a couple of abandoned tenants' crofts and cottages,' Barto said as he handed over the reins.

'Want me to take a closer look?'

Barto shook his head. 'I don't see how they could mean anything except a loss of income for Christopher Marchant.'

No wonder the moors seemed to be taking over, Barto thought, as he looked out over the land. This estate might once have been prosperous, but could it be again? A lot of work would be required, as well as efforts with the locals. The place had a bad reputation, but was that simply from neglect, the effects of an addled owner over a long lifetime, or was there more?

Barto shook his head again. The problems weren't his concern, but somehow his concerns were getting muddled the longer he remained here. Although it would be easy to fall back into a pattern of aiding and advising his former neighbours, he was here for a purpose, not to renew old companionships that he had dropped long ago.

Barto knew all too well why he had severed his relationship with the Marchants. As a part of his childhood, they had represented a life filled with adventure tales and carefree romps, of freedom from adult responsibilities and from artifice, where confidences were shared and friendships easily given.

At Eton, he had a hard lesson in the real world, where power and rank and wealth were the currency, friendships were made for gain, and nothing was shared, lest it be used against you. Barto learned to protect himself, and in the process had shed any past associates who knew him too well.

At the time, he had reacted instinctively, never really imagining that the neighbours of his youth would use their knowledge against him. But now? Barto could be sure of nothing, for nothing was what it seemed.

He had come here to look for evidence, of what, he wasn't sure. But he had found only rubbish, red herrings that appeared to have no connection to his father. He'd spoken to the servants, poked around the house, and shadowed the Marchants until he felt restless and confined by their house and their company. But where had it got him? He was no closer to answers than when he arrived.

Patience had never been his strong suit, as evidenced by last night's episode. When Sydony had tried to thrust her books on him, Barto had longed to end the charade right then and there. Indeed, one more moment and he might have shaken the truth from her. But Kit had interrupted, and Barto had finally sought the fresh air needed to clear his head.

As Barto stood watching Hob hand the horse over to Jack, he considered his former friends. Of the two Marchants, Kit had always been the easygoing one, welcoming Barto, even after all this time, with open arms. Indeed, Kit was so open, it was hard to imagine him harbouring any secrets.

Unlike her brother, Sydony seemed to seethe with a host of emotions that she made no effort to hide. Were there even more churning beneath the surface? Barto was not eager to dig any deeper; already he was finding it difficult to look at her.

Was that because of what he might see on her face? Or had she become too tempting a morsel to observe closely? Barto frowned at the thought. He was not known for his careless dalliances, and yet Sydony Marchant appeared to possess the ability to puncture his carefully cultivated composure, rousing emotions he had locked away, whether they be rage or frustration or…something else.

It was a power he did not intend to cede to her.

His eyes narrowing, Barto determined to seek her out, to question her more carefully, to look her full in the face, to master her…

'Sounds like a carriage, my lord,' Hob said, jerking Barto from his thoughts. They both stepped into the shadows of the stables as a conveyance, clearly Mr Sparrowhawk's, rattled up the drive.

'Maybe that's our two,' Hob said.

Barto lifted a hand to shade his eyes. 'There looks to be a third, another man.'

'Perhaps Sparrowhawk is pushing some of his own people on them.'

'I doubt it,' Barto said. 'He acted reluctant to hire anyone at all.'

'He's an odd duck, that one.'

'Yes, perhaps I should have a private chat with him,' Barto said. He had dismissed the solicitor as ineffectual, but now he wondered if more information on the Marchants' sudden inheritance would be useful, and he was sure that Mr Sparrowhawk would gladly share— for a price.

Moving towards the carriage, Barto saw that both Kit and Sydony were outside greeting the new arrivals, and in the confusion he was able to step behind them and listen to their low conversation.

'Are you sure we can afford so many servants?' Sydony asked her brother, a worried expression on that gorgeous face of hers, so different and yet so familiar… Barto tore his gaze away to concentrate on her brother.

'We have to have a groomsman, Syd, and this new fellow, Martin, is only to replace the man who ran off,' Kit said.

'But another maid? We already have one and a housekeeper who must receive higher wages.' The concern in her voice made Barto want to turn toward her again, but he resisted. After all, he was responsible for the additional maid. Again, he wondered about the Marchants' situation and resolved to seek more information from the solicitor.

Whatever their finances, could Kit handle them? The Marchants' father, though a kind fellow, had no head for such things, and had left them with little, according to local gossip. And yet here they were, with a house and land that could be tenant-farmed, grazed, planted to orchards. Was it all a timely coincidence?

With his usual good nature, Kit appeared to pay little heed to his sister's concerns, but welcomed the new servants, who were directed to take their belongings down to their quarters by the housekeeper. And with the movement of the new staff, the Marchants finally saw Barto.

'Good morning,' Kit said. 'I thought you still abed.'

'Apparently not,' Sydony said. 'Where have you been?' she asked, without the slightest bit of *politesse*. If Barto hadn't known better, he would have thought she was raised without any manners, but her sharp tongue seemed reserved only for him.

'I've been out riding,' Barto said. He forced himself to look at her, to appraise her with analytical detachment. He had seen more beautiful women, to be sure, and yet there was something… He felt a tug of interest and firmly quelled it.

Like her brother, she was dark, her hair a thick mass of deep browns that gleamed in the sunlight, and her flawless skin was not quite as pale as fashion dictated. But while Kit's eyes were as dark as his hair, Sydony's were a deep green, an unusual colour that Barto had thought conjured in his imagination, until he saw her again.

There were women more beautiful, Barto acknowledged, more voluptuous, more elegant, more practised, but perhaps none so fresh, so intelligent, so much a part of his past. *That was it*, Barto told himself. Like a child's cherished toy, Sydony Marchant affected him because she had once held his hand, if not his heart.

It was time to move on, Barto told himself, and he spoke to Kit of his ride, his assessment of the property, and the abandoned cottages.

'Yes, I think there's only one working farm on the property, so we'll have to lure some of the tenants back,' Kit said. 'I assume our esteemed great-aunt scared them away.'

Barto heard Sydony's low intake of breath, as though she were going to speak, but instead she turned towards the rear of the house. 'It doesn't look like rain,' she said. 'Perhaps today I'll investigate the maze.'

'It's too overgrown, Syd,' Kit said. 'You'll be scratched bits.'

'I'll wear your leather duster.'

'No, you won't! You'll ruin it,' Kit countered.

Again Barto felt a jolt from the past. How many times had he heard a similar exchange? It was tempting to slip back into the roles they had once played, tempting to embrace these two as boon companions and share some new adventure. But he could no more do that than bring back his father.

The Marchants fell silent when the new staff emerged

from the house, and Barto saw Sydony give the groomsman a curious look as he walked towards the stables. She
turned toward Barto, as if to speak, but he cut her off.

'Here's your man Martin,' he said. 'Why don't you
set him to trimming back the hedges?'

The workman, who was approaching them, stopped
in his tracks.

'Yes, he can fix the floor any time,' Sydony said. 'Let
us take advantage of the sun.'

'In order to crawl into that darkness?' Kit asked,
tilting his head toward the labyrinth. 'But I admit that
I'm curious. Although I hoped to find something about
it among the family papers, I haven't come across so
much as a mention, let alone a map.'

Barto turned toward the stables, where his man was
standing in the shadows. 'Hob, see if you can find this
fellow some clippers,' he called.

'Yes, my lord,' he answered before disappearing into
the interior of the old building.

'Uh, Mr Marchant.' The workman stepped forwards,
clutching his cap in his hands, as though nervous.

'Yes, Martin?' Kit asked.

'Uh, Mr Sparrowhawk didn't say there'd be any
outside work,' he muttered.

'What? There's probably more that needs to be done
outside than inside,' Kit said, with a grin.

Martin continued to roll his hat through his fingers.
'Well, I don't mind mowing and planting and raking.
My father was a farmer, you see. But…' His words
trailed off as he looked down at the ground.

'But what?'

'Well, it's that thing, sir,' he said, cocking his head

toward the maze. 'I don't know that I ought to be touching it. Or you either, beg your pardon.'

'What? Why not?' Kit asked. He appeared perplexed, but Sydony leaned forwards.

'Well, sir, you see…it's what happened to the last two fellows who were working here.'

Sydony blinked, as though surprised, and Barto wondered if she had expected to hear something else.

'What fellows? You mean Newton?' Kit asked.

'No, sir.' Martin shook his head. 'He's all right. As far as I know, anyway. Wouldn't say a word to anyone, but took off to live with his sister in Suffolk is what I heard. No great loss to yourself, if I may say so.'

'Who, then?'

'The two fellows who were hired by Miss Marchant,' he said. He glanced at Sydony. 'The other Miss Marchant, before she…died.'

'Who were these two men?' Barto asked.

'Clayton Blackpoole and Charlie Smith, my lord.' The workman shifted uncomfortably. 'Miss Marchant set them to digging up the maze there,' he said, with a tilt of his head. 'And, well, it's likely cursed or something.'

'What?' Kit snorted.

'Well, sir, those two fellows. They started the job, all right, but…' Again, he trailed off, as though unable to continue.

'What about them?'

'Well, sir, they were found dead that very night, drowned in the river.'

'And what would that have to do with Oakfield?' Barto asked. He was growing weary of the vague rumours that clung to the estate, like some great fog, through which he couldn't see his way clearly to the truth. 'They could have been swimming or fishing.'

'No, my lord. Not at this time of year. It was nigh on a year ago, not long before All-Hallows Eve,' he said, with a visible shudder.

'Perhaps these two had been drinking or fighting and lost their footing,' Barto suggested, thinking it more than likely. 'Or do you believe the shrubs chased them into the water and held them under?'

Kit laughed outright at that, but the workman just shook his head. 'All I know is that she—Miss Marchant—tried to cut it down, and it struck back at her.'

'How?' Kit asked, obviously incredulous.

Martin looked down at his cap. 'Well, she's gone, too, now isn't she?'

Sydony paled, and Barto eyed her closely. 'But surely she died of some ailment of old age. We can check with the physician, can't we?' she asked, looking at Kit. Was her concern real or feigned? Barto wondered, not for the first time, whether the Marchants' sudden good fortune was no coincidence.

'Of course,' Kit said, with the appropriate expression of outrage. 'I can't believe you're spreading such nonsense.'

The workman lifted his head. 'It's not just me, sir. Why, everyone hereabouts knows to stay away from the maze.'

'And why is that?' Sydony asked. Again, she seemed especially interested, though Barto had no idea why.

'It's got a mind of its own, miss, a lingering evil,' the workman said.

'How? From what?' she persisted.

'From the fellow who lived here.'

'You mean before Miss Elspeth?' Sydony prompted.

'Oh, yes, miss. But a long time back. I don't rightly know when.'

'Who was this person?'

'Well, he was a strange one, by all accounts.'

'Did he have a name?' Barto asked, drily.

'Oh, I don't know it, my lord,' Martin said. 'Can't say I ever heard it. Or if I did, I don't remember.'

'Do people think he haunts the place?' Sydony asked.

The workman shook his head. 'I haven't heard anything about his ghost walking about, miss. Why? Have you seen something?' he asked, his expression a mixture of curiosity and horror.

'Of course not,' Sydony said.

'Well, then.'

'Well, then, why should we concern ourselves with some long-dead inhabitant?' Kit asked.

'They say he was a powerful mystic, sir, that he built the house with ill-gotten gains. And that, too,' the workman added, giving the maze a dark look. 'No one knows what went on there.'

With that cryptic conclusion, Martin appeared to have finished, providing them with precious little reason to excuse him from trimming the hedge. Was the fellow full of fustian, or did the locals actually believe such rubbish? There was no denying that Oakfield had a bad reputation in the area, but did it date back as far as the building itself?

Barto's eyes narrowed as he turned to assess the

place. The original manor with the battlements was probably built in the sixteen hundreds, with some later additions. Had the builder some dispute with his neighbours that resulted in ill will that lived on to this day?

Barto wondered if the trepanned skull they had found belonged to this infamous resident. Perhaps the fellow was nothing more than a medieval surgeon, with an eye for a decorative garden…

'If you need an extra hand, I'll help.'

Barto turned at the sound of Hob's voice. His man had returned with two pairs of clippers, which made Martin step back apace.

'Thank you,' Barto said. 'Perhaps you can prevail upon Jack to assist, as well?' Hob nodded and headed back towards the stable, while Kit set Martin to some other outside chores.

'I'm sure I can find someone willing to take the position,' Barto offered, as he watched the workman hurry away.

'Let us see how he handles himself before we lose another man,' Kit said, frowning. 'If what he says is true, we won't find anyone else locally. The villagers certainly are a suspicious lot, far more entrenched in their odd lore than anyone at our old home, even old dame Higgins.'

Since old dame Higgins had been the town sooth-sayer, Sydony laughed. 'Perhaps we should seek her advice,' she said.

'I'd be afraid to hear it,' Kit said, drily.

'I wonder if any digging really was done,' Sydony said, eyeing the massive hedges.

'There's one way to find out,' Kit said, and soon they were walking towards the entrance of the maze, Sydony not far behind. But they found no signs of disturbance among the heavy growth. Turning left, they followed the outer perimeter until they reached the corner, then headed along the other side.

'Here,' Barto called when he came to the back of the labyrinth, where holes and clods of earth that had not been replaced gave evidence of some disturbance. Although part of the green wall had been removed, the hedges were already growing back, reclaiming the ground, creeping outwards, so that nothing could be seen of the interior of the maze. Perhaps it had been neglected for so long that it was just one big hedge, with the top of a tree poking out of the middle.

When Sydony stepped close to peek between the leaves, Barto moved away to a blackened strip of grass, where he found another rent in the hedge.

'Is this where she burned the books?' he asked, glancing towards Sydony and Kit.

Sydony shook her head. 'Mrs Talbot claims that the books were never burned,' she said. Barto gave her a sharp glance, and she swallowed, as though suddenly conscious of her speech. 'But she said that Great-aunt Elspeth tried to set fire to the maze itself.'

Barto lifted a dark brow, certain that there was more she could say about the books, but he left the subject…for now. 'You're lucky the whole place didn't go up,' he said, and this time it was Sydony who glanced away from his intent gaze.

'I'm surprised our new man Martin didn't mention it,' Kit said. 'One of the servants must have started the fire, so if they weren't suddenly struck dead, there goes his theory.'

'I think he meant that Great-aunt Elspeth was the one who died, so she could order no more attacks on the labyrinth,' Sydony said.

Kit frowned. 'Although I can't picture Great-aunt Elspeth tottering out here to set the hedges ablaze, maybe that's why it didn't get very far.'

'Someone could have doused it,' Sydony said.

'Maybe it just died out on its own,' Barto said. Kneeling, he stripped off his glove, and felt under the growth. 'Everything's a bit damp now.'

'But the dry autumn leaves could make for a tinder-box,' Kit noted.

'If started correctly,' Barto said, rising to his feet and brushing off his breeches. As he put his glove back on, he saw Hob and Jack trudging towards them.

'Where shall we start, my lord?' Hob asked.

Barto turned to Kit, as the owner of the property.

'The entrance, of course,' Kit said, with a grin. 'We all want to find our way inside.'

They all walked back to the narrow opening, barely visible as the entry point, and while the men took up the shears, Barto shook his head. 'It might be too over-grown for them to even find the paths,' he said.

'Can you see anything from your room?' Kit asked.

'It's really difficult to see the pattern,' Barto said. 'But perhaps you could get a clearer look from the bat-tlements, assuming they are all intact.'

He was surprised to hear the swift intake of Sydony's breath and even more surprised when she swung towards him, her eyes wide. 'The battlements! With all that has happened, I completely forgot about them.'

Barto stood still, struck silent by her outburst. Surely

no woman had ever appeared so delighted by anything he'd said, including the most tender of compliments. Her colour was heightened, and strands of dark hair escaped their arrangement to dance about her face. In that instant, she looked too beautiful to be real, a figment of his imagination, some dream conjured up in the darkest hours of the night…

'Let's go see if Mrs Talbot knows how to gain access,' Sydony said.

'All right,' Barto said slowly. Only after he had spoken did he realise she hadn't been talking to him, but to her brother.

'Yes, you two go,' Kit said. 'I'm going to see if the new groomsman is settling in.'

Barto was caught, and yet, it was just as well. He needed to speak to Sydony Marchant, and what better place to put his questions to her than on the privacy of the roofs, where there was no one to hear and no way to escape?

Sydony walked uneasily alongside Barto as they headed into the house. Truth be told, she would have liked to forgo this outing. Ever since the incident with the shutters, she was wary of being alone with her former neighbour. And although she might have imagined what had happened then, she had not imagined her reaction just a few moments ago when he had stripped off his glove.

The way he had peeled away the leather to reveal his bare hand with its long, lean fingers… Sydony had found herself staring, only to flush and look away. At the memory, she flushed again, this time with anger at herself and at Barto, who had no business coming here to affect her so…uniquely.

'Don't you have matters at Hawthorne Park that require your attention…my lord?' Sydony asked.

'Not at the moment,' Barto answered, without even glancing her way.

'I would think that such a vast estate requires management, as would your London townhouse.'

He turned his head towards her ever so slightly and lifted one dark brow. 'I have people who handle things…just as they did for my father.'

The reminder of his lost parent made Sydony's irritation melt away, to be replaced by a sudden melancholy. She had liked the old viscount. Although he'd never had much time for children, he had always treated them with courtesy. Sydony drew a deep breath.

It was hard to believe that she had once begged to trail after Bartholomew Hawthorne when now she lagged behind as though on her way to the gallows. Even the once-cherished thought of the battlements did not hearten her, for as much as she wanted to reach them, she did not want to be there with Barto. Alone.

But perhaps not. When Sydony saw Mrs Talbot inside the house, she loosed a sigh of relief. What better chaperon than the dour housekeeper to keep Sydony's mind off her neighbour?

'Mrs Talbot,' Sydony called out with a bit more urgency than was necessary.

The older woman stopped in her tracks and turned round, looking grave, as always. 'Yes, miss?'

'Viscount Hawthorne and I would like to view the battlements. Can you take us there?'

'Certainly, miss.'

The mystery that had racked the household for days didn't seem to baffle the housekeeper in the slightest. Had Kit been with her, Sydony would have exchanged a look with him, but Barto's expression was closed. And did she really want to share anything with him, even a moment's puzzlement?

In silence, they followed Mrs Talbot up to the locked door on the first floor. Before Sydony could protest that none of the keys would work, she heard a jangle and a click, and the housekeeper stepped back, pulling the door open to reveal a long, narrow flight of stone steps. Sydony blinked in surprise.

'Perhaps we should get a lantern,' Barto said from beside her, but Sydony stepped past him. Surely the boy who once had led her on myriad adventures hadn't turned into this stiff and stolid adult?

'Rubbish,' Sydony said, taking her first step up to the battlements. She turned her head to give her former neighbour a challenging look, and, as she suspected, he could not refuse.

'Very well,' he said, moving behind her.

In the excitement of the moment, Sydony had forgotten the need for a chaperon, but when Barto stepped close, she almost felt the heat from his body.

'Aren't you going to lead us?' Sydony asked the housekeeper in a voice that had lost its bravado.

Mrs Talbot shook her head. 'I won't go up there.' And without waiting to be dismissed, she walked away.

Sydony turned to Barto in surprise, but her position on the step above put her face on a level with his. Looking directly into those dark eyes, unfathomable, and yet somehow alluring, Sydony felt a sudden panic. She jerked around and stumbled up the stairs, only to feel Barto's hand on her waist. Although he was preventing her from falling, Sydony hurried upwards, away from his touch. Away from him.

'I wonder how she managed to unlock the door when we could not?' Sydony said, to cover her nervousness.

'Perhaps she has a set of keys that you don't,' Barto said.

Sydony frowned. 'How? And why?'

'She served the previous owner.'

That was true enough. Had the housekeeper held on to keys when she left? But why wouldn't she be required to turn them over? Because she left as soon as Elspeth died, Sydony thought, and the solicitor had paid no heed. Still, shouldn't Mrs Talbot have mentioned her set when she returned?

The passage that had looked dim from below grew darker the higher she went until Sydony put out a hand along the wall to help her find her way. Perhaps Barto was right and they could use a lantern, but surely it wasn't much further to the roofs… The thought had no sooner crossed Sydony's mind then she was plunged into utter blackness.

For a moment she feared she had fallen into some abyss, a broken stair leading into nothingness. But the steps were stone and hard beneath her feet, and her palm still rested against the rough surface to her left. Sydony gave a sigh of relief, only to draw in a harsh breath at the feel of Barto's body pressing behind her, a very different threat…

'Are you all right?' he whispered, his voice low and

intoxicating. He was so close that Sydony felt his breath upon her neck, against her ear, and she shivered, her heart pounding frantically.

'Mmm, yes,' she said, though she wasn't so sure now that his hand was on her waist once more, the light touch of his fingers seeming to burn through her simple muslin gown. 'What happened?'

'The door must have swung shut,' Barto answered. 'If you feel steady where you are, I'll go down and check.'

Of course Sydony felt steady. She was his fearless companion, wasn't she? She nodded before realising that he wouldn't see her assent. 'Yes,' she whispered.

Sydony felt him pat her waist encouragingly, then the movement of the air as he stepped away. She heard the low sound of his boots as he navigated the stairs with assurance, the silence as he halted at the bottom and felt for the latch, then the low thump as the heavy door rattled. But the passage was still as black as night.

'The door appears to be stuck…or locked,' Barto said, and Sydony blinked at his ominous tone.

'What?' Putting her right hand to the wall and lifting her skirts with her left, Sydony felt her way down the stairs, though more slowly and less confidently than her companion.

'It won't budge,' Barto said, grunting softly when she bumped into him.

'Let me try,' Sydony demanded, against the unease rising in her throat. Her fingers thrummed along the surface of the wood, then Barto's hand settled over hers, stilling it and leading it unerringly to the latch. Sydony swallowed hard.

Thankfully, his hand fell away, allowing her to do for herself, as he had so often in the past. But she trembled in her efforts, grateful that he could not see; ultimately, she was unsuccessful as well.

'Now, what?' she asked, turning toward him. At once, she realised they were touching, and she moved back, to put some space between them in the darkness.

'I'll go up to the top, and we'll exit on to the battlements,' Barto said.

'All right,' Sydony said. But she was not sure she wanted quite that much space between them. There was no reason to be frightened, and yet the eeriness of the house seemed to close in around her, threatening to drive her as mad as it had her poor great-aunt. Sydony wanted nothing more than to throw her arms around Barto, just as she had the day he arrived. But she couldn't. Not now. Not when she was so aware of him.

'I'll come, too,' she muttered.

He did not mock her, but took her hand in his gloved one and led her up with him. Except for the glove, the gesture was no different than countless others in the past, and yet it did not feel the same. Things were different. They were different. And her pulse pounded as it never had before.

They retraced their path upwards, Sydony blindly moving along with Barto until he halted and released her hand. Reaching out in front of her, she felt wood, but it did not give way despite Barto's noisy efforts. As a matter of course, Sydony attempted to open the door, as well, only to fail, as she had below.

'How can it be locked, too?' she whispered.

'It may not be,' Barto said. 'After years of disuse, it

might simply be stuck or painted shut, or something might have fallen in front of it—roof tiles, tree branches or other debris.'

Sydony swallowed hard against a longing for her old home, with its bright, airy rooms and no dank cellars, no bats, no locked passageways. No maze. No mysteries. *No Barto.*

Her arm brushed up against his, and, with a swift intake of breath, Sydony realised that they were trapped here together. Alone. In the darkness. Suddenly, danger thrummed in the very air, making her heart pound wildly.

That night they had spent together in the forest, Sydony had not been afraid because Barto was with her. But now she was afraid…because Barto *was* with her.

Chapter Seven

Barto lifted a fist to the lower door again. He had been pounding for some time, and though the sound reverberated in the passage, no one outside the stair seemed to hear it. He was not surprised, for the first floor was very likely deserted, unless the housekeeper or one of the maids were cleaning. The kitchen and servants' quarters were well below, muffled by the heavy beams and plaster of the Tudor building. And he had no idea where Kit was—probably outside, oblivious.

With all his senses heightened in the blackness, Barto was immediately aware when Sydony put a hand on his shoulder. The touch made his fist jerk away from the wood, and he turned towards where she must have been standing, above and behind him.

'Stop for a while,' she said. 'No one can hear you.'

'They might, if they are anywhere near,' Barto said. 'But surely no one will hear, if I cease.'

'My ears are ringing,' she complained.

'Very well,' Barto said. 'We shall sit and wait. Kit

will eventually find us, if we do not appear at supper.' Any female in her right mind would not want to be locked away until supper, but when had Sydony been typical of her sex?

Barto heard her sink down upon the step, and he sat beside her. He had planned to put some questions to her on the battlements. Should he try to get some answers here and now? But how well could he judge her truthfulness when he could not see her face?

The darkness changed everything. The air was so close, Barto could smell her perfume, some light scent of soap and Sydony. Feeling the brush of her leg against his thigh, he wondered whether he ought to move away. He was not sure of the protocol of their situation, but he suspected marriages had been made for less.

Suddenly, the suspicion that had struck him on her doorstep rose again, even more fiercely than before. Had the Marchants purposely trapped him here? Sydony certainly had not used any wiles on him, quite the opposite. But perhaps her brother was forcing her into it, hoping to tidy up things by tying the Marchants irrevocably to the Hawthornes. Would Kit lock them up together in the dark, only to conveniently cry foul hours later?

If so, he would not succeed. Barto did not care how bad the situation appeared to the gossips or whether it was shouted from the rooftops, he would not be made to wed. He let his anger sustain him, overwhelming everything else, including the enticing vision of Sydony Marchant at his side, in his life, on his bed…

The heat he had felt when alone with her earlier returned with a vengeance. If they truly were trying to trap him, then why shouldn't he take the bait? The silence was so heavy that he could hear Sydony's breathing, ragged and loud. Would she protest if he turned to kiss her, or would she welcome his embrace? Barto frowned as a memory, long forgotten, came back to haunt him like some spectre in the night.

It had been his birthday. The Marchants had been invited to partake of cake and jollities, along with the rest of the area's residents. But Barto, fresh from Eton, was feeling his oats and bragging of his conquests. He was too sophisticated to care for the homemade gifts of the locals and had downed a bottle of his father's best port. Restless, boiling over with impatience at country life, he had wandered into the gardens, where he'd found her.

Suddenly, he remembered it all too well: the thick summer air, bees buzzing about the rich flowers, and himself, a callow youth, leaning forward with reckless abandon. 'Shall I have a birthday kiss?' he'd asked.

The bold question had stunned Sydony, as well it should have. The girl who had so often played the boy probably had never even thought about such things. But lest he be met with refusal, Barto did not wait for her reply. He bent nearer and touched his lips to hers.

Rearing back, Barto had seen the astonishment on her young face, but it was only a reflection of his own. Having kissed many a maid, and more than that, he had thought himself worldly. But never before had he felt a bolt of electricity as though struck by lightning. Had it been the port? The thrill of stealing a kiss in his own garden? Whatever the reason, Barto had been jolted from his arrogant, newly won sense of control. Stripped of his cockiness, he had left her, hieing back into his parents' house, away from the gathering. Away from her.

He had never looked back.

In the stillness of the passage, Barto drew in a harsh breath. He'd put the incident behind him quickly enough after his return to school, with the certainty that he had imagined it, just as he had imagined the colour of her eyes. But Sydony's eyes really were the shade of green he remembered.

Would her kiss be the same, as well?

Thankfully, before he could act on his impulses, the door before them swung open wide, and Barto saw Kit standing in the doorway. If Sydony's brother had planned the trap, it had not lasted long enough to cause much of a scandal.

'B—er, my lord, your man wants to talk to you,' Kit said. Then he took in the sight of them sitting side by side in the darkness. 'What are you doing?'

Carefully schooling his expression to reveal nothing, Barto rose to his feet and held out a hand for Sydony.

'The door locked behind us, and we were trapped in here,' Sydony said. She let Barto help her to her feet, then dropped his hand as though eager to be rid of his touch. Would she have been so unwelcoming when they were alone?

'But the door wasn't locked,' Kit said, looking perplexed.

'Yes, it was,' Sydony insisted. She hurried toward Kit, and Barto followed, turning to watch as she shut the door, then tugged on the latch to swing it wide once more.

'Maybe it was just stuck,' Kit said. 'You know these old houses.'

'But it was standing open,' Sydony insisted. 'Someone must have shut and locked it while we were in there.'

Had the door simply been stuck fast? Barto studied Kit, but Sydony's brother appeared as guileless as always.

'Maybe a draught closed it. Or maybe it isn't hung correctly,' Kit said. 'I would guess that this door is a newer addition, probably another one of Great-aunt Elspeth's plans to keep anyone from viewing the maze.'

'Well, it worked,' Sydony said.

Kit looked as though he might laugh, but was stopped by Sydony's stony expression. Her anger seemed real enough, but was it directed at their entrapment or a plan gone awry?

'Your man wanted to speak with you,' Kit reminded Barto, and he nodded. Obviously, Hob had found something worth reporting immediately. Had his man also inadvertently ruined the Marchants' scheme?

'If you'll excuse me, I must attend to this matter,' Barto said. He inclined his head toward Sydony. 'Perhaps we can…explore the battlements another time.'

Sydony blinked at Barto's sly comment. Was he insinuating something? If so, she wasn't sure what, but he wasn't going to escape so easily.

'I'll come with you,' she said. He turned, obviously prepared to argue, but she cut him off. 'Isn't your man the one who is trimming the maze? If he's found something, I would like to know what it is.'

Barto did not looked pleased, but Kit spoke up, as

well, so the viscount nodded his assent. He could hardly keep them away when it was their house, their land and their maze. And so they all trooped back out of the house, where Barto's man was waiting.

If the servant was surprised to see all three of them, he did not show it. 'I thought you might want to see what we found, my lord, Mr Marchant,' the man said, with a nod to them all, and they followed him toward the maze.

The younger fellow was still cutting away at the hedges when they arrived, but he stopped and moved aside.

'I thought I'd cut around the entrance enough so as to try to get a little ways in,' the one called Hob said. 'If you just move past this first tangle...' His words trailed off as he ducked through the overhanging branches and disappeared inside.

Barto followed, and Sydony hurried behind him, struggling through the foliage that seemed almost too thick to pass. For a moment she wondered how Barto had gotten through, but then the hedges fell away and she stepped into a narrow opening. She paused in surprise, but felt Kit at her back, and stepped forwards.

'What the devil?' Kit asked, as he emerged and straightened.

What the devil, indeed. Although from the outside the maze seemed impenetrable, here, not far inside, a narrow pathway was clearly visible. 'But from above, it all looks overgrown,' Sydony said. 'Is that just a trick of the light?'

'I don't think so,' Barto said, his voice ominously low.

Sydony glanced upwards and saw that the hedges

were practically growing together, blocking out the sunlight and covering their heads. 'But how could these plants grow only upwards, not outwards?'

'I don't think they can, miss,' the groomsman said. Sydony leaned around Barto to see the servant gesturing toward a branch. 'Look, this end has been snipped, and not that long ago.'

'It's almost as if someone kept it maintained,' Barto said.

His words gave Sydony a chill. 'What are you saying? That someone sneaks in here and trims the walls of the hedges for easy access, while leaving the tops overgrown...'

'To hide their actions,' Barto finished.

Kit snorted. 'The place has been deserted since Elspeth's death. It was practically standing wide open, with no one to look after it, so I doubt anyone's been out here, doing the gardening on the sly.'

Sydony glanced sharply at Barto, but his face was expressionless. 'Perhaps it's just this section,' she suggested. 'Hob, can you move on? Can we go all the way to the tree?' As soon as she spoke, Sydony felt a shiver of excitement. Instead of waiting days or weeks, they might find the way now, perhaps to the very heart.

'I don't care to get lost in here. Take it to the first turn, Hob, and see,' Barto said. Sydony frowned, but she did not argue. Did it matter what course the others took? She felt a sudden urgency to press onwards, to seek out the secrets of the labyrinth, with or without them.

'If the grounds were unattended, shouldn't we be wading through weeds as high as our shoulders?' Barto asked, in a dry tone that made Sydony looked closer at the ground. There were grass and weeds and leaves, of course, but nothing was impassable.

'It's probably too late in the season for anything to flourish under these bows,' Kit said, but Sydony could hear the uncertainty in his voice. Was there more here than met the eye? But who would tend to the passageways in an old maze on deserted land? The answer came to Sydony swiftly: *the Druids*. At the thought, Sydony stumbled and fell forwards against Barto, who had halted.

'Take a look at that,' she heard his servant say ahead.

'Yes, I see,' Barto said, and, as soon as Sydony had righted herself, he dropped into a crouch to examine the path. Then he looked back towards Sydony and Kit behind her. 'The ground has been disturbed, just like the hedges outside.'

When Barto stood and moved on, Sydony could see the clumps of dirt along the path. But it didn't look as though the greenery had been uprooted. Indeed, unlike outside, whatever hole that had been made had been filled in.

They found another spot further on. 'It's almost as though someone was digging for something,' Sydony mused.

'Maybe our skull is out looking for the rest of himself,' Kit said, but Sydony did not laugh. She felt a growing unease that even Kit could not banish. Surely, even her amiable brother could not ignore the fact that something was not right in the labyrinth.

'Watch yourself, my lord,' Sydony heard Hob warn, and Barto halted again.

'What is it?' Kit asked from behind.

Sydony heard the clank of metal and moved back. She was glad of it, for when Barto turned, he held up a wicked-looking set of jaws. 'A trap, cleverly set among the undergrowth,' he said.

'What?' Kit said. 'Do you suppose it was left here years ago?'

'So we could stumble across it?' Barto asked. His tone was so serious that Sydony blinked. Had someone purposely set the trap in order to catch the unwary?

Kit did not share her suspicions. 'More likely poachers are responsible since the property was abandoned, and there's lots of undergrowth here for small game,' he said.

Sydony watched Barto lift a dark brow, but he did not argue the point. Instead, he turned to face them, his expression grim. 'I'd rather not put my man in any danger, so I suggest we continue our investigation when we are more prepared,' he said. 'Who knows what else lies in wait ahead?'

It was a quiet group that left the labyrinth. Hob and his helper went back to their trimming, with renewed caution, and Kit headed towards the stables. Glad to leave Barto talking quietly to his man, Sydony walked back to the house alone.

At first, she had wanted to argue with Barto, but when Kit fell back, she could hardly go on. Still, the urgency to reach the centre didn't leave her until she stepped out from the entrance, as though she were under some kind of spell woven by the dark bows. She no longer felt her earlier need to reach the battlements, either; after seeing all of the overgrowth, she suspected the maze would not reveal its pattern, even from the roofs.

Suddenly weary, Sydony was tempted to go to her room, but Mrs Talbot stopped her, inquiring how many would be for supper. 'Three, as usual,' Sydony said.

'Will the viscount be staying for another night?'

'Yes,' Sydony answered. Indeed, she wondered if they'd ever be rid of him.

With a nod, the housekeeper turned to go, but Sydony called after her. 'Mrs Talbot, why did you lock the door to the upper stair?'

'What, miss?' the housekeeper asked, turning back around. 'I unlocked it for you and then went about my work.'

'But someone shut it behind us and locked it,' Sydony said.

The housekeeper eyed her stonily. 'It wasn't me, miss.' She might have turned again, but Sydony stopped her once more.

'Where did you get your set of keys?'

The housekeeper's expression didn't alter. 'They're the set I've always had, miss.'

'But didn't you turn them in when you left?'

For once, the woman appeared uncomfortable. 'I suppose I didn't,' she said. Then she lifted her chin. 'But I've done nothing wrong. I left and never came back until Mr Sparrowhawk summoned me. I can go again, if you wish.'

'No, of course not,' Sydony said. 'But I'd like the keys, please.' Sydony held out her hand, palm upwards, and, for a long moment, she thought the housekeeper would refuse.

'As you wish, miss,' Mrs Talbot said, finally. And she lifted her hand to drop the set into Sydony's.

'One more thing, Mrs Talbot,' Sydony said. 'Is there anyone around here who might know more about the maze?'

The housekeeper paled. 'What do you mean?'

Sydony adopted a casual tone. 'I'm just curious about the whole garden, really. I'd like to put in some other plantings and tidy up the property. It looks like the moors are taking over.' That was true enough.

'I'm not seeking someone of the order of Capability Brown's successors, but a man familiar with the area,' Sydony said. 'Is there someone in the village or even in Sutton who does good work?'

But the housekeeper just shook her head.

Sydony did not give up. She knew there was no use talking to the cook, but she found Nellie scrubbing the tiles in the entryway. The girl was muttering to herself when Sydony spoke.

'Nellie?'

The maid paused in her chore and looked up, abashed. 'I beg your pardon, miss.'

'Is Mrs Talbot working you too hard?' Sydony asked.

'Oh, no, miss,' the maid said.

Sydony waited, and the maid spoke again. 'It's just that there are some who think they're too good for certain jobs.'

Again, Sydony waited, and Nellie eventually sat back on her heels. 'It's that new girl.'

'Yes,' Sydony prompted.

'Well, I can't like her, miss.'

Sydony didn't smile, though she was tempted to do so.

'She's not from around here,' Nellie said, with a local's wariness of all things outside her own experience.

'Where is she from?' Sydony asked.

'I don't know. She won't say, miss. She won't say anything about herself, but is always asking questions.'

'Maybe she's curious.'

Nellie eyed her askance. 'Questions about you, miss, and Mr Marchant and old Miss Marchant what died, and Oakfield. I can tell you one thing, Mrs Talbot doesn't like it. Told her to stop chattering.'

'Perhaps she just wants to know what she's getting into here,' Sydony said. 'I wonder where Mr Sparrowhawk found her?'

Nellie shook her head. 'I wish he'd take her back as I don't know what use she'll be to you, refusing to scrub the floor and all.'

'I'll keep an eye on her,' Sydony assured the maid. 'Nellie, do you know of anyone hereabouts who does garden planning?' This time, Sydony was smart enough not to mention the maze. 'Someone with a lot of experience and a history in the area?'

Nellie didn't even pause to think. 'Old Mr Humbolt. He was quite famous in his day. What he doesn't know about gardening, he's forgotten. He was born and raised in Sutton, but he's living with his daughter in the village now. She married one of our own, you see.'

'Thank you, Nellie,' Sydony said, her weariness melting away under a new urgency. At last, she might find out something more about Oakfield's labyrinth.

* * *

An hour later, Sydony was seated in a squat, neat home at the edge of the village being served biscuits and cider by Mr Humbolt's daughter, a reserved woman probably twice Sydony's age. Mr Humbolt, seated nearby, was old indeed.

Sydony had surprised her brother and his new groomsman by arriving in the stables, ready to be driven into the village. But Kit had sent her off with well wishes, and Jeremy assured them that he knew the surrounding roads.

Sydony could have sworn that she'd seen the groomsman before, but when she asked him if they had met, he had laughed. 'I doubt it, miss,' he said, handing her hurriedly into the carriage before taking his seat and the reins.

The journey had been uneventful. The weather held, but the wind was picking up, blowing the leaves about, and clouds were soon covering the sun. Her new home was part of a bleak landscape, no matter what the conditions, Sydony decided.

She was glad to reach the village, where a young boy pointed her to the small cottage housing Mr Humbolt and his daughter, the widow Carey. When Sydony arrived on their doorstep, she was pleased to have a pert maid usher her into a little parlour, where the old gentleman was eager for a consultation. They had just settled in for a chat when his daughter arrived with the refreshments, and now Mr Humbolt leaned forwards.

'So, what brings you to see me, Miss Marchant?'

As soon as he spoke, Mrs Carey appeared to choke on her cider, and he got up to pat her on the back. 'Are you all right, Anne?'

'Yes, yes, I just… Did you say Marchant?' She turned wide eyes upon Sydony.

'Yes, I'm living at Oakfield Manor.'

Mrs Carey looked horrified.

'Is there something wrong?' Sydony asked.

'No. I… We had heard that there were new owners. I just never expected…' She trailed off in confusion, but Sydony guessed that she would have liked to find a polite way to usher her guest out. Quickly, Sydony turned to Mr Humbolt, in the hopes of getting some information before she was forced to leave.

'Yes, my brother and I inherited the estate and are doing our best to improve the property. The grounds have been neglected for some time, so, of course, I would like your advice about them.' Sydony paused. 'Also, much of the rear gardens consist of the maze, and I wondered what you could tell me about it.'

'I haven't seen it,' Mr Humbolt said, taking his seat once more. He appeared not to share his daughter's wariness and spoke easily.

'You are welcome to,' Sydony said.

'Father doesn't get out much.' There was no mistaking the steel in Mrs Carey's tone.

'Meaning my daughter doesn't want me to go. And why is that, my dear?' he asked, smiling.

'I don't think it would be good for your gout, all that walking about,' she said.

'You think there's something wrong with it,' Sydony said softly. *Some lingering evil.*

Mrs Carey had the grace to blush. 'Of course not. The house has a history of odd goings-on, that's all.'

'Well, I don't think this lovely young lady is involved

in any odd doings,' Mr Humbolt said. 'And while I haven't seen your particular maze, I've heard of it—an outstanding example, from what I gather.'

'Do you know how it came about?' Sydony asked. 'Why it was planted?'

'Well, garden mazes have been around for a while,' Mr Humbolt said, obviously warming to his subject. 'They grew out of the knot gardens that were common by the sixteenth century. Of course, those first mazes weren't like yours, and I'm not talking about any odd doings,' he added, winking at his daughter. She flushed, but said nothing.

'How were they different?' Sydony asked.

'The plantings between the paths were low. Like knot gardens, they were best seen from an upper window, and their greenery gave the garden colour throughout the year.'

'Yes,' Sydony said, nodded. 'It would be delightful to see it from the battlements.'

'And those early mazes weren't made to puzzle. They were simple, and often used herbs such as thyme, rosemary and lavender, which gave off a lovely scent for those admiring the garden. But they were a lot of work to maintain, requiring too much trimming.'

He paused to stretch out his legs. 'So dwarf box came into use. It didn't require much cutting, but, again, provided only a low hedge. Floral labyrinths were also popular, using flowerbeds, sometimes along with dwarf box, and with other flowers or shrubs situated in the centre.'

Mr Humbolt smiled. 'This was back when formal, enclosed gardens were popular, before William Gilpin,

Capability Brown and devotion to the picturesque and more natural landscapes. And the mazes were larger, taking up special areas within the gardens. The floral labyrinths that were planted with tall shrubs probably began the movement towards the sort of hedge maze you have. They say there was one made of high plants at Nonsuch Palace, and there are even early books on the subject, like *The Gardener's Labyrinth*, that date to the late fifteen hundreds.

'Still and all, those mazes were all unicursal, meaning that there weren't any forks to take. Each portion of the path was walked only once. And from what I've heard you've got yourself a puzzle maze, which came later, in the seventeen century.'

'Really?' Sydony blinked in surprise, for she had imagined the labyrinth as being far older.

Mr Humbolt nodded. 'By all accounts, your maze was planted by the original owner of that property, Ambrose Mallory, when the house was built in the 1680s.'

Sydony heard the man's daughter gasp and slanted her a glance. Was she choking again? The woman was frowning and looked as though she might speak, but her father continued without a pause.

'It is only recently that mazes have become popular at pleasure gardens and spas,' he said. 'Although some are even in parks, most are part of private estates, far larger than yours,' he added.

'So this maze, the one at Oakfield Manor, isn't that old?' Sydony said.

'Well, that depends on your definition of old,' he said. 'I would say more than a century is quite a long time.'

'Of course,' Sydony said. 'It's just that I… Well, I imagined it as far older.' Ancient. *Perhaps with a lingering evil.* 'Didn't the Romans have labyrinths? I thought there are still some mosaics from those days.'

'Perhaps,' Mr Humbolt said. 'But I only know about the garden ones. Maybe you're thinking of turf mazes. There are some of those still about, gulleys cut into the turf. They aren't the art of the gardener, but of shepherds and the like. They're found on village greens or hilltops and used for festivities, such as May Day.'

He paused as if in reminiscence. 'When I was a child, we played a game where a girl stood at the centre, while we young men raced around the pathway to rescue her.' He smiled. 'We called it a mizmaze. Legend has it that there was once a large tree on the central mound, but it burned down during a celebration that got out of hand.'

'But why?' Sydony asked. 'Why were they made in the first place?'

Mr Humbolt shrugged. 'I don't know about turf mazes, but the puzzle maze is decorative, as well as entertaining, and another feature of the puzzle labyrinth is that the pathway is known only to a select few, making trespass difficult.'

Sydony nodded slowly. It would certainly be difficult to trespass in their maze, especially since the path was strewn with traps.

'As for the pattern itself, who knows? Some say the origins go back to the earliest residents of these isles, who were known to practice the disembowelling of animals or people for divinatory purposes.'

Sydony drew in a sharp breath just as a loud thump echoed upon the tile floor. She turned to see that Mrs

Carey, white as a sheet, had dropped her glass of cider. 'I think you'd better go now,' she whispered.

For a moment, Sydony simply stared, stunned by Mr Humbolt's words. Was he talking about Druids? Did they have something to do with mazes? Mr Humbolt probably did not know, and even if he did, Sydony could not ask. She could barely thank her host before his daughter hurried her to the door.

And she received no invitation to return.

Chapter Eight

When Barto heard that Sydony had suddenly called for the carriage, he decided to follow. He told himself that he wanted to know just what the female Marchant was up to, but he had to admit that he was concerned, as well.

He hadn't liked what they found in the maze. Unless the Marchants themselves had set up an elaborate ruse to keep him out, someone was endangering them. And while Barto trusted Jeremy to keep a better watch than most, he had no idea what they were up against, if anything.

He'd seen some strange things in London, but nothing as mysterious as the doings at this Tudor manor on the moors. If not the Marchants, who had set traps in the maze? Barto had no idea who would gain, if one of the family was injured. Or was the Marchants' crazy relative responsible? By all accounts, she had tried to have the hedges destroyed. Barring those attempts, perhaps she had tried to catch trespassers, real or imagined, with animal snares.

Barto hoped it was something as simple as an old woman's whims, but he couldn't be sure. Something was wrong here. He could smell it; it hung over Oakfield like the taint of bad food. But was it the Marchants themselves who reeked…or something else?

Without knowing, Barto had to be on guard, and not just for himself. He could easily picture the headstrong Sydony barging through the shrubbery only to become caught. Besides mangling her foot, perhaps irreparably, the loss of blood might kill her.

Barto frowned. He didn't trust Kit to keep her safe. Sydony's brother had left her totally alone in that strange house, and now he seemed oblivious to any threats. Kit wasn't stupid, so his lack of concern was odd in itself. Was he blind to any problems with his inheritance, or was he behind it all himself? With Sydony by his side…

Barto slowed as the family's carriage halted at a small cottage. Calling to a nearby lad, he found out who lived there and paid the youngster to run and fetch him when the conveyance left. In the meantime, he had his own visit to pay.

Mr Sparrowhawk's shabby office spoke for itself. Although he seemed to be a poor solicitor, he was sharp enough to be eager for business, so his greeting was effusive. Cutting through the welcome, Barto took a seat and wasted no time getting to the point.

'As you know, I'm well acquainted with the Marchant family and am acting as an adviser to them,' he said, ignoring the exclamations of delight and petty flattery that followed.

'Naturally, in order to properly counsel Mr Marchant, I want to be in possession of all the facts, so I was hoping that you could give me a more detailed account of his inheritance.'

'Of course, my lord,' Sparrowhawk said, without the slightest hesitation. 'Although my time is valuable…'

'I'll reimburse you,' Barto said.

It was money ill spent, for Sparrowhawk soon proved himself as worthless as Barto had suspected. He claimed to have served Miss Elspeth Marchant faithfully for years, and that when she died in her sleep, her estate went to her nearest relation, Kit and Sydony's father. By the time the solicitor had finally prepared to inform Mr Marchant of his good fortune, he, too, was dead, and left his son the heir.

'And how did Miss Marchant die?' Barto asked.

The solicitor blinked his beady eyes. 'Why, she was quite elderly, my lord. I don't know that there was a specific cause beyond old age.'

'I see,' Barto said. So no one really knew what killed Oakfield's former owner, beyond the maze theory, of course. Despite the workman's claims, Barto did not think the hedges themselves responsible. Yet there might be some truth buried in the superstition.

'But the heirs weren't aware of their coming good fortune and paid no visits to her before her death, as far as you know?' Barto asked.

'No, my lord,' the solicitor said. 'Miss Marchant was something of a recluse, so that is hardly surprising.'

Indeed, Barto was not shocked that few ventured out to Oakfield, considering its reputation, but what of the

Marchants? Had their father been too sunk in his books to keep up a correspondence?

Barto listened as the solicitor detailed the funds Miss Marchant has accrued, which should be more than adequate, as long as Sparrowhawk himself didn't dip too deeply into them. 'Are there any irregularities with the accounts?' Barto asked, lifting a brow in question.

The solicitor shook his head a bit too vehemently. If he was pocketing some change, he might well change his habits now that Barto had broached the subject. With a casual air, Barto tossed off another question, far more important to him than Sparrowhawk's activities. 'Any large amounts withdrawn before her death, or added recently?'

'No, my lord,' Sparrowhawk said, looking bewildered. 'Everything has been quite stable…for years.'

'Obviously, very little was used to maintain the house, which I understand was left unlocked and essentially abandoned after Miss Marchant's death,' Barto noted.

Sparrowhawk's eyes darted away. 'I assure you, my lord, I knew nothing of this. I thought the housekeeper was still there.'

'Because you checked?'

'Really, my lord, I have so much business to concern myself, there would not be enough time in the day to personally verify all—'

Barto cut him off. 'But you have visited the house?'

'On occasion,' Mr Sparrowhawk said, a bit nervously.

Barto wondered whether the solicitor attended his client at all. 'Then you must have seen the large library, that is empty now of books. What happened to them all?'

The solicitor blinked at him in apparent confusion. 'I'm not sure, my lord. I had heard that she wanted to burn some books, though I certainly did not condone it.'

'Apparently she did not set fire to the books, yet they are gone. Did they just disappear?'

'I don't know, my lord. I can hardly keep track of all of the possessions of all of my clients. Miss Marchant was free to do what she willed with her property.'

'So the books were gone before she died?'

'I assume so, my lord.' Sparrowhawk swallowed, and Barto was guessing the man never knew what was in the house, if he had been there at all.

'So you know nothing of any activity at the site after she died?'

'Of course, not, my lord. We went through the house together, and I thought all was to your satisfaction,' Sparrowhawk said in his oiliest tone.

'What about the property itself? The lands, surrounding gardens, et cetera?'

'If there was any vandalism, my lord, I certainly wasn't aware of it.'

Barto wouldn't call laying traps vandalism, so he guessed that the solicitor wasn't cognisant of any goings on. Still…

'The place seems to have an odd reputation,' Barto said, eyeing the man closely. 'The servants are reluctant to work the grounds or even commit to continued employment.'

The solicitor looked away again, visibly nervous. 'I'm sure that's just local gossip. You know country folk. They will cling to their primitive beliefs.'

'And what might those be?'

'What's that, my lord?' Sparrowhawk said, his gaze darting anywhere except to Barto's face.

'Those primitive beliefs. What might they be?'

'I'm sure I don't know.'

'Then why the difficulties hiring servants?'

'The place is rather out of the way, my lord.'

'What is it, Sparrowhawk?' Barto said, leaning forwards. 'What's the gossip, the bad reputation? I'll be extremely displeased if I can't get the information I want easily.'

The solicitor looked pale.

'Is there someone you're protecting? Because, if so, you'd better hope he's far more powerful than I am.'

Now Sparrowhawk looked appropriately frightened. 'I'm not… There's no one, my lord! Oakfield makes all of the locals nervous because of its odd history. That's all.'

'What odd history?' Barto pressed.

'The man who built it was thought to dabble in the dark arts, and supposedly, that makes the place one of ill luck,' the solicitor said, obviously uncomfortable. 'No one wants to get too close or stay too long.'

'And just how did this affect the previous owner, Miss Marchant, who seems to have lived well into old age?'

The solicitor blinked at Barto. 'Why, she went mad, my lord, mad as a hatter.'

By the time Sydony was able to talk with her brother alone, it was late. When he retired early, she made her excuses to Barto, then hurried to follow Kit to his room, closing the door behind them.

For once, he didn't appear too happy to see her. 'You

might have stayed below to entertain our guest,' he said, heaving a sigh.

Sydony made a sound of exasperation. 'Let Barto entertain himself. He always does anyway.'

Kit shook his head, but did not pursue the subject. 'Your visit to the village went well?' he asked, instead. He had questioned her earlier, but Sydony had kept mum in front of the viscount.

'Yes—'

'Jeremy handled the pair well?'

'Yes,' Sydony admitted, but the mention of the new groomsman triggered her memory. 'Kit, doesn't he look familiar?'

'A bit, I suppose. Why?'

'I think he worked at Hawthorne Park.'

'Hmm.'

Sydony knew that sound, which meant her brother wasn't paying much heed as he shrugged out of his coat. Sydony moved to help, trying not to remember when she had done the same for Barto... 'Wasn't he Barto's groomsman?'

Kit shrugged. 'I can't say I've been to his stables in recent years. Maybe Barto brought him along to help.'

'No. He was one of the new hires, and if he had once served the Hawthornes, why wouldn't Barto mention it?'

Kit shrugged, obviously uninterested. 'Maybe he just looks like someone else, someone you've seen before.'

'Perhaps,' Sydony conceded. After all, the fellow denied having met her. She began methodically brushing out Kit's coat, rather than leave it for the maid, even as she wondered what Barto's valet did all day. Surely he did not have enough work to keep him occupied, unless Barto had set him to other duties…

Sydony turned at the sound of Kit sprawling in a heavily carved chair. She had not been in his room since that first day, and she saw now that a nearby writing desk was piled high with materials.

'Are those the family papers you've been going through?' Sydony asked. She'd been unaware of them until her brother had mentioned them earlier today. 'What have you found?'

Kit leaned back to rub his eyes with his palms. 'Nothing interesting, just the usual property records, rents, crops, household expenditures, and that sort of thing.'

Sydony felt a pang at the carelessly tossed answer. Already cut off from friends and neighbours, she did not want Kit to shut her out, as well, intentionally or not. Did he think she wouldn't be interested? Or was he consulting with Barto instead?

'Did you pay a call on the vicar?' Kit asked with a yawn. 'He can probably fill you in on local society. There must be some gentry who hold country dances, at least. I'm surprised we haven't received any invitations.'

Sydony was tempted to tell him that she didn't think any invitations would be forthcoming, considering that everyone she met acted as though they were somehow tainted, just by living at Oakfield. But she didn't want to start another argument. She had more important things on her mind.

After hanging up his coat, she took up a small shield-back chair and placed it close to him. 'I wanted to talk to you about the maze,' she began.

Kit sighed. 'Don't start, Syd. I don't want you wandering through it, just in case there are more traps in there.'

'I'm sure there are.'

Kit lifted his head. 'You didn't go back in, did you?'

Sydony shook her head. 'I don't have to. It's obvious that somebody has been in there, maintaining the pathways and laying snares for the unwary. I went to the village today to talk to an expert on mazes, and he said one of the reasons for planting a puzzle maze is to keep its secrets among a select few.'

'And who would those *select few* be?' Kit asked, giving her a jaundiced look.

'The Druids.'

Kit shook his head. 'Don't start that again. It's absurd, Syd. You might as well claim that witches or demons or ghosts are responsible. All-Hallows Eve is coming. Do you think they're planning on having a big ball in our maze?'

Sydony flinched. She knew Kit could be cutting, but rarely was she on the receiving end of his sarcasm. 'No, I don't think anyone's having a party in there. I have no idea why, but someone wants to keep us out. And how do we know that someone isn't Barto, who arrives out of nowhere to take a sudden interest in our new property?'

Before Kit could argue, she continued. 'Barto and his man were ahead of us. How do we know that they didn't place that trap there?'

Kit looked exasperated. 'Whatever for?'

'Because he's a Druid, just like his father before him.'

Kit looked at her long and hard. 'I'm worried about

you, Syd. Maybe you should go visit Sally or Eliza. Take a whole month, if you like. We'll manage here, and maybe it will be more like home when you return.'

Sydony blinked in astonishment. *Was her brother trying to send her away?* It had always been the two of them, motherless, taking care of their bookish father more often than not, standing together after the funeral and their uprooting. Although there had been some childhood squabbles when he had sided with Barto and she had run off to her father or the servants or another friend.

But here there was no one else.

Sydony shook her head and turned away, determined not to let him see her dismay. She had reached the door before he spoke again.

'Syd,' he called after her, but his tone was more exasperated than apologetic.

Drawing a deep breath, Sydony left his room and sought the relative haven of her own. Her brother wanted to send her away, and not even the prospect of seeing her old friends could cheer her. Such a visit might well be more bitter than sweet, seeing her home occupied by someone else, her old friends moving on without her. And then what? It would be even more difficult to come back here.

And what would go on in her absence? Sydony shuddered to think of Kit totally under the viscount's sway. No matter how much her brother might like to ignore it, there was something going on here, something unnatural, and Sydony was certain that Barto was involved.

She went to bed feeling more alone than ever, far

away from her old friends and isolated from her new neighbours, without even her brother to stand by her. As Sydony lay there in the darkness, she wondered if this was how her great-aunt felt, alone except for her odd servants, battling a threat only she perceived…

When Barto went down to breakfast he found the Marchants both there, but Sydony looked pale and drawn. Although Kit was his usual teasing self, she didn't laugh, and her smile was wan. Was she under some strain beyond that of living here?

Without asking specifically about the traps in the maze or the trepanned skull, Barto had obtained no further information from Sparrowhawk. And since the solicitor's story echoed that of the workman, Barto could see no reason to delve further into the house's ill repute.

For a moment, Barto felt a bit of sympathy toward Kit. He had inherited a good living, and if he could get the estate back in working order, he should be successful. But the Tudor manor seemed a bogey house, driving away all the locals.

One glance at Sydony's tense expression made Barto dismiss those thoughts, for the Marchants weren't above suspicion. They could very well have poisoned their great-aunt and killed their own father in order to come into their tidy inheritance. And Barto's father had just been caught in the way.

Barto took only some toast as he studied his companions. If there was a breach developing between the siblings, he wanted to take advantage of it. Then, at last, he might get some answers. 'Shall we try the battlements again this morning?' he asked, turning toward Sydony.

At his words, Sydony looked up, surprised pleasure written upon her lovely features, and for a moment Barto could only stare. He couldn't remember the last time he'd genuinely tried to please a woman, just for the sake of putting a smile upon her face. *And he was not doing so now,* he reminded himself.

'Good idea,' Kit said. 'Syd, don't go haring off by yourself. There are too many hazards around this old place.'

'Hazards,' Sydony repeated, her voice rife with sarcasm.

'Yes,' Kit said, and Barto wondered what was behind the look they exchanged.

But any rift between them could only serve his ends. 'Bring the keys, and we'll see if we can unlock the top door,' Barto said.

This time Barto had the wherewithal to grab a lantern and some tools, as well as to inform Hob where he was going, just in case he encountered any further problems—or traps, animal or human. When he reached the first floor, Sydony was already waiting by the door, but Barto put down the lantern and ducked into one of the nearby rooms where he'd seen the flash of a skirt, to call for the maid.

'Bessie, isn't it?' he asked as she approached.

'Yes, my lord.'

'Would you please stand watch for us here, to make sure the door doesn't fall shut?'

With a fierce nod, she stood behind them as Sydony tried the keys and managed to swing the door wide.

Propping it open with a heavy chair he dragged from the gallery, Barto told the maid to sit there and keep watch.

'If anyone, even Mrs Talbot or Mr Marchant, tells you to move, don't leave your post,' Barto said. 'Just tell them you have your orders from the viscount.'

Barto thought Sydony might bristle at his words, but she did not, another sign that the siblings might be on the outs. He felt a certain smugness as he headed up the stairs, perhaps some remnant of those rare days past when a youthful Sydony would side with him, rather than her brother.

At the top of the stairs, Sydony tried the keys, while Barto held the lantern, but the lock soon clicked. Barto pushed the heavy door outwards and felt fresh air, crisp with the feel of autumn. Though no rain appeared imminent, the sky was overcast, casting the roofs in a stark grey glow. About him, the battlements stretched towards pitched roofs on one side and additions on the other, but, despite years of neglect, they were relatively free of debris.

He heard Sydony move forwards, and he had to stop himself from physically pulling her back from her recklessness. 'Be careful!' he said, instead, though his fingers flexed against the urge to catch her to him. 'There could be cracks in the old stone.' The warning was true enough, but Barto was alert for other, more subtle dangers.

Propping the door open with the lantern, he saw that Sydony was already standing at a machicolation, having ignored his admonition as usual. Barto stepped forwards more carefully, but the area looked safe enough, weathered, yet strong, a sheltered corner of a past long gone. And Barto realised it was a place they would have loved in their younger days. *A haunt for Robin Hood and his Maid Marian.*

Barto shook his head. There was no such place. There were no such people. Had there ever been?

He approached Sydony slowly, watching the wind take a strand of silky dark hair to whip about her face. She was leaning against one of the corbels, looking out over the land. Having unerringly chosen the rear of the property, she seemed transfixed by the maze below.

Barto stopped beside her and silently studied her profile. She really was beautiful. Once he stripped away all his memories of the child, the woman she had become was breathtaking. This new Sydony had flawless skin, a slender nose, deepset eyes under delicate brows, and a mouth that seemed far too tempting for the urchin she had been.

As if aware of his scrutiny, she shivered and turned her head away. Barto followed her gaze over the bleak landscape. No doubt someone as cheerful as Kit could learn to love this estate, but it held no allure for Barto. He preferred Hawthorne Park, with its wide lawns and carefully tended gardens, and he was struck by a sudden yearning for it. How often had he condemned country life these past few years as dull and provincial and his responsibilities there as onerous? Yet, now it seemed a haven, a trust, a place to build a life…

Sydony shivered again, and Barto realised that up here the wind was fierce, whipping at her thin gown and delineating her slender figure. One look at that outline, and Barto was seized with a desire so great that he had to put a hand out to steady himself against the stone.

'You must be cold,' he murmured. 'Here, take my coat.' It was a gesture he had made countless times before, but not to the grown Sydony and not when the very sight of her sent heat burning through him.

She muttered some kind of protest, but Barto stripped off his coat, welcoming the air that cooled him and cleared his head. Still, he had to move behind her and slip the garment over her shoulders, without succumbing to the temptation of dipping his head close and pressing his body against hers.

When he stepped away, Barto was tight with anger at a weakness that had never troubled him before. There were many among his peers who would chase after any skirt, including genteel young ladies. But Barto was not among them. In fact, most of the mamas had given up pushing their marriageable daughters at him. He was polite, no more, to them and took his pleasures elsewhere, from women who knew how to be discreet.

Sydony Marchant would never be discreet. She could not hide the simplest of emotions from her expressive face, Barto knew, and yet somehow that did not seem a drawback. In the throes of passion, she would keep no secrets, tell no lies… The thought brought him up short, reminding him that the Marchants were not to be trusted, no matter how guileless they appeared.

Barto assumed a casual stance against the worn stone of the battlements. 'All yours, to a great distance,' he murmured as he gazed out over the surrounding lands.

Sydony said nothing.

'Did you ever think to be such a landowner?'

She shook her head silently, but she did not seem pleased.

'Surely your father must have told you what you would inherit some day,' Barto said. God knew his own legacy had been drummed into him since birth.

'No. We had no idea Great-aunt Elspeth was so well situated.'

'You never came to visit her here?' Barto asked, his voice carefully neutral.

'No,' Sydony said. 'I remember her visiting us when we were very small, but after Mother died, Father never really kept up with the family.'

'Curious,' Barto commented, and she swung towards him, as if eager for a quarrel.

'Hardly so curious. You know how Father was. He was more interested in his studies than in socialising.'

Although Barto would hardly call maintaining family ties socialising, he did not argue. 'Yes, he was usually deep in a book, wasn't he?'

'Of course.' Sydony turned back toward the moors, away from Barto, and he felt a twinge of annoyance. He was tempted to take her chin in his hand and force her to pay attention to him, *only* him, to tell him the truth, to reveal herself…

Ignoring such urges, he assumed a mask of cool indifference. 'And what of the books that were once here?' he asked. 'At first you claimed they had been burned, then that they were not. What happened to them?'

Sydony swung round with a look of annoyance on her lovely face, and for a moment he thought she might tell him to mind his own business. But she was not quite so rude. 'Why?' she asked, a stubborn set to her dainty chin.

Barto shrugged. 'I am curious.'

She studied him for a long moment before answering. 'Mrs Talbot claims they were sent to my father, although he made no mention of them to us. We must have packed them back up with all his others.'

'And you did not recognise them as not his own?'

Sydony's brows lowered in a cross expression that he remembered well, but her beauty made it more palatable. 'Do you know how many books he had? How were we to know one from another?'

Fair enough. 'Did he handle valuable books, buying and selling for other collectors?' Barto asked, as casually as he could.

Sydony erupted in what sounded suspiciously like her brother's snort and glanced away. 'I'm sure he shared with other scholars, but he was not in the book business, no.'

'Curious.'

Barto threw the word out there again, but said nothing further, and, like a bear to bait, she swung toward him again. 'What? What's curious? Is there some particular book you are seeking, *my lord*?'

Barto shook his head. 'And you said that he was not particularly sociable, either?'

'What do you mean?' She was angry now, with twin spots of colour staining her cheeks. They made her even more desirable, and Barto wanted to seize her, to feed his own anger with hers. But where would that take him? Down a path he could not go. So he forced himself to concentrate on what he came here for, not some brief flirtation.

'I mean that you did not spend much time at Hawthorne Park, did you?' he asked, even though his mother had said as much.

'Of course not,' Sydony said.

'Then why is that your father was with my father when they died?' The fierce words sounded like an accusation even to Barto's ears.

Yet her expression showed no guilt. In fact, they seemed to drain off her anger, her skin now pale beneath the fading colour. 'I don't know,' she said softly. She looked up at him, her eyes searching his own with such seriousness that he wanted to take her to him and keep her safe always, Maid Marion to his knight of the forest, and to hell with everything else.

'Do you?' she asked, and Barto was brought back to himself, away from temptation and the stuff and nonsense of childhood.

'Your father never said anything to you about where he was going that day or why?' Barto asked, his tone harsher than he intended.

'No,' Sydony said. Reacting to the accusation in his voice, she glared at him. 'What did your mother know of their plans?'

'Nothing,' Barto admitted. It wasn't until later, after he'd been contacted by a third party, that the mystery had begun to unravel. *Or deepen.* 'Yet my father directed his coachman to your home, where your father joined him, and they departed for London.'

'Yes! I know that as well as you do,' Sydony said.

'And where were you when my father arrived?'

'Kit and I were at Molly Hutchinson's, celebrating the birth of her son,' Sydony said. 'Father said nothing to us about going out, so I don't know if he even knew of your father's arrival beforehand. We only learned of it when we arrived home, and the maid told us that Father had left with Viscount Hawthorne.'

She spoke the words as though by rote. Were they rehearsed, or had she simply repeated them too often already?

'And you did not know where they were going or why?' Barto pressed.

'No!' Sydony turned upon him, her eyes glittering with her intensity. 'Do you?'

'Yes,' Barto said. 'As it happens, I do.'

Chapter Nine

Sydony blinked up at the man beside her, her emotions careening between curiosity, anger and suspicion. If Barto knew more about the accident, why hadn't he spoken to them before, at the funerals for both men? Or in the months following when they were still living in the house they were forced to leave? Why wait until now, after days of arriving unannounced only to corner her on the roofs with his vaguely threatening questions?

Under the weight of Barto's heavy coat, Sydony shivered with unease. Despite the compelling warmth and scent that still clung to it, the elegant garment felt like a prison, where this new, menacing Barto might trap her. He'd always had a dangerous air about him, but she had put that down to a child's awe for an older and more adventurous boy. Now she was acutely aware of the power of his title, his imposing physical strength, and that hint of darkness just below the surface of his expressionless face.

Sydony's heart jumped to her throat as she wondered

whether it was wise to be alone here with him. Suddenly, the ground seemed a long way down, with not a soul in sight, and no one to hear her, should she call out. Her fingers dug into the cold stone, as if to gain purchase, then she drew a deep breath.

She was no coward. She had never let Bartholomew Hawthorne bully her, and she was not going to let him frighten her, either. She turned to face him, her fingers clinging to the crumbling surface she leaned against, her eyes measuring the distance to the door and the stair where the maid waited below. But would she find safety on the steps? It was the new maid, not Nellie, who sat below, with orders from Barto not to leave her post.

Sydony struggled to gain a firm hold on her runaway imagination, then forced herself to look up at the man beside her. Dangerous or not, if he knew more, she wanted to hear it. 'What happened?'

'There appears to have been a book,' he said, and Sydony felt a chill. She remembered all the instances when Barto had been interested in the library, both her father's and Elspeth's. Was he telling her the truth, or was this tale some ruse to get what he wanted?

'Your father had in his possession a volume that he thought my father would be interested in, and, apparently, they were on their way to show it to an expert to assess its value,' Barto said.

Sydony drew in a ragged breath as she tried not to relive that day when she and Kit had come home from the party, surprised to find their father out. Then the long hours that followed as they waited until a servant from Hawthorne Park arrived late in the evening to report there had been an accident…

'But why would both of them go?' Sydony asked. 'Why wouldn't Father just give the volume to the viscount?'

Barto shrugged, but it was not a careless gesture. Sydony could see the tension in the lines of his shoulders and the set of his jaw. His dark eyes bored into her, as though seeking something. But what?

'Where is the book now?' Sydony asked, her voice a low murmur.

'I was hoping you could tell me.'

Sydony nearly flinched from the words that confirmed her own suspicions. Was that all that he wanted, a book? 'But how should I know? I knew nothing of its existence.'

'And yet the volume wasn't found in the overturned coach,' Barto said.

Sydony closed her eyes against the image she had never even seen: her father and the viscount lying dead among the ruins of their conveyance. The horses had run wild, the driver unable to control them, a wheel had gone off on a hill, and all had tumbled to the bottom, broken. Only the driver had lived long enough to tell the tale before succumbing to his injuries.

And yet Barto was concerned about a book. 'How do you know it wasn't there?' Sydony, suddenly weary.

'Because everything was returned to me, as the next viscount.'

Did Barto sound bitter? Sydony tried to see something, anything, in his face, but his expression told her nothing. 'And how can you be certain that they had this book with them?'

'Because the expert they were going to meet told them to bring it. It was the sole purpose of their journey to London, to keep an appointment with this man,' Barto said. 'And yet they never appeared.'

'But I thought you didn't know where they were going or why they were together,' Sydony protested.

'I didn't,' Barto said. 'It was only recently that I was able to devote my energies to finding out more about that day.'

Sydony felt a surge of powerful emotion. 'Recently? Do you mean today? Or last week or last month?' she asked. 'Why tell me this now? Why wait until this very moment to give me information that you have withheld from Kit and I concerning the death of our father?' Sydony paused, slanting a quick glance at his rigid features. 'Did you tell Kit?'

He shook his head, and Sydony didn't know whether to be relieved or even more angry. For a long moment, she wanted to fly at him, to scratch at his dark, fathomless eyes or beat upon his unmoving chest for proving that all her suspicions were well founded, that he was far less a man than the boy he had once been.

And then she shivered, her rage dissipating, only to leave her cold and empty. 'Why are you here?' she asked. 'You wait until we move to seek us out, arrive without an invitation, and take advantage of Kit's hospitality while giving me black looks and peppering me with questions about a book I know nothing about.

'Why? Is it valuable?' Sydony asked coldly. 'I would think that coming into your title would provide you with more than enough money.'

If she'd hoped to shame him, it did not work. His expression was just as stony as ever, his voice just as threatening when he finally answered.

'I'm here because I intend to find out what happened and why,' he said. 'And if my father's death was no accident, I will have my vengeance.'

Barto had nothing. He'd tipped his hand in the hopes of taking the pot, but he'd come away empty handed. So now he could only watch as Sydony rushed to tell her brother—to tattle, to share, or to warn him? Barto didn't know. Again, he had to fight an urge to stop her, to catch her to him, but this time not to keep her safe. Instead, he wanted to shake the truth out of her, to strip away everything…

For Sydony had revealed nothing, claiming ignorance and shedding no light upon the accident. When he had questioned her, she had been alternately silent, guarded and angry.

Kit, as usual, was a different story. Barto studied him carefully, while Sydony repeated what he had told her, but this Marchant was not guarded. He accepted the new facts with sharp curiosity and immediately honed in on the pertinent information.

'What about this expert?' Kit asked. 'Perhaps he wanted this book for himself. Is there some possibility that he could have waylaid them? Is that what you're thinking?'

Barto didn't tell Kit what he was thinking, but the look on Sydony's face suggested she knew full well that his suspicions did not involve the expert.

Barto shook his head. 'He's an elderly gentleman with a reputation for honest dealings, chosen by my father for his knowledge. I hardly think he'd do murder for the sake of an interesting volume.'

'Then what makes you think it might not be an

accident?' Kit asked. 'Perhaps someone else, some shop boy or shady character, got wind of the appointment.'

And just that quickly, Barto wasn't alone in all this; Kit was with him. Barto felt a jolt as he realised that Christopher Marchant accepted his version of events without question and was ready to offer his aid, to do whatever necessary, as always. The years fell away, and Barto was looking at the Little John to his Robin, his man-at-arms, his faithful follower and companion.

It was easy to remember why they had been friends. Kit was deceptively simple, compared to his own complexities. He was eager to face anything, and yet seemed so relaxed at all times that Barto had envied him. Yes, with all his advantages, Barto sometimes wished to trade places with the poor scholar's son, for there had been times when his responsibilities had weighed heavily upon him and he had longed for Kit's carefree existence.

But Barto realised now that it wasn't Kit's existence that was carefree, so much as Kit himself. Christopher Marchant didn't let anything bother him, and Barto might still wish for that kind of ease. Of course, his social circle would mock Kit's perpetual optimism as foolish. But Kit wasn't stupid. He had learned more from his father than expensive schooling had provided Barto. But Kit didn't lord his intelligence over others, ridiculing them to prove himself. He was just Kit. Still and always.

In contrast, Barto had grown weary and wary over the years. Too many people trying to use him, too many young women throwing themselves at him, and too many mamas thrusting their daughters forwards had made him jaded. He had been forced to distance himself from others. It was necessary, or so he thought. But in the process, had he forgotten how to be real, how to be himself?

When he had travelled to Oakfield, Barto did not set out to revisit the past, a world he had thought nothing more than a memory. And yet, though the surroundings might have changed, as well as the looks of his companions, the Marchants' manners and sensibilities remained the same, a startling contrast to his usual company.

Here there was no competition to impress or ruin another, no cruel gossip spread for its own sake, and no dark manoeuvring for favours among peers. You wouldn't find the Marchants casting up their accounts after a five-bottle night or losing a fortune in some gambling hell.

How long had it been since he had spent time among such unaffected acquaintances? The Marchants' seeming disregard for his title and money and power made Barto want to let down his carefully constructed guard and resume where he had left off years ago. *Robin Hood and his merry band.*

The idea was so inviting, Barto nearly forgot that the ghost of his father was casting its dark shadow over the threesome, reminding him that his old friends might not be what they seemed. And while he was at it, he needed to stop reacting to Sydony Marchant as if she were a delicacy presented to him in one of the more elegant brothels. She was not, and her prickly attitude, well remembered from his boyhood, ought to be enough to make him keep his distance, no matter how attractive she might be. Unfortunately, that prickliness only seemed to excite him further.

Was everything upside down here? Or, if truth be told, had he come not because of some vague suspicions, but because deep down inside he sought out the only two people he could trust?

Again, Sydony had to wait until it was late in order to speak to her brother alone. For once, Barto retired first, though he took a bottle with him, and Sydony wondered whether he intended to consume it alone in his rooms. She supposed that was the way of dissolute noblemen, but better he be doing that than forcing his presence upon them. He had been moody and scowling ever since their discussion with Kit. No doubt, he wished that he'd never confessed, although now it didn't seem as if he had.

Indeed, his admissions hadn't sounded nearly as ominous when imparted to her brother. As she had so often in childhood, Sydony felt like she was a bystander while the other two spoke a language known only among males, this time one of retribution. And Sydony, remembering her fear on the roofs, had hesitated to speak out in front of him.

'So what do you think of our house guest now?' she asked, bluntly, once she was alone with Kit.

'I feel sorry for him,' her brother said.

'What?' Sydony blinked in surprise.

'He's eaten up by something, Syd, probably this suspicion his father was murdered.'

Sydony almost snorted. 'Or maybe the suspicion that we've got that book he wants so badly.'

Her brother simply shook his head.

'Kit, you weren't up there alone with him. He kept asking me about books, Great-aunt Elspeth's, Father's, in that horrid threatening tone and glaring at me, as though I were hiding the precious volume under my skirt.'

Kit barked a laugh before sobering. 'Somehow I wasn't surprised to hear his suspicions. It never did seem right—the accident, I mean. Didn't you think it odd Father never said a word to us?' He looked at her from across the small table that stood between them.

Sydony wanted to flinch from the pain in her brother's eyes, but she hadn't before and she did not now. She told him what she had told him so often since that day. 'It might have been a sudden thing, a whim,' she said softly, holding his gaze. 'Perhaps he mentioned the book to the viscount, who set up the appointment, then arrived with his usual high-handedness to cart Father away.'

'But if Father had come across something that interesting, why wouldn't he show us?' Kit asked. 'You know how excited he was upon finding some obscure volume.'

'And you know how forgetful he was,' Sydony said. 'He could have discovered the book among some shipment, perhaps even from Great-aunt Elspeth, during the early hours when we were abed, then forgotten about it by breakfast.'

'More likely he would have slept through breakfast,' Kit said wryly.

'Yes,' Sydony agreed softly. She didn't want to poke at their wounds, fresh once again, but she had to speak her mind. She straightened and lowered her voice nearly to a whisper. 'That is if we take Barto's story at face value.'

Kit shook his head as if to dismiss the very suggestion, but Sydony leaned forward with new urgency. 'How can we be sure he's telling the truth? He said nothing of this when he arrived, but lurked around, interrogating our servants, behaving oddly, asking cryptically about libraries, and never explaining himself. Then, suddenly, he beards me on the roof and practically threatens me concerning this alleged book. If he thinks our fathers were murdered, why not tell us immediately?' Sydony asked.

'Perhaps he has just begun to suspect it himself.'

'I doubt that it came on him while he was riding about our new property,' Sydony said.

Kit looked thoughtful. 'I would like to send for this expert, to talk to him myself.'

'Yes!' Sydony sagged with relief. With all that had happened, at least Kit wasn't encouraging her to leave. Now, he would have to agree it was Barto who should be going. 'Make sure you get the man's name before sending Barto on his way.'

Kit eyed her askance. Apparently, he was not going to evict their old neighbour just yet.

Sydony adopted a mutinous expression. 'Well, if he's so consumed with revenge, why stay here?'

'Oh, I don't know,' Kit said. 'Maybe because we are the only two people with whom he can share his suspicions, who are directly affected by them, having shared his loss.'

Sydony frowned. 'So you believe that he's only here to visit his old neighbours, not to search for some rare book we knew nothing about that came up missing in the accident?'

Kit sighed. 'Honestly, Syd, you're just as bad as he is.'

Sydony blinked. 'What do you mean?'

'Oh, come on, you were always two of a kind.'

Sydony's fingers tightened on the arms of her chair. 'What?'

Kit shook his head. 'And now you dance around here, glowering at each other, barely speaking, bristling with suspicion. He's an old neighbour, a friend, a viscount. Why can't you just believe him?'

'How can I?' Sydony said, her voice suddenly harsh. 'How can I trust him after what happened?'

'What happened? When?' Kit asked.

But Sydony could only shake her head, unwilling to share that long-ago experience, for fear her brother might mock her or explain it away with some glib male response.

Perhaps she had clung to it too long, made too much of it herself, but she remembered all too well that day in the garden of Hawthorne Park when Barto had kissed her and fled. Her hero, *her Robin Hood*, had turned out to be just a petty thief.

Sydony awoke suddenly, her eyes opening on to darkness and her heart pounding. Had she been caught in a nightmare, or had some noise jarred her from her sleep? She was still unused to the wind that whistled through every crack and crevice, producing a variety of eerie sounds, but when she cocked her head and listened, the howling was no worse than usual.

Rising from her bed, she slipped into a thick banyan,

one of Kit's old ones, as her feet hit the cold parquet floor. One glance at the fireplace told her that the fire had burned down, and, walking across the room, she knelt before it to poke at the embers. After watching a flame flare, she stood once more.

Restless now, Sydony did not return to her bed, but unerringly found the deepset windows that looked out over the maze. The day's clouds had passed, allowing the moon to cast a faint glow on to the grounds. Of course, the labyrinth was only a great dark mass below, but Sydony studied it none the less. Everything she had learned only made her more curious. Was it simply a pretty garden puzzle or something more sinister?

The more Sydony stared, the more she thought she saw a pattern emerge, both tantalizing and transforming before her very eyes. The twisting hedges seemed to call to her personally, to invite her to discover their secrets, to enter the darkness…

Sydony was leaning so far forwards that her forehead touched the glass, waking her from what might have been a dream. Had she fallen asleep at the window? She shook her head as if to clear it. But how could she have nodded off with both feet on the cold floor?

She looked again into the night below, as if she could somehow find the answers there, and drew in a sharp breath. Blinking, Sydony leaned forwards once more, for she could have sworn she saw lights flickering in and out, bobbing like glow worms in the blackness. Yet it was too late in the year for such things, and surely what she saw had to be bigger, like lanterns…

Just when Sydony was wondering what she should do, the lights seemed to disappear. For a moment she thought they were simply hidden by the greenery, but though she stayed at the window, watching closely, there was no further sign of anything.

Sydony shook her head again. This time she knew she wasn't dreaming, but had she imagined the lights? Or were they simply a trick of the moonlight on the leaves below? She frowned. But hadn't someone said that Elspeth had complained about lights in the maze? That's why she had closed all the shutters…

Sydony shivered, suddenly cold, and hurried back to her bed, to seek succor in its warmth. But she lay awake for a long time, wondering just what she had seen and if her great-aunt had shared her vision.

On her way to breakfast, Sydony hailed Mrs Talbot as she approached the dining room. After settling on a time to discuss menus later in the day and verifying that the viscount would still be there for supper, barring any unforeseen good fortune, Sydony normally would have let the housekeeper return to her duties. Instead, she cleared her throat.

'You didn't hear or see anything odd last night, did you?' Sydony asked.

'No, miss.' The housekeeper's face was like stone.

'I was just wondering, because I thought you had said that my great-aunt complained of lights outside.'

'No, miss,' the housekeeper said, without changing expression. 'I never told you such a thing.'

Sydony loosed a sigh of relief, but her respite was short lived.

'It's true, though,' Mrs Talbot added. 'Miss Marchant often complained about lights dancing through the maze in the dead of night. That's why she couldn't sleep.'

Sydony went cold. 'But you never saw them yourself?'

'No, miss,' Mrs Talbot said. She looked at Sydony curiously. 'Why, have you seen something?'

Sydony was tempted to lie, for fear of sounding as mad as her relative, but she lifted her chin. 'I'm not sure, but there did appear to be lights flickering on the grounds in the early hours.'

Mrs Talbot paled and shook her head. 'That's how it begins.'

'What? What begins?' Sydony asked.

'The end,' Mrs Talbot intoned before turning to go.

Sydony might have gone after her to ask just what she meant. *What end?* But she heard Kit hailing her from the dining room. Drawing a deep breath, Sydony tried to shake off the sense of dread that had descended with the housekeeper's words and stepped into the dining hall.

Barto was already seated and Kit was filling his plate at the sideboard. 'Good morning, sister dear,' he said, with a grin. 'Did you sleep well?'

He seemed inordinately cheerful this morning, which only made Sydony more gloomy. 'Not really,' she admitted. 'Something woke me in the middle of the night.'

She reached for a plate, but added only toast before sitting at the table some spaces away from Barto. If she hoped to make a point—that she well remembered his harsh treatment of her on the battlements—it was wasted, for he never even glanced her way.

'That infernal wind was probably responsible,' Kit said, taking his own seat.

'Perhaps,' Sydony said as she broke apart her toast. 'But when I looked out my window, I thought I saw something in the maze.'

'What?' Barto eyed her with sudden interest.

'I thought I saw some lights,' Sydony said.

Again, she was on the receiving end of Barto's probing stare, and she wondered what was going on behind the mask that he wore. Had he seen something? His room faced the maze, too. Or had he been the one out there in the darkness? Surely he could not think to find his precious book in the labyrinth.

'You probably saw a reflection of the moon off something in the garden,' Kit said. 'It's bright and nearly full.'

'None the less, I would like to take a look in our maze,' Sydony said, giving Barto a challenging glare. But he seemed to have lost all interest in her again.

'Should we have another go at it?' Kit asked Barto.

'Actually, I had my groomsmen go through it, just to make sure there were no other…surprises.'

Sydony blinked at the casual statement that Barto had taken it upon himself to send people through their maze, their private property, without even asking permission. She felt a surge of anger, as well as disappointment that the puzzle she so coveted had been discovered by another.

Apparently, Kit did not share her outrage. 'What did he find?'

'Two other traps, one well hidden, some more upturned earth, but nothing else.'

'Excuse me, but aren't you presuming a bit too much, *my lord*?' Sydony asked.

Again, Barto didn't even look at her.

'Better Barto's man than us, Syd,' Kit said. 'I'd hate to be responsible for anyone losing a foot in some snare, especially you.'

Sydony was not appeased. 'And just when did *your man* go through our labyrinth? Last night?'

Again, Barto seemed to address Kit rather than herself, which only annoyed her further. 'I assure you that Hob wasn't out there removing the traps in the dark,' he said. 'However, the bushes might have become enraged over his actions and decided to set themselves alight.'

Kit barked out a laugh, but Sydony found no humour in Barto's mockery. Did the viscount think she hadn't seen anything? Or did he protest too much? Either way, she had no intention of letting him have her labyrinth for himself.

'Since the way is clear, I think I'll go look for myself,' Sydony said, feeling the familiar surge of excitement. No rain or snares would stand in her way today.

This time she would go all the way to the oak.

Chapter Ten

Sydony hurried toward the entrance of the maze, her heart pounding at the realisation that she would solve the puzzle at last. Perhaps it was the delay that had fed her curiosity. First the weather, then the overgrown entrance and the traps all had conspired to keep her from her goal: the ancient oak at the centre of it all.

But this time Sydony was prepared. She wore boots, an old pair of kid gloves and a heavy cloak, and was armed with both a lantern and a ball of twine to mark her way. In this mild weather, she didn't really need the cloak and wondered whether it would get caught on the greenery. She decided to wear it for now, if only because she had secreted in its pocket a sharp knife for cutting any errant branches.

Ducking beneath the limbs at the entrance, Sydony felt almost as if she were entering a shrine, a sacred place of exotic mystery, not just a simple garden decoration. But those thoughts gave her a vague sense of unease. There was no denying her fascination with the labyrinth, a fascination that might even have gained more hold upon her, if not for the distraction of her house guest. But had Great-aunt Elspeth also had a kinship for the twisting, turning, mass of hedges, only to turn against them on her way to madness?

'Sydony.'

Sydony started at the sound of her name, spoken in a hushed, deep voice, and for a moment she thought she was hearing things, just as she might have been seeing things the night before. Was the maze itself calling to her or was she going the way of her aunt?

'Syd!' This time Sydony recognised her brother's voice and turned to find both he and Barto behind her. She felt a measure of relief, followed by a swift surge of annoyance at their interference. Did they think her incapable of finding her way? This was her maze, after all, she thought, fiercely proprietary of its secrets.

'We thought we'd take a look, too,' Kit said a bit sheepishly, and Sydony wondered if Barto was responsible for her company.

Ignoring the two men as best she could, Sydony turned back towards the interior of the maze. She had no intention of letting either of them lead, while she tagged along, just as though she were five years old again. She could hear Barto saying something about his man having marked the passages by breaking stems as he went through, but she did not listen. She moved ahead slowly, but surely, as if she already knew the route. At the first junction, she paused only briefly before choosing the fork to her right. Seven turns…

The further Sydony progressed, the more eerie the passage became, the greenery overhead casting shadows, along with the hedges themselves. The labyrinth became a separate world, rich with the scents of earth and leaves and evergreens. The shrubs muffled sound and distorted it, so she was never sure from what direction came a bird's call or the rustle of foliage. Even the footsteps of the men behind her were deceiving. If she got too far ahead of them, she began to think them in front of her as the passage wrapped around itself.

Sydony had only gone a few steps past a turn when she saw something on the path before her. It might just be a pile of leaves. Or it might not. A sudden sense of foreboding made her slow her steps. Although clumps of grass and weeds encroached upon the passageway, and dead leaves, brought in by the wind, gathered against the hedges, she had always been able to find a clear way forwards.

But now she stopped, wary of what she could not identify. It was not a trap, but what was it? Some natural collection of debris or something placed there deliberately? The memory of last night's lights returned, and she paused, reluctant to get any closer.

'What is it, Syd?' Kit asked. 'Have you lost your bearings?'

'There's something here,' Sydony said, her voice unsteady. Although there was no cause for fear, she shivered, suddenly swamped by unease. Yet what could possibly threaten her? She was not about to turn back when she was finally near to her goal. Nor was she ready to succumb to whatever foolishness had taken her great-aunt.

Sydony was about to step forwards when she felt Barto at her side. She grunted a protest as he squeezed by her in the narrow opening, his larger body brushing against her own before taking her place at the head of the party. But instead of walking towards whatever lay in the path, he stepped slowly and carefully, his tall form bent into a crouch, as though he were studying the ground for any marks. *What on earth…?*

'It's probably just some leaves,' she said, annoyed at having her position usurped.

'No, it's not,' Barto said, and though Sydony tried to push past him, he put out an arm to hold her back.

'What is it?' Kit asked.

'It looks like entrails,' Barto said.

Sydony frowned. If that was all, why wouldn't Barto let her go forwards? A child of the country, she had come across the remains of animals, whether prey to larger creatures or dead and decaying, and was not so missish as to faint at the sight. Determined to go on, she leaned against Barto's arm, straining to see.

But what lay ahead was no ordinary carcass, and Sydony put a hand on Barto's arm to steady herself. It looked like entrails, all right, but they were curiously isolated. There were no telltale signs of fur or feathers or other remains.

Behind her Sydony could feel Kit craning his neck, but she would not let him pass her. The presence of the men, so annoying before, now gave her a sense of safety, and she stayed between them.

'Was something caught in a trap?' Kit asked.

'No,' Barto said. 'There's no sign of anything nearby.'

'Perhaps we scared a fox or wildcat from its dinner,' Kit said.

Barto, bent over the mass, shook his head. 'It's too large for that. I'd guess this came from a large animal, a deer or even a cow. And although it's obviously fresh, the blood is dried, so it isn't that recent.'

'Odd that's all that's left,' Kit said.

That wasn't all that was odd. Sydony looked at the twisting mass spread out on the grass and felt a sickening sense of recognition. She swallowed hard against the bile rising in her throat. 'Does it look familiar?' she asked, her voice barely above a whisper.

'What?' Kit asked. 'If you're suggesting this is part of our man in the cupboard, I don't think so. These bits are fresher than his head.'

'The pattern,' Sydony said. 'Mr Humbolt said that some people think the original labyrinth pattern came from the practices of disembowelling…for divination purposes.'

'I suppose that was common enough in ancient Greece,' Kit said. He paused to look over her shoulder. 'But I can't really see it.'

Sydony shook her head. She did not *want* to see it, but she could not rid herself of the certainty that there was some connection, some reason beyond the random, for what they had found. And one look at Barto's dark visage told her he thought so, too.

Sydony opened her eyes to darkness, her heart thundering. Was she dreaming? The faint glow of her fire told her she was not, that again she had been awakened in the late hours of the night. But this time, she had a feeling some noise in the house was responsible, that she had heard the sound of a door. Pulse pounding, she glanced at her own door and was relieved to find it shut, but what of the room next to hers? Was Barto up and about?

Sydony slipped out of bed and moved to the window without even donning a wrap. As she looked out, moonlight cast its eerie glow upon the grounds, and, just as before, she thought she saw a flicker of light somewhere down there, perhaps even in the maze itself. Without hesitation, she began to dress, for tonight she would not wait and watch, only to be mocked by her brother.

Although she had said nothing in front of Barto, later, when she and Kit were alone, she'd reminded him of Nellie's warning. As always, Kit was sceptical.

'What are you saying, Syd? That glowing ghosts of some long-dead Celts are wandering about our property at night? You've heard so many weird tales about this place that you're imagining things.'

'I didn't imagine that bloody mess that we found in the maze today!' Sydony had protested.

Again, Kit had shrugged off what Sydony saw as a sign of something sinister at work.

'A dog probably ran off with remnants of a fallen deer or a neighbour's butchering,' he said. 'It's the time of year when farmers are putting by their stores for the winter.'

Although Sydony didn't argue, she didn't believe his rationalisation, and she didn't think Kit did either. Was he trying to keep her calm, or did he prefer to ignore what was happening on their own land? Sydony wasn't sure, but after tonight, she knew he couldn't dismiss her so easily. She was determined to catch Barto in the act, to find out what mischief he was making or hoax he was perpetrating.

Dressed in a warm gown, cloak, boots and gloves, Sydony quietly grasped the latch and slipped out of her room, shutting the door behind her. The house was eerily silent, without even the servants about, and Sydony made her way as best she could down the stairway, her hand feeling along the wall to guide her way in the darkness. She had been tempted to bring a lantern, but did not want her presence revealed, so she sought out the patches of moonlight shining through the windows to get her bearings.

Even the kitchen was silent as Sydony moved through it, casting a wary glance at the entrance to the servants' quarters below. When she heard no movement, Sydony breathed a sigh of relief and let herself out the side door.

Thankfully, the night echoed the day, with mild temperatures. And Sydony's eyes had adjusted to the darkness, so she was easily able to make her way to the corner of the house to peek around the back.

Before her stretched the old terrace, with its stone benches, and beyond that lay the labyrinth, the centre-piece of a garden long gone to seed. The grounds in between appeared deserted, but what of the maze itself? Was Barto already in there, making sure that she and Kit never reached the centre?

For a long moment, Sydony stood where she was, uncertain. Her anger at Kit and her suspicions of Barto had carried her this far. But what now? She could hardly step into the maze at night without a lantern. The moon-light would not penetrate the overgrown hedges, and the very thought of those darkened passages made her shiver.

She could not go in, but she could get closer. If she hid near the entrance to the maze, she might hear something from inside, and if she watched and waited, she might catch Barto upon his exit. After all, there was no other way out.

Sydony looked at the overgrown hedges and swallowed hard. From up in her room, it had all seemed so easy. She would expose Barto for what he was, whatever that might be, and Kit would finally have to listen to her. But here on the ground, she felt her determination ebb. The moonlight shifted and swayed, casting odd shadows across the grass and undergrowth. The wind, as always, moaned softly, sending leaves up in the air to dance and back to the earth to rustle and move.

It was an eerie landscape that would give anyone pause, especially when All-Hallows Eve approached. And crowding Sydony's mind were various warnings, along with images of skulls and entrails, mazes meant to keep people out, mystics and Druids. As Kit's younger sister, Sydony had learned to brave nearly anything, but now her hard-won courage was tested.

Drawing a deep breath, she told herself that she wasn't afraid of bugaboos and lore. What danger was there in stories? The wind and the leaves and the shadows could not harm her. Nor did she think Barto would, though she had felt threatened by him more than once. So, with great force of will, she moved around the corner and scurried across the terrace.

Sydony had nearly reached one of the stone benches when her progress was halted suddenly and violently. Seized from behind, she opened her mouth to scream, only to feel a heavy palm close over it. Panic made her want to flail at the arms that held her, but instead she slipped one hand into the pocket of her cloak, where the knife still rested. Her fingers closed about the handle and she might have reached up to slash at the hand covering her mouth, but for two things.

Gulping for air through her nose, she caught Barto's unmistakable scent just as she heard his whisper against her ear. 'What the devil do you think you're doing?'

Angry now, Sydony tried to stomp on his foot, but his grip tightened. 'Stop! Don't you realise what danger we are in? Stay still and speak softly, and I shall loose you.'

Sydony nodded and felt his warm hand leave her mouth as he turned her around to face him. 'What the devil are you doing here? Are you insane?' He gripped her arms so tightly that Sydony sucked in a harsh breath.

'I thought I saw some lights.'

'So you decided to investigate by yourself in the middle of the night?'

When stated that way, her actions did seem ill advised. But there hadn't been time to wake anyone else.

Suddenly, Barto stiffened and cocked his head. In the silence that followed, Sydony heard something, as well, something louder than her frantic heartbeat, louder than the rustling of the leaves, and louder than the moaning of the wind. With growing horror, she realised that noises were coming from the maze, the sound of movement, of footsteps… Her eyes wide, Sydony slanted a glance at the labyrinth's entrance, but before she saw anything, Barto dragged her down upon the bench.

She felt stone, hard beneath her bottom, then Barto's arms around her as he drew her close. One long-fingered hand cupped her chin, lifting her face. His own was shrouded in shadow, but she heard his words, whispered with urgency.

'Ignore everything but me,' he said.

And then he kissed her.

For years, Sydony had wondered if she'd imagined the sensations she'd felt when he'd kissed her before. It was easy to say she had been too young to know better, too shocked to understand, and so fond of her neighbour that she had romanticised what was little better than a peck on the cheek.

But now she knew. *She had imagined nothing.* As soon as Barto's lips touched hers, Sydony felt it: a fiery spark that swept through her entire body. She wanted to rear back, to see if Barto was feeling the same thing, just as she had all those years ago, but this time he held her tight against him. This time his arms encircled her, pressing her close, and heating her beyond the warmth of his body. She could feel his chest against her own, the length of his thigh moulding hers.

It was too much, too fast, too hot. Sydony tried to gasp for breath, but that gave her no respite, for his lips trailed against her cheek and down her throat. He buried his face against the curve of her neck, as if breathing her in, and Sydony made a muffled noise. She wasn't sure whether it was a cry of dismay or an urgent call to continue.

She wasn't sure of anything except the feel of Barto, the smell of him, and the heat of him as she fit to his hard frame. It seemed that she not only lost control of her thoughts, but of her limbs as well. Her head fell back, as did the hood of her cloak, loosing her hair, and Sydony felt Barto's fingers tangle in the locks. She sucked in a breath, too astonished at what was happening to do anything but cling to Barto, her sole anchor in a world of darkness and sensation.

'Enough of the moonlight. Let us to bed, my love,' he said. His words rang out loudly in the night, and Sydony had no reply. She could not even find her voice. *To bed?*

Sydony gasped in some mixture of horror and delight when he pulled her to her feet and lifted her into his arms. She had been carried by Barto before, upon his back, on his shoulders, but never like this, and her arms wrapped around his neck as he bore her away from the bench.

How many times had she and this man fought a contest of wills? Sydony remembered never giving in to him in the past, and yet now she made no protest, unwilling or unable to speak, let alone strike out against his bold handling of her person.

Sydony had no sense of time or her surroundings, she only knew that he stepped through an opening into deeper darkness and kicked the door shut behind him. She knew they must be inside the house, but her mind was slow to grasp the details as he slid her down his tall, hard body. Her back was pressed against the door, and when he stepped away, she nearly fell, her balance, like all else under her control, seemingly lost this night.

'Stay there,' he whispered.

Sydony was so dazed that she opened her eyes, uncomprehending, to watch him dart across the drawing room, hunched low to the ground, and slip behind the curtains. She sagged against the hard wood, bereft at the loss of his touch, his heat, his mouth…

'I think they've gone,' he whispered from across the room.

For a long moment, Sydony had no idea what he was talking about. And when, finally, the truth dawned upon her, it was so painful that she lifted a hand to her mouth to stop the sound that threatened to escape. She still had enough presence of mind not to loose a mournful cry of lost love when it had all been an act. A sham. A ruse. *Again.*

Barto's eyes narrowed as he tried to see as much of the grounds as he could from his place at the window. The area looked deserted, but he would not relax until Sydony was locked in her room. Alone.

He lifted his hand from the curtain only to notice that it was shaking. The movement was almost imperceptible, but Barto was aware of it. He could see it, feel it, even in the darkness. It was evidence of his weakness, and for the first time in his life, he was frightened.

He thought of his first days at Eton when he had been bullied by far bigger, older boys. Then, as always, he had possessed a cocksure confidence, even in the worst of situations. But that arrogance had deserted him tonight when Sydony had been in danger. Barto hadn't known whether he could protect her, and the uncertainty had seared his gut.

He turned around to look at the person responsible, and suddenly, his temper flared. 'What the devil did you think you were doing?' he demanded, his voice low.

'Me? I might ask you the same!' she answered.

Had he once found her fearlessness admirable, a fitting accompaniment to his boyhood pranks? Now he wanted to shake it out of her, to make her see reason, to hold her safe at all costs…

'I was trying to keep you from harm,' he said. 'To others, we looked like any couple trysting in the moonlight, no threat to anyone who might be lurking on the grounds.'

'What's happening?' The sound of Kit's sleepy voice made them both turn toward the doorway.

'I heard a door slam,' Kit said, running a hand through his hair. Then he seemed to comprehend just what he was seeing. 'What are you two up to? I'm not obliged to call you out, am I?' he asked Barto.

He might, if he knew. And how would Barto excuse himself? What had begun as a pose to fool intruders soon turned into something else entirely. Barto felt another surge of anger at Sydony and at himself, for allowing her to distract him, to endanger her.

'Don't be absurd,' Sydony said, with more vehemence than necessary.

Barto refused to look at her. Whatever was showing on her face, whether contempt or dismay, he didn't want to see it. Had she felt what passed between them out there on the terrace, or had she only been acting as instructed? His jaw tightened. He didn't care. He couldn't care.

Barto forced himself to focus on Kit. 'Let's go somewhere private, where the servants or anyone else about can't see or hear us.'

Kit must have recognised the urgency in his voice because he asked no questions, but led them up to his room, where the heavy curtains were drawn against prying eyes. Kit lit a brace of candles and when they drew up chairs into a circle of sorts, he leaned forwards, arms upon his legs, addressing them soberly.

'What is it?' he asked.

It was so like old times that Barto had to blink against sudden emotion. Where had that come from? *From the well that had burst since he touched Sydony Marchant*, he thought. And all he could do was to try to plug the holes.

'I saw the lights,' he said, without glancing at Sydony.

'In the maze?' Kit asked.

Barto nodded. He did not mention that he'd seen the lights the night before, too, when restless and angry, he'd taken a bottle to his room. He never drank to excess in public, and he had no respect for those who did, for he'd seen the consequences too many times. He did not intend to lose his fortune in some gambling den or wake up in a brothel, his head aching and his pockets let.

But once in a while, he indulged alone, safely away from temptations and responsibilities. He would not do so again, for it seemed he needed his wits about him at all times. At first Barto had thought the flashes he saw in the darkness were a product of too much drink, but when Sydony mentioned them, he'd decided to stay sober tonight. And watch and wait.

'What was it?' Kit asked.

'Not what, but who,' Barto said. 'Someone was in the maze.'

'I knew it!' Sydony said.

Although Barto refused to look at her, he could tell

she was angry. It permeated her voice. *It permeated his skin.* He wanted to show her he was just as angry…

'Why didn't you stop him from trespassing upon our property?' she demanded.

'I don't think they care much for legalities,' Barto said.

'They?' Kit asked sharply.

'Yes, I don't know how many, but I saw more than one,' Barto said. 'I suspect they are the same group that was here before, bothering your great-aunt.'

'So she wasn't mad after all,' Kit mused.

'If she was, they probably are responsible,' Barto said. *And that might not be all they were responsible for.*

'But who are they?' Kit asked.

'I don't know,' Barto said. 'They appeared to be wearing hoods that covered their faces.'

'Hoods?' Kit echoed, obviously astonished.

'So you just stood there watching?' Sydony asked, a note in her voice that raised Barto's hackles.

'I might have, if you hadn't rushed on to the scene,' he said. Tonight he'd been prepared, and he'd alerted Hob, as well. With Hob, Jack and Jeremy at the ready, he had no qualms about confronting the source of the lights. But then Sydony had stepped into their midst, changing everything. Barto had been watching from the shadows on the terrace when he saw her, and his heart had nearly stopped in his chest.

'And what did you think you were doing?' Kit asked his sister.

'I saw the lights, too,' she said. 'If you recall, no one believed me, so I was out to prove myself.'

That sounded familiar, Barto thought, but shouldn't

Sydony have matured since the days when she reck-
lessly threw herself into any situation? His fingers itched
to seize her, to force her to see sense, to bend her to his
will.

'So you were going to do what?' Kit asked, without
his usual calm. 'Confront hooded trespassers in the
dead of night?'

'No, but I was trying to see what they were doing,'
Sydony said. 'You can't have it both ways, Kit. First you
think I'm as mad as Great-aunt Elspeth and need to be
packed off to stay with friends, but when I try to prove
myself, I'm at fault.' Barto heard her draw a deep breath.
'Or is just that you believe Barto over your own sister?'

She turned toward Barto, and he could no longer
ignore her. 'What a coincidence that you just happened
to be lurking about, keeping watch in the middle of the
night,' she said. 'Or was it? Perhaps you were just
meeting your Druid friends out there in the dark.'

Barto stared for a moment, shocked dumb. Then he
surged to life, leaning forwards to seize her arms.
'What's this about Druids? What are you talking about?'

'You ought to know! Are you following in your
father's footsteps?'

Barto's temper snapped. *'What about my father?'*

Barto had no idea what he might have done, if it
weren't for Kit. Just as in the past, it was Kit who sep-
arated them, Kit who acted as the voice of reason when
his sister and his best friend quarreled.

'It's nothing, B—my lord,' Kit said. 'Ever since one
of the servants warned her to leave the maze to the
Druids, she's been convinced that they are still practis-
ing right upon our lawn.'

Barto sat back in his chair, his sense returning, while Sydony glared at him. 'And why would I be out there with them?'

'Because your father was a Druid.'

Barto shook his head. 'Believe me, he and his fellows did not don black hoods and wander through garden labyrinths. And if they did, there are many at great estates and in better condition in which to romp.'

Barto paused, unsure how much to say, but she had shaken him from his silence. 'But I find it curious that you should suddenly mention Druids when that was the subject of the book that disappeared the day of the accident.'

'What? Why didn't you say that before?' Sydony asked.

Barto shrugged. *Because I didn't trust you*, he did not say. *Because I'm not sure I should even now.* 'Presumably, your father found some tome on the subject and showed my father, knowing of his passing interest in the subject,' he said, lifting a brow at Sydony.

'Father arranged for a meeting with the expert, who said there were no known surviving copies of the book, which would be quite valuable, if proven to be genuine,' Barto said. He drew in a harsh breath. 'The book was supposed to be full of arcane lore written by a famous Druid of the time, by the name of Ambrose Mallory.'

Sydony gasped. 'The man who built this house?'

'What?'

'Mr Humbolt said that Mallory was the one who put in the maze,' Sydony said. 'He must be the mystic everyone fears, the one whose "lingering evil" hangs over the estate.'

'Do you suppose that's his head in the cupboard?' Kit asked.

'Or perhaps part of his collection,' Barto said grimly.

'But if some thieves were looking here for the book, and…arranged to steal it, they've got their money. What would that have to do with these hooded trespassers? Are they looking for more books, buried in the maze?' Kit asked.

Barto shook his head slowly. 'Maybe they weren't after the money, but the lore.'

Chapter Eleven

When Barto left Kit's room to return to his own, Sydony watched him go with an almost desperate yearning. Despite all that had happened, she wanted to run after him, to demand that he acknowledge what had passed between them, to see if he had felt anything at all.

Sydony shuddered, sinking back down upon her chair with a kind of dread as she forced herself to face the truth. Both of the times that Bartholomew Hawthorne had kissed her, years ago and now, she had felt like a firework, exploding with sensation, alight with longing. Even now, the heat seemed to linger, deep down inside of her, as if she were tinder just waiting to be set ablaze.

But all evidence pointed to the experience being otherwise for her former neighbour. While she had sagged against the wall, dazed and drunk with emotions, Barto had gone about his business with cold detachment. In fact, his complete avoidance of her afterwards made Sydony suspect that he found the whole business repugnant.

No doubt he was well used to women with more experience, more wiles and more allure than his childhood companion, she thought, flushing to the roots of her hair. And unless she wanted to lock herself away in her room or spend her days red with embarrassment, she had better learn to keep her yearning to herself.

Sydony fought against the urge to bury her face in her hands and lifted her head instead, drawing deep draughts of air in her lungs. She had lived through this before, she reminded herself. But then it had been only a kiss, not…all the rest of it. Sydony felt as though she might swoon at the memory of Barto's hard body pressed against her own, his breath against her ear, his lips upon her throat.

Ignorance was indeed bliss. For now that Sydony was aware of the power of his touch, how was she to pretend that she didn't crave it? She stared, unblinking, into the dimness of Kit's room, until he returned to his chair. Clasping her hands in her lap, she tried to appear composed before her brother when she just wanted to throw herself upon her bed and weep.

'I'm sorry for not believing you, Syd,' Kit said, with a rueful expression. 'And that whole thing about going away to visit. I was just worried about you. I was afraid you were becoming as mad as Great-aunt Elspeth.'

'Me, too,' Sydony muttered. Truth be told, she still wasn't sure how much she was imagining. Was Barto finally telling the truth, after keeping so much from them, only tossing out bits and pieces when it suited his mood? Or was his latest revelation about their fathers just another distraction? Worse yet, when he had taken her in his arms, was he trying to protect them both, or was he using her as an excuse, to distract her from what was really happening on the grounds?

'Kit, about Barto…' Sydony began.

'Yes?' Her brother met her gaze with sudden intensity.

Sydony drew another deep breath. 'Don't think I've gone mad again, but hear me out. How do we know that he wasn't with them, that he isn't some sort of de facto leader and simply whipped off his hood when he saw me approaching?'

Kit stared at her for a moment, then gave out a short laugh. 'I'm sorry, Syd. I'm trying not to dismiss your theories out of hand, but I just can't picture it. Why would a rich nobleman be tramping about our maze in the middle of the night?'

'He admitted that his father was interested in Druids,' Sydony said. 'Perhaps Barto is simply following in his father's footsteps. Maybe that's why he's here, to do…something out there, not to visit us at all.'

'But why our labyrinth? You heard him say that there are finer ones, and he's probably just as cosy with their owners.'

Sydony frowned. 'Perhaps there is something to that Ambrose Mallory business. Maybe the man who built the house is the key, book or no book, as to why anyone, including Barto, would want to use our maze for some hidden purpose.'

Kit shook his head. 'I don't know, Syd. My gut instinct says to trust Barto as we've always trusted him. I just don't think there's any reason not to…unless you can tell me differently?' He paused to study her carefully.

Sydony couldn't quite meet his eyes and looked down

at the hands in her lap instead. 'What do mean?' she asked. 'I've been telling you differently ever since he arrived, but you haven't listened.' *And he still wasn't listening.*

'Well, you have to admit some of your ideas are pretty outlandish,' Kit said. He sighed. 'And maybe I thought you were just being difficult.'

When Sydony lifted her head to glare at him, her brother leaned back in his chair and ran a hand through his dark hair. 'Why do you think I welcomed Barto into our lives again after all these years?'

'Because you are far kinder than I,' Sydony said, a hint of bitterness in her voice.

'Oh, come on, Syd, it's because you've never been interested in anyone else.'

Sydony blinked in astonishment. 'What do you mean—*interested*?'

Kit glanced at her askance.

'*What?* In Barto?' Sydony sputtered. 'He was a childhood friend, *your* childhood friend. I just tagged along.'

'Come on, Syd. You idolised him, and everyone knew it. It was there on your face every time you looked at him.'

Sydony nearly flinched. 'If I idolised anyone, it was you.'

Kit snorted. 'You were always trailing after Barto, not me. And you haven't looked at anyone else that way ever since.'

'Because I grew up,' Sydony said. *And learned better.*

'Grown or not, you never took the slightest interest in any other fellow,' Kit said.

'And why should I?' Sydony asked. 'It's not as though I was dancing the night away and turning aside offers.'

'No, but there were several gallants who would have courted you, if you had given them any attention at all.'

'What? Who?' Sydony asked, genuinely surprised. Among their small circle of friends, she had never seen anyone as a potential beau.

'Teddy Kirk, for one.'

'The farmer? You and Father always acted as though he were beneath my notice!' Sydony protested.

'Well, so did you.'

Sydony made her own sound of dismissal.

'What about the Armstrongs' cousin, who visited from London? And there was that Wheeler fellow, who composed sonnets about you.'

Sydony laughed. George Wheeler had visited the local squire and wrote poetry to all the young ladies in the neighborhood. He had hardly singled her out.

But Kit shook his head, as though it were not so much stuff and nonsense, as if he saw something she didn't. He gave her a long, assessing look. 'When I arrived here that day to find Barto on the doorstep, I nearly kissed him.'

Me, too, Sydony thought, but she did not say it. Instead, she took refuge in humour. 'I thought you were going to, you were such a toadying fool.'

'Ha! That's because I was afraid you were destined to become a spinster.'

Sydony felt a pang at hearing the words that had never been voiced between them. Did Kit fear she would hang around his neck for ever, perhaps preventing his own marriage? 'We couldn't afford a Season, you know that,' Sydony said, her voice suddenly thick.

'Shall we go next year, then?' Kit asked. 'We ought to be able to rent a place or stay with one of the Armstrongs' cousins.'

Sydony glanced down at her lap, uncomfortable when presented with the opportunity, at last. She had never really wanted to go to London, to be paraded before the eligible men like prime cattle—or *not so prime* in her case. She had no title, no dowry, no connections and no feminine wiles to speak of. How would she snare a husband?

When she said nothing, Kit laughed. 'I thought not.'

Sydony swallowed against a lump in her throat, afraid to ask, but afraid not to. 'Do you want to be rid of me, Kit?'

'Of course not,' he said, leaning forwards to take her hands in his own. 'I wouldn't let you go to some unworthy fellow, no matter if he offered the world. But when I saw Barto, I thought our good fortune was complete. Not only did we have a home, but you might have a husband and a family of your own.'

Sydony's head jerked up in shock. She felt a surge of some long-buried emotion, only to force it down again. Barto, now a viscount who moved in the first circles, never bothering to visit his own family seat, would never offer for a country nobody he couldn't even bear to look at.

'That's rubbish, Kit,' Sydony said, as evenly as she could. Her voice sank to a whisper. 'How can you even suggest such a thing?'

'Perhaps because he always looked at you in the same way,' Kit said gently.

Sydony blinked back a tide of emotion as she

searched her brother's face for some sign of a jest, but he was perfectly sober. She shook her head, denying herself even a glimpse of such an impossible future. This was her brother, after all, and he would see what he wished. If he knew the truth, he might think differently, but Sydony couldn't bear to tell him. It was too painful.

'Kit, he doesn't even glance at me,' she finally said. And when he looked as though he might argue, Sydony shook her head again. 'Now, you're the one who's gone mad.'

'Well, perhaps it's a condition of living here,' Kit said lightly, as he squeezed her hands. 'It's late. Shall I walk you back to your room?'

'No,' Sydony said, rising to her feet. 'I think we're safe in the house.'

'I'm glad that I sent for that book expert when Barto first told us about him,' Kit said, releasing her hands. 'Perhaps he can shed some light on the mysteries that seem to be dogging us.'

Sydony nodded. What else could she do? Kit was loyal to a fault, to both her and Barto, and was seeing something that wasn't there. He was not going to change his mind about his old friend without some clear evidence implicating Barto. And Sydony wasn't sure of his role herself. As she closed her brother's door, her thoughts and feelings on all that had happened were a jumble of confusion. Even now, despite everything, she felt Barto's pull.

Indeed, as she passed his room while heading to her own, Sydony knew a traitorous urge to throw herself back into his arms even though he'd pushed her away, not once, but twice.

* * *

Barto insisted that guards be put around the maze. They were his men, of course, which made Sydony wonder exactly who they were supposed to keep out. She might have confronted him about it, except for the fact that he was even more distant that ever. Acting as though she had disappeared entirely, he wouldn't look at her and would rarely respond to her conversation.

Inside Sydony fumed, and she wanted to hate him for the feelings he had unleashed, for making her eager for the sight of his face turned away from her, the wide shoulders of his back, the dark sheen of his hair… She found herself listening for his voice, wishing that it would lower to a whisper, breathy against her ear. And she would shiver before stalking away, angry at herself—and angry at Barto.

Sydony would have liked to avoid him, but his behaviour only fuelled her suspicions, so she was determined to keep track of him. During the day, she made it a point to know where he was, while she unpacked the rest of the books, looking for anything unusual. And during the night, she listened at her door for sounds from his room or slept fitfully on a chair by the window as she watched the maze below. But she could not catch Barto wandering the house, nor did she see the lights again.

It seemed as though Oakfield was quiet at last.

By Sunday, Sydony was short tempered from her lack of sleep and anger at Barto's treatment. He made his contempt for her so plain that she wanted to slap him, but what had she done to deserve it, beyond exposing his night wanderings?

'How do we even know this expert is to be trusted?' Sydony asked Kit as they waited in the library for their houseguest to join them. 'We only have Barto's word as to his identity and his claims concerning the day of the accident. What if Barto made the whole thing up?'

Sydony's even-tempered brother threw up his hands. 'I shall write to one of Father's scholar friends,' Kit said. 'No, I shall write to *all* of them, asking for any information on Father's books, Druids, mazes, Oakfield and, most of all, Viscount Hawthorne. Shall I write to Barto's mother, too? Perhaps she could vouch for him, or is she somehow involved in whatever it is you think he's doing?'

Sydony shot Kit a sulky look, but he stamped from the room. With a sigh, she leaned against the nearby cupboard, only to realise just what was in it. She lifted her fingers as if they'd been burned and wondered, yet again, what they should do with the trepanned skull. They might bury it, but the digging that seemed to go on about the grounds made Sydony hesitate.

Perhaps she should seek more appropriate advice. Maybe she could speak with the vicar after today's service. Being local, he might be able to tell her more about Oakfield, as well, and the legends that clung to it. And as a man of the cloth, he would have a unique perspective on the superstitions.

Lost in thought, Sydony heard Kit call for her from the hall and hurried to join him. When she saw Barto, she drew in a ragged breath. He was in profile, his handsome face turned toward the door, the faint light of the windows casting his features in shadow. As soon as she approached, he turned away, and Sydony fought down her boiling emotions. How could he be so distant, so cool? Because he was a viscount, a nobleman who had been to school and to town, moving among the most beautiful ladies, sunk in who knew what vices...

Swallowing hard, Sydony let Kit lead her out to the Hawthorne coach. It was a gloomy day as they set out, Sydony and Kit on one seat, Barto opposite, staring out the window. Although the temperature was still relatively mild, Sydony wore a heavy cloak against the drizzle of rain, which dampened even Kit's mood. Surely no Druids would be tempted by the maze on a day like today. Sydony suspected the poor fellows set to guard the hedges were miserable.

The village church was a rather nondescript small stone building, its only interesting feature some lovely arched windows that might have been fitted in a later addition. A few people were entering when the coach drew up outside, and Sydony saw them eye the crest with interest. But they did not linger to greet the new arrivals. Nor did anyone inside approach them. Indeed, when Kit asked a passing boy if one of the high square pews were reserved for Marchant, he showed them to a spot near the front of the church, and quickly left them there, without the slightest comment.

As they took their seats, there was no denying the covert glances in their direction, and Sydony felt her face flame. She remembered the kind, elderly vicar of their old parish and the neighbours who gossiped and greeted each other warmly. The reception here made Sydony feel more cut off than ever from everything she had known before.

Even the rector made no acknowledgement of the

new faces before him. His sermon was brief and lack-lustre, and he seemed in a hurry to escape his own par-ishioners. They, too, moved quickly toward the doors. Either they were well accustomed to his ways, or else everyone, including the churchman, wanted to get away from the Marchants.

Sydony tried not to let her imagination run wild, but if she did catch someone's eye, she was met with the cut direct. And when she finally reached the rector, he barely glanced her way.

'Talk to my curate, who should be here later in the week, making his rounds,' he said in gruff dismissal.

Struck numb, Sydony stood there for a long moment, jostled by the people passing by, until she felt a hand on her elbow. She looked up to see Barto, his handsome face bending toward her with a nod. Putting her gloved hand through his arm, he led her through the building with a subtle grace that made him stand out from anyone else.

It was obvious that he was the only nobleman in the little village church. And against all good sense, Sydony felt a swell of pride in his elegance, in his bearing, in the power that throbbed through him. She lifted her head, his composure bolstering her own, as they pro-ceeded toward the doors.

There, they found Mr Sparrowhawk, who did not flee, but greeted the viscount with his usual eagerness. Still, Barto kept Sydony by his side, including her in the conversation, so that the solicitor inquired about her health.

Sydony was too dazed to respond very coherently. She didn't know which was more shocking: the behaviour of the congregation or the behaviour of Barto. The man who had ignored her for days was acting as a buffer between her and the unfriendly locals, the perfect gentleman, the ideal companion, *Robin Hood to her Maid Marian.*

But had Marian ever felt like this? Once she got over being startled at Barto's solicitous treatment, Sydony became aware of the feel of his arm beneath her fingers, the heat of his body next to hers. As much as she tried to ignore the warmth that crept through her, Sydony had only to slant a glance at Barto and she felt faint—and rather indecent, considering that they were in church.

As if sensing her gaze upon him, he chose that moment to turn his head toward her, and Sydony saw his eyes widen ever so slightly as something leapt to life in the dark depths when they met her own. Sydony might have stared, breathless, but his lashes lowered and he looked away, leaving her to wonder whether she had imagined the brief exchange.

'Miss Marchant had hoped to speak with the rector, but he seemed to be in a rush,' Barto said, so smoothly that Sydony knew he could not feel what she did. She clutched at one hand with the other in order to still its sudden trembling.

Mr Sparrowhawk shook his head. 'I suspect he was anxious to get home to his comfortable lodgings in Burley.' He leaned close to Barto. 'The man has several livings and bestirs himself only to preach the Sunday sermon, while his curate is run ragged.'

The solicitor straightened and hailed a passing gentlemen. 'Wolsey, have you met our esteemed visitor?'

'My lord, Squire Wolsey serves as justice of the

peace and arbitrator of our local society,' Sparrowhawk said to Barto, as he snared a seemingly reluctant older man. 'Viscount Hawthorne,' the solicitor said, preening in Barto's reflected glory.

But either the squire did not like the introduction or even Barto's title could not bring him to be gracious. He nodded in a most perfunctory manner. 'My lord.'

'And this is Miss Marchant. She and her brother have recently moved to the area,' Barto said, putting Sydony forwards.

Again, the squire's greeting was clipped, and when Kit arrived, the man took the opportunity to excuse himself, rather than press an invitation upon his new neighbours. As she watched him go, Sydony felt Barto's arm stiffen beneath her gloved hand, but he gave no other sign of the slight and paused to make sure she was still beside him before heading towards the door. Was he protecting her from the snubs of the populace or putting on a show for them? Sydony didn't know, but it would be easy to fall into the habit of leaning upon his arm, letting him lead her, looking up to him again…

Maybe Kit was correct. Maybe there had been a time, right before their first kiss, when Sydony had imagined some kind of future with Barto in it. He had been such a part of their lives, why would she think differently? In those simple days, she pictured them together always, growing up to go to the local dances and maybe some elegant balls at Hawthorne Park. Her dreams always involved the three of them as friends, Barto perhaps more so, in the way of Robin and Maid Marian.

Of course, Sydony had imagined herself growing up

to be Maid Marian, wealthy, beautiful and wise, with maybe a bit of her own daring thrown in. Then, perhaps, Barto wouldn't dismiss her, or leave her behind when he went off with Kit, or argue with her. In that far-off future, he would be transformed into a man who would be gracious, attentive and kind—rather more like Kit than himself, she had to admit now.

But no matter what Kit might say, Sydony had never imagined herself in Barto's mother's position, as mistress of Hawthorne Park. Even as a child, she knew her place and could not see beyond its boundaries. Just last year, she had read Jane Austen's book about two country girls who vaulted into the upper reaches of society with advantageous marriages, but Sydony's impressionable girlhood was over by then. And Barto was long gone, off to school, off to London, out of her life for ever.

Until now.

If the weather had been better, Barto might have lingered, manoeuvring the locals into conversation, despite their disinclination. But no one wanted to stand in the rain outside the church, and the Marchants seemed just as eager to be gone as the villagers. Even gregarious Kit looked grim, and Sydony… Barto helped her into the coach with a carefully controlled expression that masked the anger simmering inside him.

When he'd seen the way her neighbours treated her, Barto's temper had flared. The look on her face as she stood among people who should have been glad to be able to know her had torn at him. He'd charged through the village idiots to her side, tempted to take the rector by the neck. But the churchman was long gone, leaving Sydony lost and alone amidst strangers.

Barto had wanted to make every one of those people acknowledge her, to realise how beautiful she was, great of heart, brave and brilliant. Taking his seat, Barto glared out the window. Although he had rushed to her rescue, he hadn't been able to do much, and the realisation gnawed at him, like some canker. Barto had never flaunted his position, and he certainly did not crave the sycophancy of men like Sparrowhawk. But neither was he used to being cut by those who were not his betters.

He frowned at the memory of the averted faces. And while the peasants might be forgiven, Squire Wolsey knew better. What was his excuse? Surely the justice of the peace did not fear to associate with someone just because they lived in a particular house. And even if he was so ignorant as to believe in local superstitions, then his wariness should not extend to a visiting viscount.

It had been a long time since anyone had dared to treat Barto with so little regard, and he wondered whether he ought to have a little chat with Wolsey. Perhaps the squire's aversion had something to do with his own activities, rather than the Marchants'.

Barto heard Sydony move and had to stop himself from glancing toward her, seeing to her comfort, checking on her mood. It came easily enough after his gallantry in the church, when he had taken her arm, let her take his, stood beside her, and presented her to the world as though she were…someone to him. But that dangerous behaviour could not continue. His anger had only taken him so far, and then he had begun to notice everything about her: her subtle scent, the curve of her cheek, the slender fingers reposing on his arm. And then he had made the mistake of catching her eye…

Only iron control had kept him from responding. Barto stirred restlessly in his seat, flinching from the memory and the desire that went along with it: of slaking his thirst for Miss Sydony Marchant in one long night of passion. Barto drew in a sharp breath, dismissing such thoughts, but they nagged at him, flitting in and out of his mind ever since that night on the terrace, the night that had changed everything.

He rued what had happened with a fierceness that kept him grim and angry, his concentration gone, his focus wandering, and his nights fitful. For how would he ever be able to sleep again, when every time he closed his eyes, he felt beautiful, reckless Sydony in his arms again?

Chapter Twelve

Sydony was not surprised that Barto's attentiveness did not last. As soon as he took his seat stiffly across from her, she knew that the gracious gentleman inside the church had been replaced by the sullen, distant boor that was Barto these days. But if he couldn't bear to look at her, why had he come to her rescue? Was it just another pose, or was there something else going on that she knew nothing about?

It all made her head ache. But better that than her heart, Sydony told herself. The incident was a well-timed reminder not to trust Barto, not to let herself get too close, not to let herself fall in love with him.

Sydony flinched from the word, just as though it were some foul curse Kit had spoken aloud. Even her brother had not dared to mention it the other night when he'd spouted all sorts of other rubbish. Indeed, she couldn't remember the last time she'd even thought about such a thing—perhaps when Molly had married.

Hers was a love match, and she had glowed with *something* that all the other girls envied.

But Sydony hadn't shared that envy because she'd never considered falling in love. Was it because she didn't think of any of the available males as a beau? Or was it because she'd already given up, her heart long broken by the man across from her when he was hardly more than a boy?

The thought filled her with a bleak sadness, and she blinked against the sudden moisture behind her eyes. It would have been better if she'd never seen Barto again. At least then she would have avoided all this introspection, the painful memories and Kit's mad speculation.

Sydony was tempted to turn to her brother and ask him what he thought of his theory now, as Barto stared out the window, grim and silent. But she never wanted to have that conversation again and preferred not to even think of it.

For once, Sydony was glad to reach Oakfield; she hurried out of the close quarters of the coach, as cold and elegant as its owner. Holding her skirts, she ran through the intermittent drops, eager for the relative warmth of the hall. Even Mrs Talbot's dour face was welcome after the trip to church.

The housekeeper silently took Sydony's cloak, while a maid hurried forwards to take the gentlemen's coats. Sydony was as eager to escape the company as Barto looked to be, but Mrs Talbot stopped all three of them with the announcement that a visitor was waiting in the library.

Sydony glanced at Kit in surprise. Hadn't they just

been cut by every person who lived in the parish? Or so it seemed.

'He says his name is Scrimminger and that he has travelled here to see you according to your request,' the housekeeper said. She appeared to disapprove, whether of visitors in general or Mr Scrimminger in particular Sydony didn't know. She thanked the housekeeper, who gave a curt nod before slowly moving away.

'I hope you don't mind, but I wanted to speak to your expert myself,' Kit said to Barto. 'Perhaps he can shed some additional light on matters, especially after all that's happened here.'

Sydony wasn't sure what a book dealer could tell them about entrails in their maze, but she was glad for the distraction. Although Barto did not object, she wondered what he really thought. Perhaps they would discover this fellow wasn't even who he claimed, but some charlatan hired to pretend the part.

'He's in the library,' Sydony said aloud, as the re-alisation struck her. Was the man even now searching the shelves for some volume whose import she had missed? But that fear was soon overtaken by another.

'So?' Kit asked.

'So I hope he didn't open the cupboard,' she whis-pered.

To her relief, when they entered the room, their guest wasn't crouched before the skull or lying on the floor in a faint, but seated on one of the mahogany step chairs. Mr Scrimminger was a small man, balding and pale, who resembled a scholar or someone who spent most of his time among books. *At least he looked the part.*

Kit stepped forward. 'Hello, Mr Scrimminger. I'm

Christopher Marchant. This is my sister, and I believe you know Viscount Hawthorne.'

The elderly gentleman rose to his feet and acknowledged Barto with a bow. Although Sydony watched them closely, she could see no secret signals pass between them.

'Thank you for coming to meet with us all,' Kit said, as he gestured for the man to sit once more.

'Think nothing of it,' Scrimminger said. 'It was a pleasure, for I have looked forward to seeing this famous site.'

Sydony blinked at him. 'Oakfield?'

The elderly gentleman appeared surprised. 'Why, yes, it has long been associated with Druidic activity. Quite a famous practitioner once lived here.'

'You seem to know a lot about Druids,' Sydony said.

'Well, that is my area of expertise,' Scrimminger said, looking a bit perplexed.

'I thought you were a book dealer,' Kit said, echoing Sydony's thoughts.

The elderly gentleman looked from Barto to the Marchants and shook his head. 'I'm sorry if there was some confusion. When I contacted the viscount,' he said, nodding toward Barto, 'I was concerned about a book, which was the reason for my appointment with the two gentlemen.'

He paused, as though reluctant to discuss the accident, before continuing. 'They were interested in an evaluation of the volume's authenticity, which I hoped to give them because of my studies of the subject. Although I do some collecting, it is only of those editions that catch my interest, so my own library is small, and I would never pretend to deal in books, per se. Nor would I attempt to buy the book they purported to have in their possession. If authentic, it would be far too valuable for me to purchase,' Scrimminger said.

Sydony glanced toward Barto, but, as usual, she could read nothing from his closed expression. Had he been unaware of Scrimminger's history, or had he deliberately misled the Marchants? 'And you never spoke of this book or your meeting to anyone else?' Barto asked.

Scrimminger shook his head. 'I might have mentioned the fact that I had a meeting to others, but I wouldn't tell anyone about finding a Mallory, without having actually seen it.'

The old fellow looked rather offended, and Kit, as usual, stepped in to smooth his ruffled feathers. 'Well, you are just the man we wish to talk to, then, for we know nothing about Druids.'

Scrimminger smiled. 'You aren't alone, for there isn't much information about them. They kept no written records, as far as we can tell, so our knowledge comes from outside sources, sometimes of questionable validity. Indeed, no one can say what they actually practised.'

'What of these outside sources, then?' Kit asked.

'Most of what we know comes from the Romans, who vilified the Druids, perhaps because of a campaign to conquer them. And by the time the Celts began writing their own history, they were working from a Christian viewpoint, which obviously changed their perspective on what had gone before.'

'But you're speaking of the original Druids. What of

the modern ones?' Sydony asked, with a pointed glance toward Barto.

Scrimminger smiled. 'Like the medieval revival, this supposed return to Druidism has little to do with history. People have a tendency to look back on earlier times as more chivalrous or more in tune with nature and adopt what they see as good in those earlier societies.'

'So the group that the viscount belonged to didn't necessarily adopt the practices of the old Druids?' Kit asked.

'Doubtful,' Scrimminger said. 'The Ancient Order of Druids revived by Henry Hurle in 1781 was his own creation, a Masonic society that did charitable work. They are much to be admired, but not accurate.'

'What about the man who built this house, Ambrose Mallory, the one who is supposed to have written the book our fathers had?' Barto asked.

'Oh, he's a different kettle of fish,' Scrimminger said. 'His work is definitely based on the Romans' version of the Druids. Whether or not his writings are rooted in other sources is unknown because no editions of his book survive, only references to it.'

'So this book, the one our fathers supposedly had, is well known?' Kit asked.

Scrimminger smiled. 'Well, among those who study Druid lore, it would be. It is referred to by various titles, but is supposed to consist of the secrets of auguring.'

'Auguring?' Sydony echoed.

Scrimminger nodded. 'According to Diodorus, the Druids used human sacrifice to tell the future, stabbing their victims and auguring from their death-throes.'

Sydony blanched, and even Kit looked a bit queasy.

'And Tacitus claims they slaked their altars with

captive blood and consulted their deities by means of human entrails.'

'Entrails.' Sydony barely got the words past her lips.

'But you discount the Romans' reports as propaganda?' Kit asked.

'Not necessarily,' Scrimminger said. 'You must remember that our ancestors were a brutal people. The Irish poet Dindschenchas tells of children being sacrificed at Samhain to an idol known as the lord of the mound at Mag Slecht.'

'Samhain,' Sydony echoed in a whisper.

'Yes, Samhain being one of the four great quarter days celebrated all over the Gaelic areas. Of course, Samhain legends more often refer to the slaughter of animals, probably because of the practice of putting by winter stores rather than ritual killing.'

'Winter stores? So Samhain is approaching?' Kit asked.

'Oh, yes. It's nearly upon us. It begins at dusk on All-Hallow Eve, a holiday that probably is derived from its predecessor.'

Scrimminger did not look the least bit fazed by this information, but Sydony shivered.

'But you don't know anyone among the modern Druid groups who would do such things,' Barto said.

Scrimminger's expression was a mixture of outrage and surprise. 'Certainly not! Those practices died out centuries ago.'

'Except for Mallory,' Barto said.

Scrimminger frowned. 'Well, yes, if the rumours about his writings are true.'

'So there might be others that you aren't aware of,' Barto said.

'My lord, I assure you that no one these days is engaged in ritual killing,' Scrimminger said. 'We cannot even know if that was an actual Druidic practice.'

He looked as though he were going to continue, but Barto held up a hand to forestall him. 'I understand,' Barto said. 'However, if you should hear of any…unique groups or anyone who's especially interested in Mallory, I would ask that you write to me immediately.'

Scrimminger nodded, stiffly, perhaps leery of Barto. And, if so, who could blame him?

'Mr Scrimminger, please beg our pardon if we seem a bit zealous, but the author of the book, Mr Mallory, seems to have left quite a legacy hereabouts,' Sydony said. 'Most people are wary of Oakfield.'

'Well, if they think they're going to be murdered for some fortune telling, who can blame them?' Kit asked, his expression grim.

'Yes, but that was more than a century ago,' Sydony said. 'It's not as though this Mallory put a curse on the place, is it?' she asked, despite herself.

Although Kit snorted, Scrimminger did not laugh. 'While the Druids used a *geis*, or what some might call a curse, to assert authority, it was placed on a particular person, and mainly used to maintain order and authority. Even if one believed in the *geis*, it would have little application beyond Druidic society,' he said.

'However, I don't doubt that you are facing some superstitions concerning your property, like those sites where murders or hauntings are purported to occur.' Scrimminger shook his head. 'Once a house gets that kind of reputation, it is difficult to change it. And, of course, the very name Oakfield tells a tale.'

'How?' Kit asked.

'Oaks were revered by the Druids as a source of food and knowledge. Some say they not only venerated the trees, but worshipped them.'

Sydony thought of the ancient sentinel of the maze and felt a sudden chill. 'And did they worship labyrinths, as well?'

Scrimminger glanced at her with an expression of puzzlement. 'I've never heard of such a thing.'

'Mallory is supposed to have put in the decorative garden maze that stands behind the house,' Sydony said.

'Really? I would be most interested in seeing it,' Scrimminger said.

At his eagerness, Sydony felt her suspicion return. She eyed the old man carefully, but there was no reason to believe that he was anything other than a scholar. Even if he wasn't, what could he hope to do in the labyrinth, dripping with rain and guarded by Barto's men?

Chances were that he was genuine, not only because of his knowledge, but because Kit had summoned him, not Barto. And, as Kit noted, it would be easy enough to inquire in scholarly circles concerning his reputation.

'We can certainly show you the maze, but I'm afraid it's too wet to enter today,' Sydony said. *Not to mention the possibility of deadly traps and entrails littering the paths.* Mr Scrimminger might not know of any connection between Druids and mazes, but Sydony thought it no coincidence that entrails and auguring had a part in discussions of both.

'What about skulls? Did the Druids worship those as well?' Kit asked.

Sydony drew in a sharp breath, but Scrimminger did

not appear startled. He paused, as though considering the question, before answering. 'Not that I know of, but the ancient Celts thought that the soul was located in the head, so it was venerated.'

Sydony's eyes were drawn to the cabinet, where a certain head reposed, but she refused to ask about the holes bored into it. And the silence from Kit told her he, too, did not care to bring up that particular subject.

Mr Scrimminger seemed imperturbable, but a trepanned skull was enough to send anyone running from Oakfield.

It had stopped raining when they stepped outside, though the grey sky cast a gloom over the grounds, and the maze looked unappealing to all but Druids perhaps, Barto thought with a certain bitterness.

Scrimminger's admissions about the book had left him angry with himself—for not thoroughly questioning the fellow—and angry with his father. No doubt his sire had thought to profit from the volume. Oh, not in cash, perhaps, but in cachet when he revealed its existence to someone among his so-called Druid group. Currying favours and jockeying for position and prestige had driven him, and Barto resented that those venal qualities had caused his death.

Lost in his dark thoughts, Barto stood on the terrace while Kit and Sydony and Scrimminger walked through the damp grass. It had not rained much here, but the greenery was slick with moisture, and Scrimminger appeared content to view the labyrinth from the outside. 'You say Mallory commissioned this?' he asked.

'That's what I've been told,' Sydony said.

Barto shook his head. How many women would trudge the grounds to discuss the less-than-savoury habits of Druids? How many would even be interested in anything beyond their own complexions? Barto frowned. Maybe there were other women who were intelligent and amusing and admirable, and he had just never sought them out. Maybe he had never wanted to find any others…

'I will have to contact my colleagues to see if anyone is aware of an association between Druids and mazes,' Scrimminger said. 'Normally, I would dismiss such theories outright, but not when dealing with a legacy from Mallory.'

Barto's ill mood made him surly. Sydony was affecting his concentration, and he was no closer to discovering his father's murderer. Thieves and assassins were one thing, but ancient cults and superstitions were as elusive as the wind. How could he catch them?

'Perhaps this Mallory just wanted a decorative planting,' Barto said.

Scrimminger turned and smiled. 'Of course, that is always a possibility, my lord. In looking at the past, one never knows what might be important, does one?'

Barto nodded in answer to the question that might be applied to his personal history, as well, especially the days spent with the two people nearest to him.

Scrimminger turned back towards the Marchants. 'If not for the inclement weather, I might have a peek inside,' he said.

'You are welcome to stay with us,' Sydony suggested, and Barto felt a twinge of annoyance at the graciousness she bestowed on another.

'Thank you, but I promised my daughter I would not linger,' Scrimminger said. 'I should like to get on the road as soon as possible, now that my horses have rested.'

The old gentleman began walking to the house, Sydony at his side, and Barto moved forwards, taking the opportunity to catch Kit's eye.

'Shall the knights meet this evening?' he asked.

Kit sent him a startled glance, looked toward his sister, who was already stepping inside, then nodded.

After retiring early, Barto waited until he heard Sydony open her bedroom door before slipping back out, whatever noise he made lost in the sound of her own movements. Making his way silently down the stairs, he found Kit in the library with a bottle of port. The male Marchant glanced up when Barto entered and silently held out a glass.

With a nod, Barto accepted the drink and took a seat in one of the worn upholstered chairs.

'I must admit, it took me a moment to understand what you were saying earlier today,' Kit said as he poured for himself.

Barto leaned back in his chair, a smile playing about his lips. He could have just asked Kit for a late meeting, but the phrase had slipped out, a remnant of their shared experiences.

'Our Knights of the Round Table era. It followed the Merry Men period, didn't it?' Kit asked, flashing a grin.

'But it was the merrier, if I recall.'

Kit snorted as he sank down in the opposite seat and propped his feet on one of the library step-chairs. 'I'm not sure if it was merrier, but the pursuits were more suited to a gang of thieves than noble knights. Obviously, we had the whole thing backwards.'

Barto chuckled. Before he'd gone off to school and sometimes when he'd been home for a visit, they would sneak out late at night to sample his father's finest port or get into some other mischief.

'Remember when we tried to smoke that cigar?' Kit asked with a groan.

A smile played about Barto's lips. 'How about the snuff?'

'I had a headache for a week,' Kit said. 'I kept asking Syd if I had a bloody nose.'

At the mention of Sydony, both men became quiet. She hadn't been included in those midnight jaunts, so that they could feel free to swear, discuss the finer points of the female anatomy, practise their boxing techniques and generally play at being manly. With sudden, sharp clarity, Barto recalled one night when he had spilled all of the horrors of Eton to his friend.

Flinching from that memory, Barto eyed the wine in his glass. 'What did you think of Scrimminger?'

'He seems genuine enough. You say he contacted you?'

Barto nodded. 'Actually, he wrote to my father. The missive got buried in the stack of correspondence that accumulated after his death.'

Barto did not add that it was his own failure to immediately grasp the reins passed to him that led to that accumulation. After the funeral, he'd been tempted by all the frivolities that could make a man forget his grief, his duties, himself. Eventually, he had decided that it was time to return home, to take over the responsibilities that he must assume.

And that's when he had found the letter that had given him a new purpose. If Barto couldn't bring his father back to his rightful place, then at least he could see that some justice was done. That quest for vengeance had driven him to Oakfield, and it drove him still, though not quite as fiercely.

There was something about the company here that toned down his intensity, that made his initial urgency seem excessive, that had led him to this moment of easy familiarity with Kit, former best friend, partner and peer in all but position. The longer he remained here, the more it felt like old times—when the three of the them were friends and the Marchants could be relied upon to keep his secrets and to share his goals.

Only one thing was different now: his lust for Sydony.

Barto shifted, uncomfortable with the thought, and cleared his throat. 'After sorting out Scrimminger's letter, I went to meet him. Maybe I wasn't thinking as clearly as I should have been,' Barto admitted, swirling the wine in his glass. Indeed, he was so intent upon his mission that he'd probably scared the old man to death. 'When he kept referring to the missing book, I assumed he was in the book business. Not very thorough.'

'What's the difference?' Kit asked, in a casual tone.

Barto glanced up at him sharply, and Kit shrugged. 'It doesn't really matter, does it? Obviously, our fathers had a book by Mallory. But what happened to it?' Kit shook his head. 'After meeting the old fellow, I withdraw my theory that he had anything to do with it.'

'Since he's not a book dealer, that rules out any of his staff, too,' Barto said. 'Unless someone came across his correspondence.'

'Or your father's letter to him,' Kit said.

Barto frowned down at his port. It was less complicated when he'd thought the Marchants responsible, but his initial furious suspicions had burned out. Even in his darkest moments, he found it hard to believe that Kit and Sydony had done murder for a volume few people thought existed. And they could hardly be to blame for what had happened since. It had become apparent to everyone, including Hob, that the mystery had not ended with the accident. Indeed, now it seemed as if the deaths were only the beginning. But of what?

'It was easier when I thought it was just a simple theft for money,' Barto said.

'And why couldn't it be?' Kit asked. 'Maybe someone came across the accident and took the book.'

'And left my father's gold watch fob and rings?' Barto asked.

'A petty thief might not desecrate the dead,' Kit suggested, but he appeared unconvinced.

'Kit, there's just too much going on to put down to coincidence,' Barto said. 'The book, the maze intruders, even what's in the cupboard.'

Kit looked like he might snort, but stopped himself when he saw Barto's face. 'You can't tell me you think that trepanned skull had anything to do with our fathers' deaths?'

Barto sighed. For a moment, he rued the exclusivity of the Round Table meeting. Perhaps Kit would be more convinced by Hob's unbiased opinions or Sydony's sharp observations. Kit's sister seemed to be suspicious of everyone and everything.

'All right,' Kit said, taking his silence for an answer.

He leaned forwards to rest his arms on his thighs and eyed Barto intently. 'Let's go over what we have.'

Barto nodded. 'Your great-aunt is plagued by various problems here at Oakfield and wants to burn both the books and the maze. But the housekeeper sends the books to your father. He finds one on Druids, and, knowing of my father's interest in the modern version of the so-called religion, he contacts Hawthorne Park. Whether Father stopped to look at the book beforehand, I don't know, but he made an appointment with Scrimminger to assess the volume. But they never got there, dying instead in a violent accident that should never have happened. And when the bodies are retrieved, the book is gone.'

Kit nodded, with him so far.

'But that's not the end of it. Now you find signs of searching in the house, the skull beneath the floorboards, traps and entrails in the maze.' Barto paused. 'And, worst of all, trespassers.'

Kit shook his head. 'Yes, these are all pretty strange events that don't make for a delightful housewarming, but I don't see how you can connect them with the missing book. If someone actually planned the accident to steal it, they have it. What else could they want?'

Barto didn't reply because he didn't know the answer. But the thieves wanted something more, something from Oakfield. He could feel it in his bones.

'It's dangerous, Kit,' Barto finally said. 'You know I'm not one to imagine things, but I sense a threat here.' He drew a deep breath. 'I think you should send Sydony away until it has passed, to one of her old friends' homes. She could even stay at Hawthorne Park. My mother would welcome the company.'

'You want to send her away?' Kit repeated, as though he hadn't heard Barto correctly.

Barto nodded. Of course, his main concern was to protect Sydony from whoever or whatever was behind the incidents here at Oakfield, and that's what he would tell her brother. She had already narrowly escaped animal traps and hooded intruders; he wanted to avert any future perils. Certainly, his men afforded some safeguards, but Sydony was not like other women. Her own recklessness would be the death of her—or himself, Barto thought grimly.

Although he could hardly admit as much to Kit, by sending Sydony away, Barto could also protect her from himself. And without the constant temptation Sydony Marchant presented, perhaps he could focus all his energy on finding out just what was happening here, conclude his business, and return to his life. *What life?* he wondered suddenly, only to push the thought aside. Now was not the time to assess his own lack of direction.

Kit leaned back in his chair, an odd smile playing about his lips. 'Gad, you're even worse than she is.'

'What?'

Kit shook his head, his usually open expression turning grim, as he looked down at the glass in his hand. 'I won't send her away.'

Barto felt a surge of surprise, followed by a spark of anger, but he carefully schooled his own features to reveal nothing. 'Kit, our fathers are dead.'

'Yes, but why would anyone kill any of us? We don't have the book they apparently wanted.' Lifting his head, Kit wore a stubborn expression reminiscent of his sister, reminding Barto that his agreeable friend could be pushed only so far.

Obviously, Kit was determined not to send Sydony away, and Barto did not argue. In fact, he was seized by a traitorous kind of relief, along with something he did not recognise, at the knowledge that she would remain here, within reach.

'As for the other things you mentioned, the skull has certainly been here a while, and the marks in here might not be recent either,' Kit said. 'The traps could have been left from years ago. And even though all the business about Druids and ritual sacrifice sounds ominous, it doesn't go on in this day and age. Only the trespassers are a threat, and the guards seem to have put a stop to their visits.'

Apparently, easygoing Kit was satisfied with that conclusion, but Barto wasn't. He'd come here for a reason, and he wasn't leaving without finding out who was responsible for his father's death. And the happenings here were somehow related. Setting down his glass, he leaned forwards.

'Maybe we're going about this the wrong way,' Barto said, eyeing Kit intently. 'Instead of guarding the maze, we need to catch them in it.'

Chapter Thirteen

Several days later Barto leaned against the wall of the house, watching the maze. There had been no more than that single sprinkling of rain, so the wind sent leaves swirling across the terrace. And, for once, the sun shone brightly upon Oakfield's grounds, alleviating the usual gloom. Conditions were perfect for a visit to the labyrinth, but Barto doubted anyone would dare trespass during daylight hours, even without any visible guards.

He had convinced Kit that the men should be moved to different stations around the property, so they weren't as obvious to intruders. As always, Kit seemed careless about the whole business, unconvinced that the trespassers were connected to the murder of their fathers. But even if he was right, Barto wondered how the Marchants could safely settle into their new home until they found out who was wandering their property and why. As much he admired his old friend's equanimity, there were times when Barto thought his own, more forceful, approach was necessary.

Nodding to Hob, who lounged in the shadows of the stables, Barto turned his head at the sound of a door opening. He knew a guard was just inside the drawing room, and he wondered if the fellow had something to report. But it was Sydony's slender form that emerged from the house. She moved across the old stone, her cloak caught by the breeze; since she hadn't noticed him, Barto watched her.

He felt like some bow-window gawker, ogling the females on the street, but he couldn't help himself. The curve of her slender body, the dark hairs that escaped from the simple arrangement upon her head, and the graceful glide of her steps—all worked some kind of magic on him, more powerful than anything the Druids had conjured.

He had seen women who were more beautiful, but never had one filled him with such longing. More than desire, more than passion, the sensation was like a soul-deep yearning. Not one for self-examination, Barto did not dwell on the cause or the source, and, indeed, he tried his best to thwart it. He hated anything that was beyond his mastery, so such feelings were not welcomed. He should turn away, look away, *go away*, Barto thought, with a kind of desperation, but instead he stared, putting a grown Sydony Marchant to memory.

As if sensing his attention upon her, Sydony turned and Barto looked into the distance, where the moors rose in a lonely landscape. He waited, oddly tense, for her to move, but he heard nothing and finally glanced towards her again.

The force of her gaze, the bright green intensity of it, made him want to flinch…or pull her to him. They had not been alone since that night, and Barto's attention un-willingly drifted toward the bench, not far from where she stood. He shifted uncomfortably. It was time to go in.

'Since it's such a beautiful day, and your men have pronounced the maze free of any surprises, I thought to go through it today,' Sydony said.

Barto eyed her in surprise. He opened his mouth to protest, but what he could say? There had been no activity since they had put guards on the hedges, so how could he refuse her passage through her own garden? And what could happen to Sydony in there, with his men around the grounds?

Nothing. It was not as though Sydony would disap-pear inside, never to be seen again. And yet, that very thought raised the hairs on his neck. 'I'll go with you,' he said, even though that was the last thing he wanted to do. The thought of being alone with Sydony inside the close passages made him tense, and he lifted a hand to call Hob to join them.

But Sydony stopped him with a touch on his sleeve. Feeling the contact like a burn, Barto stared down at it, trying not to picture her touching his skin. It took all of his will not to look at her face, to see if she felt what he did, if desire clouded those green eyes and parted her luscious lips. Instead, he focused on the fingers that lingered just a moment too long before she snatched them away.

'You are welcome to join me,' she said. 'But I hardly think we need a phalanx of guards…unless you feel ill equipped to pass among the greenery, *Sir Robin*?'

Her snide comment hit its mark, for what could

menace them inside the maze that Hob and Jack had already cleared? Bloody entrails, though disturbing, were hardly dangerous. There was no need for Hob's company…except as a chaperon, a role for which the hardened fighter was ill suited.

'Very well,' Barto said. Without waiting for a reply, he strode toward the entrance and pushed aside some errant limbs so that she could enter. He barely glanced at her as she passed, then ducked in behind her.

Sydony had brought a lantern, but it was not needed. Hob and Jack had made more progress, so that the sun shone through the openings, lighting the path in patches. For the first time, Barto could see how the labyrinth might be appealing, especially for an outing on a summer's day with a beautiful woman. There were plenty of spots for dawdling among the privacy of the plants.

As his thoughts wandered along those lines, Barto's attention drifted to the gently swaying hips in front of him. And soon it seemed as though the mild day had turned hot, the air under the greenery stifling, tempting Barto to remove his coat. Even in his current state, he realised that was not a good idea. Wresting his gaze away from Sydony, he tried to focus on his surroundings. Should he lead the way in case Sydony met with something ahead? But then she would be unprotected from the rear.

Barto shook his head in an attempt to clear it of irrational thoughts. This wasn't a trip through the back alleys of old Westminster, but a simple garden maze. Nor was he a child, trying to keep his neighbour safe during a night in the woods, Robin and his Marian.

The memory came back to Barto, perhaps bidden by Sydony's taunt. He hadn't been fearful of the night or its dangers, only that he would be unable to keep Sydony Marchant from harm, a sensation not so different from what plagued him today. Now he had bouts with Gentleman Jackson under his belt and a dagger in his boot. Then he had been armed only with a pocket-knife and a big stick, and he had stayed awake, keeping watch, long after her cheek rested against his chest, the even breathing of sleep upon her.

With sudden sharp ferocity, Barto wanted to feel her head pillowed against him again, to hear the gentle flow of her breath, to touch the stray strands of her hair and know that she rested safely with him. The vivid image of sleep, not sex, was more disturbing than his growing desire for her, and Barto wanted to recoil from the woman in front of him.

But when a twig cracked, Barto reached for her, his heart pounding as he drew her close. Sydony was silent within his grasp, her back pressed to him, and the sound of their breathing was loud in the ensuing quiet. For a long moment they stood silent, but nothing came at them out of the greenery, and gradually Barto relaxed his hold.

Only then did he become aware of the heat of her against his body, the dark hair so close he could smell its delicate scent, the curve of her neck that tempted his lips. He had only to dip his head…

'It was probably just an animal.' Sydony's breathless voice woke him from his trance, and Barto dropped his arms even as his body screamed in protest.

She stepped away and moved forwards, more slowly,

and Barto forced himself to alertness. The sun must have gone behind a cloud because it was darker now, the hedges looming above them more ominous than just a while ago, and he felt a new unease. He was not the fanciful sort and dismissed the superstitions of the locals, but there was no denying the eeriness of their passage. Perhaps well trimmed in summer, the maze would be a pleasant refuge. But now it seemed a tunnel into a dark abyss, a reflection of his own turmoil.

Sydony seemed unaffected by her surroundings, and Barto followed her as she made her way through the twists and turns ahead. She never appeared to hesitate at a fork, making him wonder whether she had taken this path before, by herself.

'How do you know where you're going?' Barto asked, the question coming out more harshly than he intended. Although he had sworn not to suspect the Marchants any longer, the habit was hard to break.

'I don't know,' Sydony answered. 'Whatever feels right.'

Whatever feels right? Barto frowned. Had he still been suspicious, he might have thought she was leading him into a trap. More likely, she had learned the way, as he had, from Hob, who had mapped it. Though why she declined to admit as much was yet another mystery.

Brooding on Sydony's eccentricities, Barto was unprepared when they broke through the narrow passage to a wide opening, a clearing where the hedge walls formed a circle around a huge oak.

'The centre of the maze,' Sydony said, her voice low.

Barto watched as she moved forwards, her cloak dragging upon the dry grass, her head held high, her hand outstretched to touch the gnarled wood. With her natural grace, she might have been a Druid priestess approaching the revered tree.

If he believed in such things. Barto looked away, annoyed at the whimsy that struck him. It seemed as if all the tales he'd heard had eroded his good sense, making him no better than a villager catching falling leaves for good luck.

'It's amazing,' Sydony said.

Trying not to picture her stroking the bark, Barto walked the perimeter, looking for any traps or holes.

'This tree must be hundreds of years old.'

Barto heard the awe in her voice and bit back a comment about Maid Marian and her love of the greenwood. Along the edge of the hedges, he found evidence of past digging, and there were even some spots between the huge roots erupting from the ground that looked to have been disturbed, as well. Though what anyone could have been looking for in here mystified him.

The tree itself was undefiled, as far as Barto could tell. He moved around it slowly, searching for signs of any primitive markings or evidence that someone had been here, but found nothing except some natural indentations, one beneath the roots and one further up, filled with dried leaves that might have made a good home for squirrels.

'Do you see any sign of rot in there?' Sydony asked, and Barto realised she was at his shoulder. Too close.

He stepped aside. 'I don't know.'

'I'd hate to see it die,' Sydony said, her voice so wistful that Barto was tempted to turn toward her, but he didn't. Instead, he strode towards the passage that led back to the entrance. There was something about this space that felt confining, suffocating and eerie. It seemed like he couldn't even hear the birds any more or the rustle of leaves. Had the wind died down?

'You don't have to stay here and mind me like a nursemaid,' Sydony said, her tone sharp.

'Well, I'm not leaving you alone,' Barto said.

'Why? Unless you think the tree is going to attack me, there is no point in you putting a damper on my mood with your sullen brooding.'

Ignoring her complaints, Barto glanced down the path they had come. Would he hear anyone or anything following? But none except Kit could enter, without Hob stepping in, he reminded himself.

'Are you even listening to me?'

'Yes,' Barto said over his shoulder.

'My lord,' Sydony snapped, 'can you at least have the courtesy not to ignore me? Look at me,' she demanded, as he heard her hurry towards him. 'Why won't you look at me?'

Barto turned towards her and gazed right into the face that was but a few inches from his own. Her cheeks were flushed, her chest rising with the force of her emotion, and he could no longer keep himself in check.

'Because of this,' he said, reaching for her.

Barto pulled her to him roughly, impatient with all the restless desire that had been building inside him for too long. He took a moment to see the shock in her green eyes before he covered her mouth with his own, silencing any protests.

As always, the kiss was a surprise to him, jolting his senses like a sudden spark and sending heat coursing through his body. He deepened it immediately, hungry for more, and pressed her close. When he felt her arms link around his neck and the first tentative touch of her tongue, he stiffened. Had it only been a few days since he had held her? It seemed like he had waited a lifetime for this, to feel her slender shape against him, to run his hands down her back, over the curve of her hip. To claim her as his own, *Marian to his Robin.*

With only a few economical steps, Barto carried her along with him to the great oak and pushed her against the surface of the tree. He managed to free her hair, and the thick waves falling over his fingers made him shudder. If he'd had his senses about him, he might have recoiled at the power she had over him. But he could think of nothing except the smell and taste and feel of her.

And far from protesting, reckless, passionate Sydony met him, kiss for kiss, pulling his head down for more, sighing into his mouth in a way that fed his urgency like dry leaves in an inferno. When he finally lifted his head to look down at her, the sight of her face made him catch his breath. Her cheeks were flushed, her tender lips parted, and thick lashes fell over green eyes so dazed with desire that he returned his mouth to hers, taking it again and again.

In some dim recess of his brain, Barto realised that he had never spent so much time simply kissing a woman, but the pure joy of it kept him going until need finally drove him further. Then he moved his lips along her cheek, down her throat to where her cloak opened, and lower. Nudging aside the top of her gown, he tasted the silk of her skin, before taking her into his mouth.

She cried out, in surprise and passion, and he felt his

own body leap in response. He drew one hand down her side, along her gown, and lifted the fabric, his fingers brushing against the softness of her thigh. His heart was thundering in his chest, pounding out a beat all the way to his head, making it hard for him to think.

In this state, he realised it would be easy to take her—not against the tree, of course. But the weather was mild, and her cloak would pillow her upon the dry leaves. She would not stop him. That thought alone made him wild, and he pulled away to tug off his coat, when a noise penetrated his muddled brain.

The blood that had drained to Barto's lower body returned to his head in a rush. Abruptly, he remembered just where they were and how vulnerable he had made them. Pressing a hand to Sydony's trembling lips, he froze, listening.

When he heard Hob's voice, Barto exhaled in relief. He turned, to hide Sydony's dishevelled form, until he realised that the man had not followed them into the maze, but was outside the hedges, calling for him.

'You all right in there, my lord?'

Barto felt Sydony whimper beneath his fingers, but he drew a deep breath and shouted. 'Yes, Hob. We're going to head back out now.'

With cool efficiency, Barto straightened Sydony's bodice, concentrating on nothing but getting them out of the maze. Taking her hand, he led her toward the passage, grateful to Hob for keeping watch. Now that he could think clearly, he recognised just how much he owed the man for his timely interruption. While his mind was in his breeches, Barto could have found himself with a knife in the back.

Worse yet, he might have found himself buried deep inside Sydony Marchant, with no thought to his responsibilities, her gentle birth, or his friendship with her brother.

Sydony let Barto drag her through the passages, dimly aware that he must have carefully noted the route they had taken. Sydony was glad of it, for she was not sure she could find her way back out, at least not now. Not when she was reeling from what had just happened.

What had just happened? One moment she had been furious with Barto for all his snubs and slights, and then he was kissing her, touching her, *putting his mouth to her*. Sydony stumbled as the hot memory flooded her, and Barto paused to pull her upright. But soon he was moving again, striding along the narrow path as though the hounds of hell were after him.

Surely, he wasn't taking her to…bed, Sydony thought, with a mixture of horror and delight. The desire that had fled in the awkward moments following Hob's call came surging back. But one glance at Barto's grim visage told her he had no intention of continuing where they had left off. And Sydony struggled against a feeling of disappointment at the knowledge.

What had just happened? Sydony took some deep breaths to try to clear her spinning thoughts. If not in haste to bed, why was Barto pulling her through the maze so carelessly? With a sharp pang, Sydony wondered if it had all been a pose again. But a man couldn't pretend something like that, could he? Sydony had to admit that her own lack of experience provided no answer. Nor could she ask her brother about such an indelicate topic.

She was tempted to do so, for perhaps then Kit would abandon his hopes for her future. Sydony didn't need a book on auguring to deduce that Barto was not planning on offering for her. And with that realisation, the euphoria that had filled her in the centre of the maze disappeared entirely, to be replaced by the bleak, dark weight of suspicion.

What had she let happen? Once again, she had proven herself unable to resist Barto's charms. Tugging her fingers from his grasp, Sydony marched behind him towards the exit of the maze, just as eager to escape this ignominy as he seemed eager to be rid of her.

Swallowing hard, she tried to keep a rein on her rioting emotions, lest she break down here and now. She knew that her friends and former neighbours would say that motherless Sydony Marchant had grown up to be strong and independent and competent. She might not be able to play the pianoforte or dabble at watercolours or flutter a fan, but she could cook and clean and run a household, ride as hard as her brother, read Greek, form an opinion and speak her mind. She wasn't easily frightened or intimidated. Some might even call her stubborn and wilful.

But weak? Sydony had never considered the word. Until now. Blinking hurriedly against the threat of tears, she realised they had reached the opening of the maze, and Barto held back the greenery, so she could step out from the wall of hedges. Slanting a glance at his face, Sydony felt her heart sink even further at his cold expression.

'Excuse me,' he said, giving her a curt nod before striding off to where Hob stood between the maze and the stables.

'Yes, excuse you,' Sydony whispered as she watched his back.

What had just happened? Sydony didn't know. She only knew that she had a weakness, and its name was Bartholomew Hawthorne.

For a long moment, Sydony stood dazed, as though waiting for the ground to swallow her up, or, better yet, that it swallow up Barto. When it did not, she lifted her chin and headed towards the house. She entered through the kitchen, in the hopes of avoiding everyone, especially her brother. Shutting the door quietly behind her, she turned to find the cook staring at her sullenly.

'Mrs Talbot's looking for you,' she said.

'Thank you,' Sydony said, though she was not grateful. Now she would have to search for the housekeeper instead of taking to her room to gather her composure. She imagined that Barto's scent clung to her, making her want him still, and if she could wash up, that feeling might go away…

In a rare shirk of duty, Sydony did not look for the housekeeper, but moved through the rooms towards the stairs, but she had only reached the first step when she heard the older woman call her name. Better it was Mrs Talbot than her brother, she realised, for Kit would know, with one look at her, that something was wrong.

'Yes?'

'There's a gentleman here to see you, miss.'

'To see me?' Sydony echoed, puzzled.

'To see the owners of the estate. But I can't find Mr Marchant. He appears to have gone out.'

'Very well,' Sydony said, aware that, at any other time, she would have been eager for a visitor.

'He's in the library, miss. Says his name is Mr Malet.'

Thanking the housekeeper, Sydony composed herself and walked to the library, where she found a tall, slender man standing in front of one of the bookshelves, his hands clasped behind his back. He looked to be in his late twenties, with neatly trimmed black hair and the clothes of a gentleman, though they were not as elegant and well cut as Barto's.

Angry with herself for bringing her old neighbour into every thought, Sydony hurried forwards. 'Welcome to Oakfield, Mr Malet,' she said.

He turned, his dark eyes intense before a smile broke upon his handsome features. 'A lovely greeting—Miss Marchant, is it?'

'Yes,' Sydony said. 'My brother is about somewhere, but if you are not particular about which Marchant you wish to see, I may endeavor to help you.' Gesturing for him to take a seat, Sydony perched on the edge of one of the library step-chairs.

'Thank you, but perhaps I am the one who can help you,' Malet said. 'You see, I have been endeavoring to research and map labyrinths of note throughout the country, and that undertaking has led me here. To Oakfield.'

Sydony blinked in surprise. Usually, the maze drove people away instead of luring them here, but she decided not to share that information with this man. Although his face was not as beautiful as Barto's, he had a compelling air about him that drew her attention and held it. Unlike Barto, he wasn't afraid to look her in the eye. Nor did he carry himself with the arrogant entitlement of the viscount. Still, Sydony had grown wary since moving into her new home, and the friendliness she once extended to strangers was no longer automatic.

'I see. Are you a gardener, or a designer of gardens, Mr Malet?'

'Oh, my, no,' Malet said, with a self-deprecating smile. 'I am only a simple researcher with an interest in the patterns that have been part of our country's landscape for so long. Currently, I am undertaking a study, with the purpose of creating a written record of many of these unique mazes, for future historians.'

Where was this fellow when she had been desperate for information? 'I can see why you would find the subject fascinating.'

'Ah, are you enthralled yourself, Miss Marchant?'

Sydony wasn't sure she would use that word, but there was no denying the maze had a hold upon her. 'I admit our labyrinth has stimulated my interest.'

'As well it should,' Malet said. 'I wanted to see this particular maze as there is so much history there.'

Did this man know something she didn't? 'I thought that puzzle mazes only dated to the seventeenth century.'

A flash of surprise or annoyance seemed to cross his expression at her words, and Sydony wondered if, like so many scholars, he didn't like anyone else pretending expertise in his area of interest.

'I can see you already have done some studying,' he said, nodding his head towards her. 'And you are quite right, Miss Marchant. But your labyrinth is much older. According to my own research…' he paused to give her another self-deprecating smile '…I believe that the garden maze that you see is only the latest incarnation.'

Sydony felt a leap of excitement at the confirmation of her own suspicions. 'Of an earlier turf maze?'

Again, he appeared taken aback, but this time he gave her an approving nod. 'Yes, indeed. Although garden mazes are all the fashion now, turf labyrinths remain, older, and, if I may say so, more mystical.'

'Mystical?'

'Why, yes,' Malet said. 'One in North Yorkshire that dates from Norman times is known as Fairy Hill because children who run through it claim to hear the fairies singing from the ground.' He paused to flash her a smile.

'Other tales are not so whimsical. One medieval maze lies next to a well whose waters are known to petrify bones,' he said. 'To run that labyrinth three times is to court death.'

For a moment, he looked so serious that Sydony shivered. Then he shrugged, as if to dismiss the story.

'Oh, there are many interesting legends,' Malet continued. 'One that crops up in various accounts is that of a virgin placed at the centre of the maze, waiting for a young man to reach the centre.'

Sydony blinked at his casual use of a word usually not heard in mixed company. 'To rescue her?'

'Perhaps to dance with her,' Malet said, with another shrug. 'There are many versions. The old turf mazes are steeped in lore from times long past.'

'But if Oakfield's was once a turf maze, why change it?' Sydony asked.

'They become difficult to maintain, and there is

always a chance of a mistake,' Malet said. 'Or perhaps the owner wanted to keep people out, instead of drawing them in.'

At Sydony's surprised look, he continued. 'Turf mazes attract children and gawkers, while a hedge maze is more forbidding, especially a puzzle maze,' Malet said. 'People could get lost and never come out.'

He spoke with such an odd note in his voice that Sydony glanced at him sharply, but his expression was bland, and scholars, as she well knew, were an eccentric bunch.

In the ensuing quiet, Sydony heard the sound of someone approaching, and her traitorous heart began beating wildly at the thought that it might be Barto. She turned, eager, despite all, to see his tall, elegant form in the doorway. But it was Kit who appeared.

Sydony told herself she was relieved, for she had no idea how to face Barto after what had happened between them. It might have been just a pose or a jest or a lark for him, but to her it was much more, something deeper, something nearly frightening in its intensity, something she was not ready to examine.

She stood, as if to escape her own thoughts, and spoke rapidly, introducing her brother to their visitor.

'Mr Malet is undertaking a study of mazes,' she explained.

'Excellent. You will have to take a look at ours,' Kit said. 'In fact, I was just thinking of going through myself. Would you care to join me?'

'Of course,' Malet said with a dip of his head, and Sydony was glad to have Kit act as host, leaving her free to repair to her room.

'Will you come, too?' Kit asked, turning to Sydony.

Mutely, she shook her head, shrinking from the thought of retracing her earlier steps, of returning to the golden circle at the centre of the labyrinth, where the great oak stood sentinel, a rough anchor against her back.

Indeed, after what had happened today, Sydony didn't know if she ever would have the heart to explore the maze again.

Chapter Fourteen

Sydony didn't remain long in her room. Her hasty wash did not have the desired result, and she soon grew uncomfortable alone with her thoughts. Restless, she looked for a distraction, anything that would not involve Barto. So when she saw from her window that Kit and Mr Malet were exiting the maze, she went down to meet them in the drawing room.

The room was empty, but for herself, and when Kit entered through the tall doors from the terrace, he glanced around, as if looking for something. 'Have you seen…Viscount Hawthorne?' he asked Sydony.

Trying to keep her expression as cool as Barto always did, she shook her head. 'Not since before Mr Malet's arrival. Why?'

'One of his men's gone missing, and I wondered if the fellow was with him. I'll see if I can find them,' Kit said. He turned to Mr Malet. 'Please excuse me.'

'Of course,' Malet said. 'Thank you again for your

hospitality. I assure you that I shall include a prominent mention of Oakfield in any published work.'

Kit exited to the terrace, leaving Sydony to escort Mr Malet to the front of the house. Normally, a gentleman guest such as the visiting scholar would be invited to dine, if not stay with them, but Sydony did not feel equal to entertaining, and Kit obviously had other concerns. The atmosphere at Oakfield was tense enough without an outsider adding to the strain, and Mr Malet had seen what he'd come to see.

'And how did you find our labyrinth?' Sydony asked.

'Most enlightening,' he said, but his face had clouded over, and Sydony wondered if he'd found something amiss in the maze, perhaps felt a sense of the lingering evil purported to cling to it.

However, when he spoke again, it was not about the hedges. 'I beg your pardon, but did your brother say that Viscount Hawthorne is here?'

'Yes,' Sydony said, in surprise. 'Do you know him?'

Malet shook his head. 'No, but I have heard of him.' He paused as if he intended to say more, then waved a hand in dismissal. 'I would not carry unwanted gossip to your ears,' he said as they continued walking.

Sydony was not sure how to respond. Although not one to condone scandal broth, she was certainly anxious to learn anything being said about Barto, especially since he was staying with them, ordering his men about, and generally directing their lives. So when the new maid appeared to show Malet out, Sydony sent the girl away, lest anyone overhear her conversation with the visitor.

Her precaution was wise, for when they reached the front door, Malet turned towards her, his dark eyes suddenly intent. 'And yet, situated as you are in such a remote location, perhaps you would welcome the sharing of news.'

That was certainly true. London seemed a world away, and even letters from their old neighbours were long in coming. 'We are far from town,' Sydony admitted. 'What is it that you have heard?'

Malet sighed. 'It is most disturbing, I fear, especially considering your situation here.' Looking down at his feet, he shook his head, as if loathe to go on, and Sydony felt her nerves stretch taut.

'Yes?' she prompted him.

His dark gaze lifted to her own, and his voice rang with intensity as he spoke. 'They say that the current viscount was in a hurry to assume his title, so much so that he may have brought it about himself...'

Sydony felt her jaw drop open. Of all the half-formed suspicions she'd had about Barto ever since his surprising appearance at their new home, she had never really let herself think this—that he had arranged to kill his own father in order to come into his inheritance.

Sydony felt as though all the air had been sucked from her lungs. She gaped at Malet, her eyes wide and mouth working, but she couldn't form any words. She couldn't even seem to take a breath.

'Perhaps you should be wary of welcoming him into your home,' Malet said. 'Good day, Miss Marchant.'

Sydony watched the visitor walk out the door, wondering whether she should call him back or let him go. Having given her his warning, he seemed eager to be on his way. Did he fear Barto himself? He could not know that Sydony had but recently left the arms of the man he advised her against, and she shuddered, unsure what to think.

Only one thing was clear: gossip was painting Barto as a murderer.

Sydony walked Oakfield's battlements, taking deep breaths full of the smell of crisp leaves and a freshening wind. Her first thought after hearing Malet's warning had been to find Kit, to prove to him, once and for all, that Barto was not to be trusted. But instead of looking for her brother, she had found herself heading upwards, as though the air up here might clear her head, helping her think straight for the first time this day.

As she approached the edge of the roof, looking out over the front of the property, Sydony saw Mr Malet striding away from the house. Had he come back? She wanted to call down to him, but he was hurrying, and Sydony didn't know if her voice would carry. If he'd thought of something else to add to his cautions, she wouldn't be able to catch him. And did she really want to know?

That was the question.

As Sydony leaned against the cold stone, she tried to work out the answer. She started at the beginning, although she couldn't recall her first meeting with Barto. He had simply been there, an integral part of her childhood. But memories that she hadn't visited in years came streaming back.

Slowly, Barto the boy in her visions grew older, until the day he had kissed her and she had put aside all thoughts of him. Perhaps, unknown to Kit, she hadn't looked at anyone else because she was afraid of being rejected and hurt again. Or maybe her brother was right, and there was just no one else like Barto. The object of all her youthful admiration had been strong, bold, stubborn, intelligent and prepared to meet any experience. How many other men had she met who were so vital, so full of life?

No wonder she had resented Barto's reappearance in her life to reawaken all that she had forgotten. And no wonder she had tried to shut him out, attempting to avoid another hurtful rejection with dark suspicions and whispers to Kit. But it had done her no good, she realised now. Clear eyed as she looked into the distance, Sydony admitted what she'd been trying to deny since the moment Barto had arrived.

She loved him.

Perhaps she always had, her childish devotion turning to a more grown-up admiration that had culminated painfully with their first kiss. But the moment she'd crashed into his tall form on her doorstep, all those old sentiments had been dredged up, only to evolve into something new and stronger and deeper. And no matter how black she painted him, how oddly he behaved, or what dark rumours swirled about him, Sydony could not help herself.

She loved him.

Sydony drew in several deep breaths as the emotions that had rioted within her for weeks settled down to that one simple fact, and she felt a certain peace in the acceptance. No longer would she hide it from herself or from Kit. Whether she hid it from Barto didn't matter; obviously, he did not share her sentiments.

But that did not stop her from loving him. And while

he was here, she would take what joy she could from his presence to hoard over the long years after he was gone. Yes, she anticipated his departure, sooner or later, even though she had no real understanding of why he had come. But she refused to believe he was a murderer, and she vowed not to mistrust his motives any longer.

Since she had finally had come to terms with her love for the man he had become, maybe it was time that she took the leap of faith and trusted him as well.

Kit walked through the house with growing impatience. Although he had felt an immediate kinship with the old manor, even he noticed that it seemed emptier than usual this afternoon. Finally spying a flash of black, he strode towards the hall, where he found Mrs Talbot standing near the front doors.

'Is someone here?' he asked.

'No, sir. I was just letting out Mr Malet.'

'I thought he had left already,' Kit said. Or had the man monopolised poor Sydony's time? Curious fellow. Having grown up in a scholar's household, Kit thought he'd be cooped up in the maze with the visitor for hours, but they had walked in and out with surprising speed. Perhaps the man had seen all he needed in that quick trip, for there really wasn't much to study or observe beyond the twists of the pathways.

'Yes, sir, but he came back. Said he'd left his satchel in the library,' the housekeeper said. 'I hope I did nothing wrong, sir.'

'Of course not,' Kit said. 'Do you know where my sister is?'

'No, sir,' she said, her dour expression unchanging.

'What about the viscount? Have you seen him?'

'No, sir,' she repeated, as if sounding a death knoll. The woman really was rather odd. Once her brief tenure ended and she went back to her daughter, Kit was personally selecting a new housekeeper. Someone who smiled wouldn't be amiss.

'Very well,' he said. 'If you see either one of them, tell them I'm looking for them.'

'Yes, sir.' She nodded grimly, and Kit was tempted to caper about or lead her into a dance just to shake her out of her stoic demeanour. But good manners forbade him from abusing the servants, so he simply watched her move away, her dark garb making her look like a giant beetle scuttling back into the woodwork.

After she left, Kit stood in the hall for a long moment, wondering where else to search for Sydony. He had been surprised not to find her within the lower rooms, and her absence coupled with Barto's made him wonder whether they had gone off together, a not unwelcome prospect, depending on exactly where they were and what they were doing.

Kit frowned. Lost in thought, he stirred from his spot at the sound of a noise, a hiss of some sort. When he glanced around, he saw one of the maids, Nellie, standing at the entrance to the library. She looked as though she might furtively motion him over, then thought better of it and stepped forwards.

'Er, Mr Marchant, sir, I can't seem to find Miss Marchant, and I was wondering…' She trailed off, her round face flushing, then took a deep breath. 'Well, my father wants me to come home, just to help out, you know.'

'We'd be sorry to lose you, Nellie,' Kit said, sincerely. He knew that Sydony especially liked the maid, and servants were hard to come by at Oakfield.

'Oh, it's just for tonight, sir,' she said. 'He's worried what with the dry weather and all.'

Kit eyed her blankly.

'It's the bonfires, sir. He's worried they might get away from the revellers and burn up something they shouldn't.'

'Bonfires?' Kit echoed.

'Yes, sir. They'll be celebrating in the village tonight, being that it's All-Hallow Eve.'

'Oh! Of course, you may go,' Kit said, feeling foolish at forgetting the annual holiday.

Her head downcast, Nellie thanked him profusely before heading towards the kitchen.

It was only when she had disappeared into the bowels of the house that Kit wondered what possible assistance the girl could be in preventing the spread of bonfires.

After looking through the house once more for Sydony, Kit headed back outside, where he saw the new workman standing with Nellie. When the fellow spied Kit, he nervously fingered the cap he held in his hands.

'Uh, Mr Marchant, sir, I thought I'd take her into the village,' he said.

From the way neither one of them would meet his eye, Kit suspected superstition was behind their sudden urge to leave. According to Mr Scrimminger, one of the days that were important to Druids began at dusk on

All-Hallow Eve. The sun would be setting soon, and Kit might have said something to the two who stood before him, but for his vow not to abuse the servants.

'Very well,' he said, instead. 'Have Jeremy take you in the carriage.'

Martin nodded gratefully, before turning toward the stables, Nellie right beside him. With a shake of his head at the whimsy that drove their lives, Kit stood gazing over the grounds, looking for any signs of movement. According to Barto's tiger, he had taken his horse out earlier, but did not say where he was going. The boy, Jack, said Barto had been alone at the time, so Kit was no closer to finding out the whereabouts of the two guards.

The disappearance of all three made Kit wonder whether Barto had stumbled across something, only to hare off suddenly, without bothering to inform him. Barto had always been independent and eager to pursue some new adventures, with or without company. And now he was even more private, arriving at Oakfield with a heavy burden of secrets it had taken him some time to share. But lately Kit had sensed a gradual thaw of the icy reserve the viscount had acquired, and he welcomed the return of his old friend.

That was one reason why Kit let Barto do whatever he wanted. Although Kit wasn't convinced that the deaths of their fathers had been anything more than an accident, he recognised that Barto might need to take action in order to work out his grief. And if Barto and Sydony wanted to chase at shadows, Kit wasn't about to stop them. Personally, he thought the maze intruders were probably young locals looking for a dare. Hell, it was something he and Barto might have done years ago.

Shaking his head, Kit heard the sound of wheels upon the gravel drive and wondered whether the carriage was returning for yet more passengers. But when he looked up, the arrival appeared to be a horse pulling a small cart, probably driven by one of the local farmers. Kit strode to meet the fellow, a young man dressed in work clothes, who jumped down from his perch.

'You Mr Marchant?' he asked.

Kit nodded.

'Farmer Jobson sent these along to you, on account of the holiday,' the young man said, gesturing toward the rear of the cart, where two small casks lay among some straw. 'One for you and one for your groomsmen what helped him out of a ditch the other day,' the young man said, jerking a thumb toward the stables. He leaned close, giving Kit a whiff of strong drink. 'Part of Jobson's special home brew,' he said, with a wink. Apparently, this fellow had already begun celebrating.

Shouldering one of the casks, he carried it to the stables. 'You Jeremy?' he asked when Jack walked out to greet him. The boy shook his head.

'Well, this is for all of you, with Farmer Jobson's compliments,' the young man said.

Jack looked toward Kit, a question on his face, but when Kit nodded, he took the barrel inside. Then the farmer's young man returned to the cart, hefting the second cask for the trip to the kitchen. He had obviously been to Oakfield before, but Kit followed, holding the door as the fellow set the keg on the work table with a loud thump. Thankfully, the sour-faced cook was not there to scowl in disapproval.

The young man wiped his hands on his dark coat. 'That's thirsty work,' he said, his eyes glinting.

Kit caught the hint. 'Indeed. Would you like a glass to tide you over for the trip back to the farm?'

'Why, thank you, sir,' the young man said, just as though the thought had never crossed his mind, and Kit swallowed a laugh. 'Will you join me?'

'I suppose I should give it a taste,' Kit said, grateful for Farmer Jobson, one of the few tenant farmers who remained at the estate.

Instead of calling for either the cook or housekeeper, who would certainly cast a pall over the proceedings, Kit found two glasses himself and filled them with the strong, dark liquid.

'Cheers!' the young man said, downing his in one long gulp.

Echoing his sentiments, Kit took a more cautious sip. It was a potent brew that smelled of apples. 'Cider,' Kit said, with a smile.

'Best in the county,' the young man said, with a grin that revealed two missing teeth. Wiping his mouth on his sleeve, he gave Kit a nod. 'I'd best be on my way.'

Opening the door, he paused to turn back toward Kit. 'Pardon me, sir, but I forgot that a gentleman on the road gave me a message for you. Said he was Viscount… er…something or other, and to tell you he was off to the Hart and Hound to sample the local revelry.' With that, the young man went out the door and hopped back upon his wagon, no doubt eager to get back to whatever celebrations were going on in his absence.

Kit stood in the doorway, watching him go, as the sun sank below the horizon. It cast a golden glow over Oakfield's grounds, his lands, and he felt an answering glow inside. He had never thought to be a landowner. Indeed, not long before his father's death, he had been duly considering his opportunities, eager neither for a military nor religious career, the two most available to young men of his class. And after their father's death, he hadn't wanted to leave Sydony, but the financial situation was becoming strained.

Until Oakfield fell into his lap. And from the moment he set eyes on the place, dark and whipped with rain, he had loved the old Tudor manor, with its battlements and ivy-covered walls. With hard work and proper investment, he knew the estate could be prosperous, and he intended to do all that he could to make it so.

Downing the rest of his cider, Kit closed the door behind him and headed towards the stables to let Hob know where his master was. The groomsmen had seemed especially concerned, far more than Barto's valet, who spent most of his time sequestered in his cellar room.

Kit found Jack already on his second glass of cider.

'Be careful with that. You don't want to become befuddled,' Hob said, with more sharpness in his tone than Kit thought necessary.

'Here, I'll join you,' Kit said, pulling up a chair to the makeshift living area the men had made past the stalls. 'It's just a sip of cider.'

'Mighty strong cider,' Hob said, with a huff, but he was persuaded to have a glass with them.

'Farmer Jobson's boy said he saw the viscount on the

road. Seems he's decided to join the revelries at the local tavern,' Kit said.

Hob slanted Jack a dark glance, as though uneasy with the news, though Kit could see no harm in it.

'I told you he just took his horse and rode off without a word to me,' the boy said.

'To a tavern? It's not like him,' Hob said.

Kit smiled at the groomsman's fierce loyalty to his master. 'Perhaps he felt the need for a change of scenery,' he said. Kit could certainly picture Sydony driving Barto to drink. The two of them were either at each other's throats or avoiding each other with dark looks. It was enough to make even Kit take to the bottle.

'And what of the two guards? Did he take them with him?' Hob asked, rather sharply.

The groomsman was talking to Jack, but Kit felt the weight of his scorn as well. He shrugged. 'Perhaps.'

Hob did not look convinced. 'Still and all, I'd like to make sure all's well,' he said.

'I'll go,' Jack said, rising unsteadily to his feet.

'Go? You've had enough already without stopping by the tavern,' Hob said.

'I'll go,' Kit said, yawning. 'The ride will do me good.'

'Are you sure, sir?' Hob said, looking like he'd overstepped his bounds. He probably had, but Kit wasn't a stickler for boundaries.

'I'll go,' he repeated.

Hob quickly readied his horse, and Kit had soon mounted. 'Just make sure my sister is told that I went to the village to join the viscount,' he said, and Hob nodded. 'And tell them about the keg of cider in the kitchen.'

Kit paused, thoughtfully, and frowned. 'I don't know whether we'll be back for supper,' he added, glad that he would not be giving Sydony that message in person.

The evening chill finally drove Sydony down from the battlements. She had stayed to watch the sun set behind the maze and was tempted to linger until the stars came out. But it was growing cold, and she had no lantern. Rubbing her arms, she walked across the roof to the door that led back into the house. But when she pulled on it, she saw the steps were barely visible, the opening a black chasm before her feet.

Sydony's heart picked up its pace at the realisation that the door she had left open at the bottom of the stairs was closed now. Ignoring a twinge of panic, she told herself that it had just fallen shut. And there was no reason to think it was stuck again, like last time when she and Barto had thought it locked against them.

Still, she took up a fallen branch to wedge beneath the upper door, just in case. She had no desire to be trapped upon the stairway again, especially without Barto to comfort…and distract her.

Now that the sun had set, the approaching night seemed to gather around her, settling over the ramparts like a heavy weight and making her blink into the gloom. Her heart pounded again, but Sydony ignored it, taking the time to prop the door open before carefully stepping on to the stairs.

With one hand upon the wall beside her, she squinted and felt her way down, the wind following her with an eerie wail. Perhaps it was making the door rattle below, as well, Sydony thought. Or maybe that was just the sound of her heart beating too loudly in her ears.

When she finally reached the bottom, Sydony lifted a hand to the latch anxiously, but it gave way easily beneath her fingers. She swung the door wide, releasing the breath she didn't even realise she had been holding, and stepped on to the carpeting of the first floor with a sigh of relief. Shutting the door behind her, she leaned against it, taking a moment to compose herself.

A bubble of laughter escaped her throat, but it sounded more like a shaky groan. Just as she had done with Barto, Sydony had assumed the worst, inventing a frightening situation where there was nothing except natural forces at work. Oakfield's infamous wind had struck again.

Smiling weakly at her folly, Sydony straightened. Perhaps, along with her decision to trust Barto, she should vow not to see bugaboos around every corner of Kit's beloved house. This was her home, too, and she needed to make it so.

Nodding at her new vow, Sydony decided the time had come for her to act like an adult.

Chapter Fifteen

Sydony headed down to the ground floor, only to find it deserted. Again, she felt a twinge of anxiety, but keeping to her new vow, she refused to become suspicious. Just because Barto and Kit were not in the library or the drawing room was no reason to become distressed. Perhaps they were outside. In the dark.

Again, Sydony dismissed her own whimsy. More likely, they were in their rooms, resting before supper. And perhaps the fires had not been lit because someone, probably Barto, was monopolising the servants. For an instant, Sydony allowed herself to imagine the viscount in his bath, and she flushed, resisting the temptation to interrupt his privacy, for she knew she would not be welcome.

When she had nearly reached the kitchen, Sydony caught a glimpse of Mrs Talbot, and she smiled, eager for a greeting. Even the grim housekeeper was welcome in the seeming emptiness of the dim house.

'Miss Marchant!' The housekeeper's face actually

registered something as she moved into the dining room. Was the dour woman startled or relieved to see her?

'Yes, what is it?' Sydony asked, her concern returning.

'Nothing, miss,' the housekeeper said. 'It's just that Mr Marchant was looking for you for some time, and I feared, or rather, the staff… We couldn't find you.'

Perhaps that explained the absence of the fires. Had Kit been so worried that he'd sent the servants out to look for her? Sydony felt a sharp pang of guilt. As upset as she had been at the time, she shouldn't have disappeared without letting anyone know where she was going. But in her own defence, she had thought the open door to the battlements would serve as notice of her whereabouts. Given Oakfield's infamous quirks, she should have known it would close behind her.

'I'm sorry to have caused any trouble,' Sydony said. 'Where is Mr Marchant now? I'll go directly to him.'

'He went into the village,' Mrs Talbot said. 'He and the viscount are at the Hart and Hound.'

'*What?* Why?' Sydony asked, momentarily forgetting herself. But if Kit was so worried about her, why would he take off with Barto for some ale?

'Perhaps he wanted a spot of supper,' Mrs Talbot suggested. Her tone was so odd that Sydony eyed her askance, and only then did she realise that the housekeeper was not herself. Indeed, the woman seemed barely able to control her agitation.

'What is it? Why would they go out for supper?'

'The cook,' Mrs Talbot said. 'She's gone. They've all gone, deserting their posts, the cowards.'

'Mrs Talbot, are you all right? Perhaps you should sit down,' Sydony said.

The housekeeper shook her head.

Sydony took a steadying breath. 'All right. Then tell me who has gone. My brother and the viscount are at the tavern…'

'Not them. It's the servants, miss. Nellie and Martin left for the village, and cook went with them, too craven to remain at her post,' Mrs Talbot said.

Craven? Sydony thought that the housekeeper was reacting rather strongly. Mentally, she totted up the staff. 'And what of the other maid?'

'She's floored with the viscount's valet!'

Sydony blinked. 'Floored? You mean dead drunk? She and Mister…' Sydony trailed off, unable to recall the valet's name, then slanted a startled glance at Mrs Talbot. Had the housekeeper found the two in some kind of compromising situation? 'Where?'

'Right there in the kitchen,' Mrs Talbot said, her voice rising.

Sydony felt like patting the poor woman, whose nerves were obviously stretched thin, but the housekeeper did not invite comfort. Instead, Sydony headed towards the kitchen, where she found an extremely well-dressed older man seated at the work table, with Bessie slumped nearby.

For one startling moment, Sydony thought they were dead, and she stepped forwards to check for signs of life. But she could see the rise and fall of the man's chest, while Bessie, whose head was on the table, could be heard emitting low snores.

Sydony blinked. Although she had heard of boozers

and castaways, she'd never seen any up close. She glanced around the room in puzzlement, looking for a bottle. 'But what did they drink?'

Mrs Talbot let out a sound of disgust. 'Farmer Jobson's cider,' she said, gesturing to a cask that sat on the table. 'He's famous for it, so the locals know not to have too much.' Her contempt for the valet and the maid, whom Nellie said wasn't from around here, was obvious.

Sydony grabbed a fresh glass and poured herself a bit of the brew. It certainly smelled strong, and when she took a sip, she found it pleasant, but too hard. She could not imagine drinking so much as to become insensate, but perhaps the more you had, the better it tasted.

Sydony set down her glass. 'So there is no one to cook supper,' she said.

'There is no one in the house except for us,' Mrs Talbot said, and Sydony realized the poor woman was wringing her hands.

Sydony took them in her own. 'What is it?' she asked, trying to understand what could move the normally stoic housekeeper to such a display. 'Why did the other servants go?'

Mrs Talbot refused to meet her eyes, but she finally muttered something. Sydony leaned close to listen and thought she heard the housekeeper blame All-Hallows Eve. It was so unexpected that Sydony nearly burst into laughter. But Mrs Talbot obviously was not amused; she was frightened.

Sydony squeezed her hands. 'We aren't alone. The groomsmen are all in the stables.'

Mrs Talbot shook her head. 'That boy Jeremy took them away in the carriage, cook and the rest of them.'

'All right,' Sydony said, releasing the housekeeper's hands and stepping back to assess the situation. 'Jeremy is gone. That leaves several others.'

In fact, besides Barto's groomsman and tiger, his two guards were standing watch somewhere. And Kit and Barto wouldn't have gone off drinking, if there was any danger, All-Hallows Eve or not. The sudden realisation that it was Samhain made Sydony falter, as did a white-faced Mrs Talbot.

'I should have never come back. I should have stayed with my daughter,' she muttered, shaking her head and wringing her hands.

'Rubbish,' Sydony said, lifting her chin. 'If it makes you feel any better, lock all the doors, and I shall go bring back Hob or one of the other fellows.'

Mrs Talbot just shook her head, as though she'd lost all pretence to good sense, and Sydony had to nudge her. 'Go lock the doors, and I'll fetch my cloak.'

Once out of the kitchen, Sydony hurried towards the hall and took the stairs up to her room. Quickly, she found the heavy cloak she had worn into the maze and turned to go. But something made her pause. Suddenly, Kit's words came back to her, from their very first day here at Oakfield: *Grandfather's duelling pistols are up in my room.*

Mindful of her vow not to see bugaboos behind every door, none the less Sydony turned towards Kit's room, where she found the pistols, balls and powder. Automatically, she filled the pan of one as Kit had taught her long ago. Then she secreted the weapon in her cloak, along with the powder and balls, before hurrying down to the kitchen.

The house was dark now, and Sydony saw no sign of Mrs Talbot. Hopefully, the housekeeper was locking the doors, and when Sydony came back with one of the men, they could start the fires and light the candles. And when Barto and Kit returned, Sydony would have a few choice things to say to both of them. She knew Kit was oblivious to the bizarre quirks of his property, but she had thought Barto more in tune with her, at least on that level.

With a sigh, Sydony took up a lantern. Although she could see lights in the stable, it was full night now, but the moon had yet to make its way into the sky. Stepping outside, she shut the door behind her and began walking the black expanse to the stables. Comfortably warm in her cloak, nevertheless she pulled it close, for the wind had picked up, swirling leaves into the air and howling through the barren trees.

The eerie atmosphere was definitely evocative of All-Hallows Eve, and Sydony tried not to think about Samhain, Druids or the great mass of the maze that rose to her right. At least she could see no lights flickering within, she thought, swallowing hard. But why should she with Barto's men standing guard? She squinted into the blackness, trying to find where they were, but they remained well hidden.

When she reached the stables, Sydony released a pent breath in relief, especially when she saw Barto's groomsman and tiger sitting at a small table at the other end. Walking past the empty stalls, Sydony called out to the two, but they did not respond. Her voice seemed to echo loudly in the old building, and she fell silent. Yet her footsteps rang out upon the stone floor, and, despite her vow, her heart began pounding at a furious pace. If one were prone to see bugaboos, now would be the time to fear them, she thought, as she made the long trek toward the men.

They did not rise or speak or react in any way, and Sydony began to wonder if she was locked in a nightmare, but she did not need to pinch herself to dismiss that notion. As she approached the table where they were slumped, Sydony thought their positions seemed familiar, and she soon saw why. Nearby stood a cask similar to the one in the kitchen.

Setting down the lantern on the table, Sydony lifted a glass that had fallen on its side and sniffed. Immediately, she recognised the strong apple scent of Farmer Jobson's cider. She let out a nervous laugh of relief, but it sounded more like a groan, even to her ears.

Reaching out, Sydony nudged Hob's shoulder, but he only snorted and wheezed. Was this the way of heavy drinkers? Sydony wondered. Her father had never taken more than a glass or two of wine, and Kit had never been a two-bottle man, like the London blades. But she knew that some of the villagers near their old home had enjoyed any excuse to celebrate, and she had seen more than one of them fallen over the bar in the local inn.

Yet, something didn't seem right. It seemed more than coincidence that all four servants had drunk to excess. Were Barto's guards still stationed about the grounds, or were they lying somewhere dead drunk, too? Mrs Talbot's shrill warning that they were all alone at Oakfield came rushing back to haunt Sydony. Should she be fearful, or was she seeing bugaboos?

'Good evening, Miss Marchant.'

The sound of a deep voice made her jump, and Sydony whirled around, her heart in her throat, only to sigh in relief that someone was still awake. But the man who stepped out of the shadows was not one of the guards.

'What are you doing here?' Sydony asked, blinking at Mr Malet. Stupidly, she wondered whether he had left something behind or returned with another warning. But one look at his face told her that he was not here to help her.

'I'm so glad you didn't have any cider,' he said.

'What?' Sydony took a step back, shying away from the handsome visage that now had a dark and menacing aspect.

'The cider. Farmer Jobson's delightful brew,' Malet said. 'I had hoped that you wouldn't drink any.'

'I wasn't thirsty,' Sydony said, backing into the table behind her. The glass she had righted fell to its side once more, the noise loud in the stillness, but a quick glance told her that Barto's men did not stir. She realised then that they weren't simply drunk.

'You put something in the cider,' she said.

'A clever girl. But then I knew that when you offered up your little facts on the maze,' he said, and this time there was no mistaking his contempt for her. 'They probably won't die, if that's what concerns you. They are simply taking a well-needed rest, long enough for me to accomplish what I need to do.'

If his expression did not give away his ill intent, his

words made it very clear, and Sydony reached for the pistol in her cloak. But just as her hand closed around the butt, her arms were seized in a harsh grip. She tried to turn, only to be held fast by someone standing behind her. And even as she stamped on her captor's foot and kicked at his shin, she saw more figures step out of the shadows. Her already hammering heart seemed to skip a beat as she realised the figures wore black hoods, just as Barto had said.

The thought of Barto gave her a certain calm, banishing the panic that threatened to take hold. How many times had they been caught in some youthful mischief, and she had watched him use a clear head to get them out?

'You had better let me go,' Sydony said. 'Viscount Hawthorne and his men are hidden all over the grounds.'

Malet laughed harshly. 'No, we are the ones who hold this land. His men met with some accidents, I'm afraid. And your carriage lost its wheel, not in such a dramatic fashion as the one that killed your father, but it will keep young Jeremy busy. And your maid and cook and workman are with him, all too terror-stricken to remain here on Samhain.'

At the mention of her father, Sydony pulled against the hands that held her, then forced herself to relax. There was no point in wasting her strength. She must watch and wait for an opportunity to use her wits and escape, as Barto would have done.

Malet gestured toward the sleeping men. 'And the rest won't wake until it's all over.' He smiled evilly. 'It's your own fault, really. I tried to buy the property outright, but you refused.'

'For a paltry sum!'

Malet's face darkened. 'For all that I had,' he snapped. Then he seemed to compose himself. 'No matter. We have what we want, and, after tonight, perhaps your brother will be more eager to sell.'

At the mention of Kit, Sydony felt some measure of hope. Surely, he and Barto would be returning soon...

As if aware of her thoughts, Malet smiled again. 'That is, once he wakes up.'

Sydony's heart sank. 'Why? Why would you want Oakfield so much?'

'If you're that clever, you must know,' Malet said. 'This was the home of Ambrose Mallory, a powerful mystic whose spirit lingers here, waiting to be tapped, to be used to obtain great power.'

So Mallory had been the key. 'Then you are some kind of Druid, like the viscount's father?'

'Ha! Hawthorne was a fat old fool who thought that his name made him special. We worship the oak, not the hawthorn. And as for him and his friends, they were nothing but a Masonic order with a Druidic name, full of helpers and philanthropists that have nothing to do with the real religion. I follow the true Druidic path, not the romantic nonsense spewed forth by that carpenter Hurle and his ilk.'

Religion? Sydony swallowed hard. She had been just as wrong about Malet as she had been Barto. The scholar she had thought quiet and unassuming was a madman.

'Mallory was a real Druid, not a fat old squire traipsing about under the trees for the sake of fellowship. And even after his death, there remained followers who were faithful, keeping his secrets, passing along the knowledge that certain items of power resided here, waiting for the next great Arch-Druid to rise.'

'The book,' Sydony said, as she realised what he was talking about. 'You tore up the floor in the library.'

'After all these years, there were bound to be misdirections, false leads,' he said. 'How was I to know that the book was in plain sight, bound in a cover that disguised its true nature? And your relative was no help, always trying to hinder us, sending the books away. When she dared touch the labyrinth, I'm afraid I had to dispose of her.'

Sydony drew a sharp breath in horror.

'I didn't realise where the books had gone until that idiot Hawthorne babbled about it, so he did provide a service of sorts to the true Druids, despite his own inadequacies.'

'So you killed my father and the viscount, as well, just for a book,' Sydony said, her voice rising shrilly. Barto had been right all along, but it was still difficult to believe anyone could be that vile, even when he was staring her in the face. 'And you've been in the maze, digging and setting traps.'

'Again, a misdirection,' Malet said, with a gesture of dismissal. 'Rumours indicated that the great man's head was buried by his followers, so I searched in the ground near the oak, when, apparently, all I had to do was look in your cupboard.'

Sydony gasped. She remembered Mrs Talbot leaving Malet in the library, and later Sydony herself had seen him from the roof. Had he returned to steal the trepanned skull?

'Perhaps his devoted few feared the elements or out-siders and moved it to a safer location,' Malet said. 'I admit that I despaired of finding it, but you provided me with the last piece of the puzzle, the third prerequisite to my ascent to power.'

'Third?' Sydony echoed.

'With the skull to channel the spirit of Mallory, the great oak to lend me power, and the book's secrets of divination, all that I need now is to perform the ceremony within the sacred labyrinth. And you, lucky girl, will participate.'

Sydony could barely hear over the hammering of her heart. 'What kind of ceremony?'

Malet smiled so fiercely that Sydony wanted to look away. 'You're a clever girl. What did the Druids do, but ritual sacrifice? In your case, we shall have a virgin in the centre of the maze, which will make for especially powerful magic.'

The dark thought that had shadowed her ever since Malet had begun speaking now became a reality, and Sydony swayed, tempted to succumb to her fright. Instead, she thought of Barto and righted herself, standing straight and tall. 'But I'm not a virgin,' she lied.

Malet eyed her closely. 'So you've been busy with your viscount?' he said, practically spitting his venom. His face darkened, and for a moment, Sydony thought he might fly into a rage. But then he gestured dismissively.

'No matter. It's too late to find another, and I sense strong magic in you anyway,' he said. 'Just like your relative, you are obsessed with the maze, aren't you?'

Sydony did not bother to answer, though she knew the truth. She might have been, if not for Barto.

* * *

When Barto left Sydony to march toward the stables, he'd thought only to clear his head. Kicking his mount to a gallop, he just wanted to get away, to breath some fresh air far from the tensions at Oakfield. But after a while, even he became aware of the fact that he was riding in one direction. Away from the estate.

When the realisation struck, Barto felt a spasm of guilt. He had no business leaving the Marchants when the mysteries that plagued them remained unsolved. But the stresses of the last few weeks weighed on him, making him want to escape, if only for a few days. Perhaps a trip to London was in order; he could easily send for his valet and coach once he reached town.

Barto knew that his rage over his father's murder had been driving him for a long time, but now that fury had abated somewhat, and he was tired, weary of being cooped up at the small manor house for so long. He could visit friends who looked no deeper than his waistcoat, who required no introspection. And perhaps easing himself on his former mistress would cleanse the taste of Sydony from his lips, make him forget about her.

Barto let out a laugh that held no amusement, for he knew nothing would ever make him forget about Sydony Marchant. She was in his blood, a part of his past—and his future? Barto shook his head. He just needed to visit his old haunts: White's, the races at Newmarket, his tailor in Bond Street…

Why? he thought suddenly. Was that really what he wanted? Did he so enjoy the life he'd made for himself, or was he just ignoring his duty again as he had once refused to take up the reins of his title? Was the once-brave Bartholomew Hawthorne taking refuge in the trivial because that's what he could control?

Barto slowed his mount as he faced the painful truth—he was running away, fleeing Sydony Marchant and what she meant to him. *Just like last time.* And why? Because he couldn't control his feelings for her. But would he rather live without those feelings?

That was the choice he'd made then when young and foolish and feeling his oats. Having built the walls around himself, he chose to maintain them, so that no one, not even Kit or Sydony, could touch him.

And he'd done a fine job of it. No one in his circle of so-called friends knew him well. Certainly no woman could claim any personal knowledge of him. He picked them carefully for their lack of interest in anything except pleasing him in the most superficial ways, certainly not for the knowledge and wit and bravery that came as naturally to Sydony as breathing.

Safe within those walls, he had let nothing touch him until his father's death. And even then, he had been soon embraced the rage that had replaced his grief. It had driven him to Oakfield, where he was determined to believe that the treasured friends of his childhood had betrayed him in the most heinous fashion, had betrayed even their own father. And he had fed that fury even in the face of the Marchants' display of duty, loyalty and goodness, things that had been missing from his own life for some time.

Although he had slowly begun to trust them, by default, what he needed to do was lower the walls that were no longer serving him well, but containing him, stifling him like the hedges of the maze. Built to keep others out, they had become his prison.

It was time to tear them down and open himself up to friendship and…more. Instead of emulating his distant father and mother, Barto could take a cue from Mr Marchant. His parents had viewed the gentle scholar with amusement, but the man had been a devoted husband and father, his life full of all the things he loved.

Suddenly, that simple existence didn't appear unfashionable, but something to be treasured far more than London intrigues with their endless cycle of parties and meaningless relationships with expensive mistresses. For so long Barto had dismissed Hawthorne Park as a place to be buried in the country, but now the estate seemed an idyllic setting in which to enjoy the wonders of nature, to raise a family of his own, to search for the kind of adventures to be had on his lands. To play at Robin Hood. *With his Maid Marian.*

The thought of Sydony, not as his enemy, but as his partner, *his wife*, made Barto jerk on the reins. Perseus danced around, and Barto urged him on again, back the way they had come, towards Oakfield.

Although Barto was tempted to kick his mount to a gallop, twilight was setting over the countryside. Indeed, when he saw one of the abandoned tenant farms, Barto decided to stop there to water and rest his horse before the moonrise would light his way. Swinging into the farmyard, he found an old cistern, where he dismounted and let Perseus drink his fill. But anxious to move on, he wondered if he might find a lantern in the old cottage.

After some rooting around in the dark interior, Barto finally found what he sought, and, using the brimstone match he kept in his saddlebag, he set it alight. He was surprised that it held any oil, especially since the building looked long abandoned. But the glow showed him an interior at odds with what he had seen outside.

Everything in the small house was neatly arranged, including a table and several simple chairs, which wasn't so surprising. It was the lack of dust and the neatly swept floor that caught Barto's attention. Even the fireplace was swept clean. Stepping closer to take a look, he also began to notice an odd smell. Turning, he saw a bucket by the fireplace and held the lantern over it, only to stare in shock at the contents. Why would an abandoned cottage contain a bucket of entrails, fresh with blood?

Barto began searching the place in earnest then. His worst fears were confirmed when he opened a cupboard to find a couple of heavy black cloaks with hoods. The separate hoods would cover the head, allowing only a small slit through which to see.

Beating back the panic that threatened with cool efficiency, Barto stuffed the garments in his saddlebag, along with the brimstone match, then put out the lantern, leaving everything else as he had found it. Outside the moon was just visible, and though he wanted to urge Perseus to a gallop, he knew better than to push the horse in the darkness. Instead, he set a slower pace and turned Perseus towards the road, an easier path.

Barto had not travelled far when he heard the whinny of a horse. Slowing, he urged Perseus into a copse of trees that would provide cover and peered out into the night. He saw no lights, but finally was able to pinpoint the animal, standing in a ditch off the road, with what looked like a cart behind it.

Barto knew he could take another route away from the road. He had no time to waste, and there was always the possibility that this was a trap. But whoever was there might know something about what was happening at Oakfield, so he drew the pistol he had taken to carrying in his bag and approached the odd scene, barely visible under the rising moon. At first Barto thought the cart abandoned, but he found a boy lying among the straw, not visibly injured but smelling of strong drink.

With a frown, Barto realised he had wasted precious time on some reveller who did not know his limit. Still, he led the horse from the ditch with the help of Perseus, and tied the reins to a tree, lest the animal wander. It was all he could afford to do.

The odd experience only heightened Barto's alertness, and he kept careful watch for anything unusual. When he heard another horse, he was ready, stopping to search the darkness before sighting the animal not far off the road ahead. This horse was not in a ditch, but standing still and apparently riderless. Yet Barto approached with pistol in hand, ducking low over Perseus in case he provided a target for some unseen rider.

When Barto drew closer, he discovered there was a rider, lying prone at the horse's feet. The figure did not stir, and Barto wondered if the man had been thrown. Was he dead or as dead drunk as the boy had been?

But something about the horse looked familiar, as did the body at its feet, and Barto dismounted quickly, bending over to turn the man over. With a harsh exhalation, he realized it was Kit, and Barto's decision to let himself feel proved ill timed, for he reeled as though someone had kicked him in the gut. With a trembling hand, he reached out to touch his old friend's chest, sinking back on his heels in relief when he felt the rise and fall of his breath.

Where was he headed? Had he come after Barto? Guilt knifed through Barto at the thought. Or, even worse, had Kit been riding for help? Running his hands lightly over his friend's limbs, Barto was reassured to find no signs of broken bones. Nor did he see any open wounds that indicated Kit had taken a bullet. But Kit was too much a horseman to be thrown, so what had happened? He had a torn sleeve and a gash on his head. Was that why he remained unconscious? Barto tapped his cheek, but Kit did not respond.

Finally, Barto rose to his feet and retrieved the brimstone match from his pack. Lighting it once more, he waved it under Kit's nose until his friend coughed and sputtered and finally opened his eyes.

'Hmmm?' Kit mumbled, blinking in a gesture so like his sister that Barto felt a sharp stab of pain. Then his heart slammed in his chest as he realised that if Kit was here, fallen in the night, what of Sydony?

Chapter Sixteen

Some time during her passage into the maze, Sydony stumbled and fell to the ground, pretending to faint. Although she hated the touch of the hooded man who lifted her up to carry her, she suspected that her captors would pay less attention to her, if they thought her unconscious. In a struggle with one or more of them, she could never hope to win. But if left on her own, there was a chance…

When she felt herself being lowered to the ground, the roots of the great oak poking into her back, Sydony did not stir. Only after she heard the man who had carried her step away did she peek out from under lowered lashes. In the shadowy light of a lantern, she could see that Malet stood nearby, easily recognisable as the only one not wearing a hood, though he had donned a multi-coloured cloak. Sydony might have laughed at his appearance had he not been discussing the advantages of leaving her unbound to another man who held a rope.

Malet argued that the death throes needed to be natural in order to properly augur the future, and Sydony swallowed back the bile that rose in her throat. If she'd been any less stubborn, she would have fainted in truth. Instead, her mind worked furiously. Unfortunately, she did not know how much time she had, so she couldn't afford to wait until the men were distracted. And there were men. She could see more dark figures filing into the clearing.

Think, Sydony! Barto had always said she had the wits to get out of any situation. Now was the time to use them. She glanced upwards at the oak that soared overhead and considered climbing the tree. She knew that there were holds that would allow her to reach the huge branches, but how far could she go before someone came after her, sacred wood or not?

Even if she reached one of the massive limbs that stretched far out over the maze and dropped into the darkness, how could she hide or escape from so many? At least one had a lantern, which he was using to light torches, the flickering lights that she had once seen from the safety of her room.

Sydony's fingers closed around the pistol she had hidden in her cloak, but there were too many of them. She could shoot one, at best, which would do her little good unless… If she killed Malet, perhaps the others would run scared. *Or they might do worse*, she thought grimly.

Her gaze lingered on one of the torches, which seemed an odd choice over a lantern. Perhaps they were required for the ritual, she thought, with a shudder. But even in the clearing, they seemed dangerous after the recent dry weather and the constant wind that swirled dead leaves through the air and against the surrounding hedges.

Those piles of leaves could easily be ignited by a stray spark, Sydony realised, her heart pounding at the thought. But how was she to wrest the torch from the man? Her fingers tightened on the pistol again. If she shot him, would she have time to grab the torch and set a fire before she was seized by the others?

It seemed an impossible task, and her mind rebelled against choices that were all too difficult. Clenching her other hand in an effort to keep her composure, Sydony felt her fingers close over the crackling remains of leaves. Discreetly feeling around in the dark, she realised that she was by the large crevice that lay at the base of the tree. And that crevice was full of dry leaves.

Sydony glanced sharply toward the Druids, but no one seemed to be watching her. And why should they? Even if she awakened, they could easily subdue her. They saw no threat from a helpless female, so she lay in darkness among the roots of the tree, unobserved.

Under cover of that darkness, Sydony slipped the pouch of gunpowder from her cloak and emptied it upon the pile of leaves in the opening under the roots of the oak. Then, carefully removing the pistol, she laid it on its side, pointing into the leaves, and fired.

Because there was no ball in the weapon, there wasn't a loud crack, only the sound of the leaves igniting. As they burned, Sydony filled the pan again as best she could and loaded a ball, all the while silently thanking her brother for a game that had involved handling a pistol while blindfolded. Now she had one shot. Who would it be for? One of the torchbearers or Malet himself?

The leaves burned quickly, the fire shooting up through the hollow to the core that Sydony had suspected was rotten. Although she lay in front of the opening in the shadows, smoke soon poured from the inside of the tree. When a shout of discovery went up, Sydony rolled away, knocking into the nearest man who held a torch. Slicing at his hand with her knife, she snatched his torch and tossed it into the upper crevice, for good measure.

It was only after she'd thrown the torch that Sydony realised the Druids had placed the trepanned skull in that opening, perhaps as some sort of shrine. She had an instant to see Mallory's head grinning at her like a jack-o-lantern lit from within before she dove for the hedges.

With the moon to light their way, Barto and Kit returned to Oakfield as fast as they could. Riding in the night air seemed to revive Kit, who claimed he was fine except for the aches and pains of falling from his horse.

But Barto could tell he was not quite himself, his thoughts still sluggish, his movements slow. The realisation was no comfort when Barto considered what might lie ahead. His first concern had to be Sydony, but he wasn't sure that Kit could fend for himself, let alone lend any aid.

That worry lay heavy on Barto as he directed Kit to follow him off the road into some trees before they reached the drive that led to Oakfield. 'I think we have to assume the house is being watched,' he said. 'And we don't know how many of them there are.'

'But what of the groomsmen and the guards?' Kit asked.

Barto's jaw tightened. 'We have to assume that they drank the same cider you did, perhaps more of it.' He did not like to think that the men he had hired had met a worse fate, but Kit's report that the guards were missing earlier in the day was not encouraging.

When they reached the edge of the trees, they could see that the house was completely dark, and Barto's heart slammed in his chest. All the vague fears that had been dogging him since he left the tenant farm coalesced into one stark truth: Sydony was in danger. And he realised, in that dark instant, that he loved her, not as a neighbour or a friend or Kit's sister, but with passion and need and more than anything in this world. Perhaps he always had.

'Where's Sydony?' Kit asked, his own concern evident.

'She might be hiding in the dark. She's intelligent and resourceful and brave,' Barto said, in an effort to calm himself as well as his friend. But he knew they had to be prepared for anything. 'Do you have a weapon?'

'Just my knife,' Kit said. 'And Grandfather's duelling pistols.'

'Can you get into the house and find them without lighting any candles or making any noise?'

'I think so,' Kit said, his voice growing more firm.

'Then let's leave the horses here,' Barto said. Dismounting and tethering Perseus to a tree, he opened his pack and withdrew the cloaks. 'Here, put these on,' he said, handing one set to Kit.

'I'm going to take a look around,' Barto said. 'I'll

meet you outside the door to the kitchen. The terrace may be watched.'

'There's a light in the stables.'

Barto shook his head. 'That may be nothing—or a trap. We have to assume they're in the maze.'

'But how are we going to find our way through the maze without any light and with these hoods blocking our sight?' Kit asked, holding up the material with its single slit over the eyes.

'I have the turns memorised. Just hold on to my cloak,' Barto said. Pistol drawn, he watched as Kit's black form flitted through the moonlight towards the front of the house, slipping under the arched entrance and through the door. Then he scanned the grounds for any sign of movement, of figures that might be hiding in the shadows, marking their presence.

Finding the cloaks and the entrails at the abandoned farmhouse had filled Barto with foreboding, but discovering Kit had been drugged and the house itself was deserted racked him with dread. Fear for Sydony threatened to undermine his efficiency, and he pushed aside his newly acknowledged feelings to concentrate on nothing but his own grim purpose. After all his preparations and hired men, it had come down to him and him alone. And there could be no mistakes.

Barto did not go near the stables. He figured the light was a lure or a lantern left burning in an empty building. If Hob wasn't incapacitated, the manor would not be dark. And Sydony would be safe. Still, Barto circled the house, looking for signs of life, before settling into the shadows by the kitchen door. Only a few minutes later, it swung out slowly, barely perceptible in the gloom cast by the house. Then Kit emerged before carefully easing it shut once more.

'One of the pistols is gone, as are some powder and balls,' Kit said. 'I didn't go searching, but perhaps it means a servant is awake and alert.'

For the first time this night, Barto felt a surge of hope. 'I think it means that Sydony is alive,' he whispered. Surely, he would know if she weren't, he thought suddenly. Their connection, forged so long ago, was so strong that surely he would know…

'What do you mean? Why shouldn't she be alive? What do you think is happening?' Kit's whisper was sharp.

'I don't know,' Barto said. And he didn't. But he had his suspicions. 'Someone was after the book, Mallory's book on auguring from death throes, and that lore was based on the Druid's practice of ritual sacrifice.'

Hearing Kit's indrawn breath, Barto regretted his blunt words. 'They might have been looking for something else, as well, or waiting for something,' he added.

'For Samhain.' Kit spoke in an anguished whisper. 'For *tonight*.'

They exchanged one long glance, the kind they had once shared as Knights of the Round Table or as Robin Hood and Little John. But this time their actions were no game, their goal no adventure, and they both knew what hung in the balance. Silently, Barto motioned for Kit to move forwards and stood still, watching, until his old friend reached the entrance to the labyrinth. And then Barto joined him.

Inside the maze it was black as night, with only patches of moonlight making its way through the trimmed portions of the hedges. The going was slow, too slow, but Barto could not risk losing his way. Behind him, he felt Kit's grip on his cloak and he inched forwards, following the twisting path toward the centre.

The wind made eerie sounds within their muffled world, but above the rustling of the leaves and the greenery Barto could hear nothing. And as they moved deeper into the passages, he began to question his own judgement. He had been so sure the Druids had been using the maze and would use it again, that he had not even considered other possibilities. What if they had taken Sydony from the property where they would never find her?

Pain knifed through him, but Barto forced such thoughts aside and forged on until at last he heard voices, whispers that echoed through the hedges, making it impossible to tell their direction or their number. And then he smelled fire, as though something was burning. He prayed that it was not Sydony.

Only sheer will kept him from rushing ahead, held him to the path and the pace and the shadows. Garbed as they were, Barto hoped that he and Kit could slip into the clearing without attracting notice. What they would do then, he didn't know, with only two pistols and knives between them. But they had the advantage of surprise and the strength of will.

They were getting close now, and Barto saw that the path ahead was bathed in light, whether lantern or fire. He stopped just short of the opening, ready to peer through the edge of the hedges as best he could, when all hell broke loose.

Shouts erupted, along with the sounds of movement,

stamping feet and jostling bodies. Smoke filled the air, the light grew brighter, with an orange glow, and someone burst through the hedge at his feet. Barto reached for the figure automatically, lest it alert the others to his presence, but as soon as he touched the form, he realised this was no black-hooded Druid.

'Sydony,' he whispered, jerking her to him. Barto wanted to take her in his arms and never let her go...until he felt the barrel of a pistol digging into his gut. Then he realised that he was wearing the costume of the Druids whom she was trying to escape, and he remembered all the times that she had looked on him with suspicion and questioned him sharply. Did she think he was one of them?

'Sydony,' he repeated, his voice cracking.

Either she heard him this time, or she cast aside her doubts, because she made a little sound, turned the gun aside, and threw her arms around him.

Then Kit was beside them, reaching out for his sister, and the sounds from the clearing grew louder, the light brighter, drawing Barto's attention. In just a few steps, he was at the opening, where he saw several dark figures silhouetted against roaring flames. The great oak was ablaze, lighting the night sky like a giant bonfire.

Among the shouting, he could hear one voice, rising above the others. 'Get the skull! Get the skull!' But the hooded shapes milled about frantically, as if confused or overcome by smoke, until finally, one fantastically garbed figure leapt forwards, towards the very tree itself, only to be engulfed. The Druid's screams rang out into the night, eerily triumphant, just as Barto realised that the fire had spread from the branches of the oak to the hedge itself.

Turning around, he grabbed Sydony's hand and called to her brother, 'Run!'

As Sydony stood alone on the battlements the next morning, she was greeted by an even bleaker landscape than usual. In addition to the gloomy pall cast by the overcast skies, the grounds below were blackened and scarred, the maze nothing but a smouldering ruin of ash and brush. Prevailing winds had saved the house, but the stables had not been so lucky. Only the stone foundation remained, yet no horses had been inside, and Barto had managed to rescue his groomsmen.

Sydony shivered at the knowledge of just how close they had all come to death. She wasn't sure how Barto had got them out of the maze. She only knew she would never have been able to remember the twists and turns, taken at that speed, with fire at their heels.

Thankfully, everyone who had downed the cider awakened none the worse for their experiences, though Mrs Talbot, the maid and the valet had all left this morning, the housekeeper for her daughter's and the other two for less dangerous employment. It was an empty household, and Sydony would not be lingering long, either.

She pulled her cloak tighter around her tender body, flushing at the memory of Barto taking her to his bed last night. The man who had been unable to look upon her refused to let her leave his side after the fire. And in the darkness of his room, they had stripped themselves of all that stood between them.

Sydony drew in a sharp breath at the memory. The restrained façade Barto presented to the world had dropped, unleashing a man fierce in his passions, but tender in his touch. And the silence that had marked these last weeks disappeared, as well. His deep voice had whispered intimacies throughout the night about how beautiful she was, how good she felt, how good she *tasted*, how much he wanted her, how much he *loved* her. It was like drinking a heady wine that made her breathless, giddy and overheated.

Sydony had never known that people did such things, but it had taken little persuasion for her to embark on this new adventure with Bartholomew Hawthorne, *Maid Marion to his Robin Hood*. For a lifetime or more.

At the sound of footsteps, Sydony whirled, her breath catching in anticipation, but it was only Kit who walked across the roofs towards her. Only the brother she loved so dearly. Reaching towards him, she hugged him close.

'What's that for?' he asked, when she finally released him.

'Thank you for saving my life.'

'Don't thank me, thank Barto,' he said, and Sydony dropped her gaze.

I already have, she thought to herself with a certain devilish delight, as she turned back towards the parapets. 'It looks rather bleak, doesn't it?' she asked.

To her surprise, Kit shook his head. 'I'm glad it's gone,' he said, leaning against the stone. 'Whatever shadows and ill rumours that clung to Oakfield were vanquished with the maze. I plan to plant an entirely new garden, *sans* labyrinth.'

He grinned, and for the first time since arriving at the manor house, Sydony could see the possibilities. Some remodelling and a new landscape would make this a home. Kit would make it a home. But not for her.

'You'll have to invite me back to see it,' she said, looking out over the grounds.

'And where will you be going?' Kit asked, but Sydony could tell that he knew the answer.

'Hawthorne Park,' Sydony said, unable to deny the bubble of happiness that filled her with the thought of her new home. And her new husband.

Kit snorted. 'It's about time. Didn't I leave you two alone often enough?' He slanted her a glance. 'I hope that means congratulations are in order.'

Sydony laughed, a light and lovely sound that even the wind at Oakfield couldn't snatch from her. 'Being a far more astute observer of human nature than I, you were right all along,' she said. 'I am to be Viscountess Hawthorne.'

Epilogue

Sydony glanced lovingly across the gardens to where her husband knelt beside their son. Like his father, Max was the solemn sort. He gazed intently at a nearby butterfly before reaching a pudgy hand toward it, already seeking adventure. Just like his father.

As if he knew her thoughts, Barto looked towards Sydony and smiled. The curve of those generous lips and the soft light in his dark eyes still had the power to make her melt. They had married at Christmas, which seemed appropriate considering the significance of an earlier holiday in their lives. She'd already been pregnant, but not far enough along for the gossips to notice when she delivered Max the following autumn. Now, the baby was taking his first steps and bending over to look at the world upside down.

And what a world it was. Sydony could hardly believe she was on the grounds of Oakfield. Gone was the ivy that had once given the old manor house such a forbidding cast, purged when Kit decided the place didn't need character, after all. Stripped of the dark vines that had once covered its walls, the building looked warm and tidy, the old stone burnished in the sunlight.

The terrace had been rebuilt, with elegant balustrades and steps leading down to neat lawns that stretched out in every direction. Well-tended gravel walks curved among the grass that was dotted with trees, clusters of shrubs and round beds of flowers. In the distance, sheep grazed behind a low fence that marked one of the tenant farms. Around the house itself, gardens abounded in the manner of landscape designer Henry Repton, the whole flowing together with a harmony of colour on this summer's day.

Since Kit had no patience for the strict formality of old-fashioned gardens, he had been determined that the plantings be arranged to make the grounds inviting, a place where the pleasures of the out of doors could be enjoyed. And he had succeeded in striking a perfect balance between the old formality and the new picturesque movement, which called for uncultivated settings that were too wild for Sydony's taste. As far as she was concerned, Oakfield had seen enough wildness.

Every once in a while it came back to her. Even now, seated on one of the new stone benches in the bright sunlight, surrounded by her loving family and Kit's dogs, which gambolled just out of Max's reach, Sydony felt a stray shiver. Was she sitting where the great oak had once stood sentinel over the dark hedges of the maze?

Again, Barto caught her gaze, a question in his eyes, and Sydony smiled in reassurance. But he stood anyway, scooping Max into his arms and striding towards her, a tall, elegant figure who never ceased to make her heart hammer with joy. And in that moment, basking in her happiness, Sydony was thankful for it all, even the mysterious labyrinth that had brought the two of them together again.

For who could say what magic was?

* * * * *

*Here's a sneak peek at THE CEO'S CHRISTMAS
PROPOSITION, the first in* USA TODAY *bestselling
author Merline Lovelace's* HOLIDAYS ABROAD
trilogy coming in November 2008.

American Devon McShay is about to get the
Christmas surprise of a lifetime when she meets
her new client, sexy billionaire Caleb Logan, for
the very first time.

Silhouette

Desire

Available November 2008

Her breath whistled out in a sigh of relief when he exited Customs. Devon recognized him right away from the newspaper and magazine articles her friend and partner Sabrina had looked up during her frantic prep work.

Caleb John Logan, Jr. Thirty-one. Six-two. With jet-black hair, laser-blue eyes and a linebacker's shoulders under his charcoal-gray cashmere overcoat. His jaw-dropping good looks didn't score him any points with Devon. She'd learned the hard way not to trust handsome heartbreakers like Cal Logan.

But he was a client. An important one. And she was willing to give someone who'd served a hitch in the marines before earning a B.S. from the University of Oregon, an MBA from Stanford and his first million at the ripe old age of twenty-six the benefit of the doubt.

Right up until he spotted the hot-pink pashmina, that is.

Devon knew the flash of color was more visible than the sign she held up with his name on it. So she wasn't surprised when Logan picked her out of the crowd and cut in her direction. She'd just plastered on her best businesswoman smile when he whipped an arm around her waist. The next moment she was sprawled against his cashmere-covered chest.

"Hello, brown eyes."

Swooping down, he covered her mouth with his.

Sheer astonishment kept Devon rooted to the spot for a few seconds while her mind whirled chaotically. Her first thought was that her client had downed a few too many drinks during the long flight. Her second, that he'd mistaken the kind of escort and consulting services her company provided. Her third shoved everything else out of her head.

The man could kiss!

His mouth moved over hers with a skill that ignited sparks at a half dozen flash points throughout her body. Devon hadn't experienced that kind of spontaneous combustion in a while. A *long* while.

The sparks were still popping when she pushed off his chest, only now they fueled a flush of anger.

"Do you always greet women you don't know with a lip-lock, Mr. Logan?"

A smile crinkled the skin at the corners of his eyes. "As a matter of fact, I don't. That was from Don."

"Huh?"

"He said he owed you one from New Year's Eve two years ago and made me promise to deliver it."

She stared up at him in total incomprehension. Logan hooked a brow and attempted to prompt a non-existent memory.

"He abandoned you at the Waldorf. Five minutes before midnight. To deliver twins."

"I don't have a clue who or what you're..."

Understanding burst like a water balloon.

"Wait a sec. Are you talking about Sabrina's old boyfriend? Your buddy, who's now an ob-gyn doc?"

It was Logan's turn to look startled. He recovered faster than Devon had, though. His smile widened into a rueful grin.

"I take it you're not Sabrina Russo."

"No, Mr. Logan, I am *not*."

* * * * *

Be sure to look for
THE CEO'S CHRISTMAS PROPOSITION
by Merline Lovelace.
Available in November 2008 wherever books are sold,
including most bookstores, supermarkets, drugstores
and discount stores.

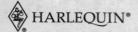
HARLEQUIN®

American ★ Romance®

LAURA MARIE ALTOM
A Daddy for Christmas
THE STATE OF PARENTHOOD

Single mom Jesse Cummings is struggling
to run her Oklahoma ranch and raise her
two little girls after the death of her husband.
Then on Christmas Eve, a miracle strolls onto
her land in the form of tall, handsome bull
rider Gage Moore. He doesn't plan on staying,
but in the season of miracles, anything
can happen….

***Available November
wherever books are sold.***

LOVE, HOME & HAPPINESS

REQUEST YOUR FREE BOOKS!

 Harlequin® Historical
Historical Romantic Adventure!

2 FREE NOVELS PLUS 2 FREE GIFTS!

YES! Please send me 2 FREE Harlequin® Historical novels and my 2 FREE gifts (gifts are worth about $10). After receiving them, if I don't wish to receive any more books, I can return the shipping statement marked "cancel". If I don't cancel, I will receive 6 brand-new novels every month and be billed just $4.94 per book in the U.S. or $5.49 per book in Canada, plus 25¢ shipping and handling per book and applicable taxes, if any*. That's a savings of 20% off the cover price! I understand that accepting the 2 free books and gifts places me under no obligation to buy anything. I can always return a shipment and cancel at any time. Even if I never buy another book, the two free books and gifts are mine to keep forever.

246 HDN ERUM   349 HDN ERUA

Name _____ (PLEASE PRINT)

Address _____ Apt. #

City _____ State/Prov. _____ Zip/Postal Code

Signature (if under 18, a parent or guardian must sign)

Mail to the Harlequin Reader Service:
IN U.S.A.: P.O. Box 1867, Buffalo, NY 14240-1867
IN CANADA: P.O. Box 609, Fort Erie, Ontario L2A 5X3

Not valid to current subscribers of Harlequin Historical books.

Want to try two free books from another line?
Call 1-800-873-8635 or visit www.morefreebooks.com.

* Terms and prices subject to change without notice. N.Y. residents add applicable sales tax. Canadian residents will be charged applicable provincial taxes and GST. Offer not valid in Quebec. This offer is limited to one order per household. All orders subject to approval. Credit or debit balances in a customer's account(s) may be offset by any other outstanding balance owed by or to the customer. Please allow 4 to 6 weeks for delivery. Offer available while quantities last.

Your Privacy: Harlequin Books is committed to protecting your privacy. Our Privacy Policy is available online at www.eHarlequin.com or upon request from the Reader Service. From time to time we make our lists of customers available to reputable third parties who may have a product or service of interest to you. If you would prefer we not share your name and address, please check here. ☐

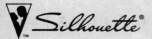
Romantic
SUSPENSE

**Sparked by Danger,
Fueled by Passion.**

Lindsay McKenna
Susan Grant

Mission: Christmas

Celebrate the holidays with a pair
of military heroines and their daring men
in two romantic, adventurous stories
from these bestselling authors.

Featuring:

"The Christmas Wild Bunch"
by *USA TODAY* bestselling author
Lindsay McKenna

and

"Snowbound with a Prince"
by *New York Times* bestselling author
Susan Grant

Available November wherever books are sold.

COMING NEXT MONTH FROM

HARLEQUIN®
HISTORICAL

- **ONE CANDLELIT CHRISTMAS**
  by **Julia Justiss, Annie Burrows and Terri Brisbin**
  (Regency)
  Have yourself a Regency Christmas! Celebrate the season with three
  heartwarming stories of reconciliation, surprises and secret wishes
  fulfilled....

- **THE BORROWED BRIDE**
  by **Elizabeth Lane**
  (Western)
  Fully expecting to marry her childhood sweetheart, Hannah Gustavson
  is torn by his sudden disappearance. With Hannah desperately needing
  the protection of a man, Judd Seavers cannot stand by and watch
  his brother's woman struggle alone.... So begins their marriage of
  convenience....

- **UNTOUCHED MISTRESS**
  by **Margaret McPhee**
  (Regency)
  Guy Tregellas, Viscount Varington, has a rakish reputation, and when
  he discovers a beautiful woman washed up on the beach he is more
  than intrigued. Helena McGregor must escape Scotland to anonymity
  in London—for the past five years she has lived a shameful life, not
  of her choosing. But she needs the help of her disturbingly handsome
  rescuer....

- **HER WARRIOR SLAVE**
  by **Michelle Willingham**
  (Medieval)
  Kieran Ó Brannon sold himself into slavery for his family, but despite
  steadfast loyalty, he cannot deny the intensity of his feelings for his
  master's betrothed—Iseult. She, too, must decide if succumbing to her
  fierce desire for the captured warrior is worth losing what she prizes
  most....